Quench
My Thirst

usually spent the first two minutes on foreplay, rubbing her clitoris to get her wet for his entry. Then he would mount her; after penetration, he was good for about five strong strokes, and then he would ejaculate. At first she tried to be sympathetic to his problem. He was apologetic and promised to do better. Then she began to get more and more frustrated as she realized this was his regular routine, and as a grown man he couldn't seem to hold off his orgasm more than two minutes. Occasionally they would exchange oral sex. It seemed he could do that for a long period of time, but whenever they stopped and shifted to intercourse, it was guaranteed the lovemaking would be over in a flash. She missed the feel of his penis inside her. They'd been married for ten years now, and nothing ever changed. She just learned to live with the depressing fact: she had married her worst lover. There were a few lovers before him. Some were good lovers, and some not. Each man seemed to have a different style. But they all exhibited more stamina and staying power.

She fell in love with Greg during a six-month courtship. He never rushed her into sex, and it was almost three months before they finally made love. She didn't suspect anything at the time. Naomi loved everything about Greg: he treated her with respect, he was caring and tender, and he helped around the house and cooked meals for her. The only area in which he wasn't perfect was the bedroom.

In the beginning she often initiated the sex between them. After a year or two of frustration and tears, she stopped trying. They would still have sex now and then. Sometimes a week or two would pass and they would not have sex. Greg never seemed to mind. She could count the times on her hand when he would actually initiate sex. She chalked it up to him having a low sex drive. Because it seemed to be his only shortcoming, she tried to dwell on all his other good qualities. Eventually her desire for sex waned, and she no longer missed it or wanted it as much as she used to. Lately, though, she was experiencing cravings for fulfillment she had thought were long buried.

She rolled over onto her side and pulled the covers around her shoulders. She knew it would be at least another thirty minutes or more before she would be able to go to sleep.

Naomi awoke the next morning to the smell of Jamaican Blue coffee brewing in the kitchen downstairs. It was Sunday morning, and Greg was already out working in the yard. She had lain in the bed until three in the morning, wide awake and unable to sleep. She looked around her bedroom and sleepily wiped her eyes. She could hear the lawnmower going outside. Greg was an early riser, and he preferred to get the yard work done before the blistering heat of the midday afternoon. Wrapping her bathrobe around her, she slipped on her socks and made her way downstairs to the kitchen. She loved this kitchen. The cabinets were made of natural oak, and the granite countertop was a mixture of black and tan flecks. There was a center island with a mini sink. Greg wanted plenty of counter space for food preparation, and she wanted a pantry. This kitchen accommodated both of those needs. There was a built-in computer desk at the far end of the counter. They had placed a flat-screen computer monitor there to save on space. It worked out fine. They spent many hours in the kitchen with a new recipe on the computer screen while they prepared gourmet meals together.

She retrieved a coffee mug from the cabinet and filled her cup from the coffeepot. She added a dash of half-and-half and one pack of sugar-free sweetener. Collecting the newspaper from the center island, she sipped her coffee as she headed into the family room to read.

Moments later, Greg came into the kitchen. "Good morning, baby," he said as he walked behind the sofa and planted a kiss on her upturned face. "You didn't sleep too well last night?" he asked.

"No, not really," she replied, sipping the coffee.

"Why? Is there something on your mind?" he asked with concern.

"No, I just couldn't sleep," she replied.

"I'm sorry, you should have awakened me," he stated.

"Why? So we could both be awake? You need your rest, too," she said.

"I could have stayed up and watched TV with you or something," he offered.

"No, baby. It's okay. Just remind me to take a sleeping pill tonight. I hate taking them after ten at night because it makes me too groggy when I wake up in the morning."

"Okay. What do you want for breakfast?" he asked.

"That's okay, I'll make it. What would you like?" she asked in return.

"Grits, eggs, sausage, and muffins?" he suggested.

"Okay, let me shower first, and I'll start breakfast." She smiled as she got up from her seat and headed back upstairs. As she passed him, she kissed him again briefly and wrapped her arms around his waist. He squeezed her back and then turned away to pour himself a cup of coffee. She looked back at him wistfully as she ascended the stairs. *I really do love him*, she thought.

BUSINESS TO BUSINESS—Agnes Garfield pushed through the revolving door and walked determinedly to the reception desk. "I have a nine o'clock appointment with Stanley Greenberg," she said to the receptionist. The receptionist looked up and took in the woman standing before her. She was nattily attired in a navy-blue Donna Karan suit with a crisp white silk boatneck blouse and a single-strand pearl necklace and matching pearl-drop earrings. Her hair was coiffed to perfection in a French roll. Freshly manicured red nails at the end of slim brown fingers drummed the counter while she waited for the receptionist to announce her. It was eight forty-five.

"If you'll have a seat, Ms. Garfield, Mr. Greenberg will be available in just a moment," the receptionist said, indicating the waiting area off to the side of the room. Agnes clutched her black Coach briefcase and turned away huffily. She hated to be kept waiting, even though she was fifteen minutes early. Time was money. She proceeded to the waiting area and laid her briefcase on the sofa. She reached in and pulled her cell phone from the side pocket. Pacing the small empty area, she punched in the speed code for her secretary.

"Pamela," she said briskly into the phone when her secretary picked up on the first ring. "Call Martin Havenburger and see if he can see me today at one o'clock. If he says yes, tell him I will meet him at Houston's for lunch. I should be out of here no later than twelve, and that will give me enough time. Leave me a message to confirm. I'll check it as soon as I am done here." She snapped the lid back into place, effectively ending the call. Putting the phone on vibrate, she stuck it back in the pocket of her briefcase. She straightened up just as the receptionist walked up to advise her that Mr. Greenberg was ready to see her. Agnes glanced at her watch; it was eight fifty-nine. She smiled to herself; let the games begin. She collected her briefcase and followed the receptionist to the office.

DIVA DIVINE—Rolling out of bed at five in the morning, Nina Carter was still groggy from partying the night before. She was going to look like death warmed over at the photo shoot this morning. Half tempted to put off the shoot for another day, she stumbled to the bathroom to relieve herself. Her hand flipped the switch as she entered the room, and the bright glare from the lights forced her to cover her eyes. Groping in the glare, unable to focus, she felt her way to the toilet seat. Sliding down her underpants with her free hand, she sat down and breathed a sigh as the sound of the urine striking the water resonated in the quiet of empty bathroom. She sat there a few moments longer with her head cradled in her hands. Reluctantly she arose and faced her reflection in the mirror. Her hair was matted on the right side of her face, and her eyes were slightly bloodshot. Her face was puffy from sleep. Nina turned on the faucet and splashed water onto her face. Pulling a hand towel from the rack, she dabbed her face. *Not that bad*, she thought. *I've given them worse to work with.* She padded over to the huge glass-enclosed shower. Reaching in, she turned on the shower. Seven gold-plated jets—two above her head, two at shoulder height, one mid-back, two lower down near her knees—spurted to life, quickly filling the shower with steam. She stripped off her clothes and stepped into the multiple streams of hot water.

Fifteen minutes later she emerged from the shower; wrapping her long black hair in a towel, she tied her robe around her waist. She took a few minutes to smooth moisturizer on her face, spread skin-toning lotion on her body, and brushed her teeth. Nina returned to her bedroom and selected a pair of jeans and sweatshirt. It took her a few moments more to call the concierge and tell him to make sure her car was waiting downstairs. Her long wet hair loosely gathered with a scrunchy at the back of her neck, she wore dark sunglasses and an oversize army jacket as she strode quickly through the hotel lobby and out to the waiting limousine.

ESCAPEE—Marissa pulled her car into the garage and turned off the engine. She sat there for a few minutes, quietly thinking. The overhead light on the garage-door opener began to dim, casting the garage into total darkness. Still, she sat motionless. Toby was working tonight, and she need not fear having to deal with his tantrums, but she felt no motivation to move from her seated position.

The cell phone trilled in her purse, startling her out of her trancelike state. Hastily she grabbed her purse and rummaged around in the bottom until her hand touched the cold metal. She checked the caller ID and recognized her husband's number. *Please don't let him be pissed, please don't let him be pissed*, she silently chanted. Nervously, she answered.

"Where are you?" he demanded.

"I'm home," she replied.

"No, you're not. I just called the house. Where are you?" he repeated.

"I am home. I mean. I'm in the garage. I just got here. I'm still in the car," she said quickly. *Oh, God*, she thought. He was constantly tracking her down again. She could barely go to the store without his timing her return.

"Where the hell were you?" he demanded.

"I was over at my mom's. Remember, I told you I was going to drop by to pick up the plants for the garden," she explained, praying he would remember the conversation from early this morning.

"Yeah, whatever," he said, "I forgot to set the VCR for *NYPD Blue*. Set the one in the living room. Do it now before you forget. You always forget shit."

"Okay," she replied, climbing out of the car and feeling her way toward the mudroom door. She silently prayed this was his only request. Fumbling with the key, she opened the door and stepped into the kitchen. "Is there anything else?" she asked.

"No, I gotta run," he said and disconnected the call. She stood inside the kitchen door for a minute to allow her heart to slow its accelerated beating. She placed her purse on the kitchen table and proceeded to the living room to set the tape as instructed. She would have only four hours of peace before he got home.

She picked up her purse and pulled out a handful of folded bills. Quickly she went to the bookcase and found the book she was looking for. It was hollowed out in the middle and contained two compartments. Popping off one of the covers, she removed the bills already there, wrapped the new bills around it, and rubber banded them together. She shoved them into the compartment, replaced the cover, closed the book, and slipped it back into its slot on the shelf.

She was stealthily collecting money for the past several months. Her job had initiated a bonus program for sales reps exceeding their monthly quota. She never mentioned the bonus plan to Toby. The checks were being mailed to her mother's house. When the checks arrived, her mother would call her at work to let her know. Marissa would then stop by on her way home, sign the check, and her mother would cash it at her bank and hold the money until Marissa could stop by to pick up the cash. Between the bonus and what she could siphon out of the house account, she had managed to save almost six thousand dollars in the last eight months. It was her escape money.

The phone rang in the kitchen, rattling her nerves again. She peered at the caller ID. The words PRIVATE CALLER illuminated. She picked up the receiver and answered. A short click and then a dial tone buzzed in her ear. It was Toby; she knew without him even saying a word. He was checking to make sure she really was at home. Angrily she slammed the phone back down on the base. "I hate you!" she yelled aloud. She was a prisoner in her own home, and she was tired of it, tired of him. "Soon," she said aloud, "soon," and then walked down the hall toward her bedroom.

2

Desmond watched Olivia out of the corner of his eye. She shifted nervously in her seat next to the aisle. He reached over and squeezed her hand, assuring her that everything would be fine before returning his gaze to the fluffy white clouds outside the airplane window. They were still a good hour out from the Chicago airport. He had debated all night and the following day about giving her more information about Trevor. He still did not have all the details. A brief search on the Internet the following morning allowed him to peruse the *Chicago Sun Times* newspaper. The story wasn't the headline, but it still nonetheless made front-page news. FORTUNE 500 EXECUTIVE ARRESTED IN LOVE-TRIANGLE MURDER. The details were yet to be disclosed, but one victim remained comatose, and another was dead. Trevor was arrested at the scene of the crime.

Olivia had walked into his office while he was reading the article, and at the sight of Trevor's face in the grainy newspaper photo, tears had filled her eyes again. They weren't able to get a flight out the next day and had to wait an additional day to travel. The extra time gave them a day to advise their jobs and family where they were going and why.

Olivia's parents told her to give Trevor their best and assure him he was in their prayers. She tried to contact his family to find out if they were going to see him. His older sister answered the phone and said no, they were not going to get involved. Olivia, surprised by the sheer venom in his sister's voice, questioned why. Edith, the eldest of the Calhoun clan, snidely remarked they knew his sinful ways would catch up with him one day. Just like chickens coming home to roost, this was bound to happen. Olivia was appalled by her lack of concern and puzzled by the "sinful ways" comment. When she pressed her about it, she simply told her to ask Trevor or the other demon, Damian.

Olivia didn't mention her comments to Desmond. She told him due to some family issues, the Calhouns would be unable to assist Trevor. She pondered the comments now as she waited for them to arrive in Chicago. What did Trevor get involved in, which led to all this trouble he was in? She knew he would never kill anybody; of this she was certain. She closed her eyes and said another silent prayer for Trevor.

Trevor sat quietly in the tiny cell at the Cook County Correctional Facility. He looked around his surroundings and wondered how he had messed up so badly to end up here. What clues had he missed because he'd gotten "soft"? Damian had warned him, but he was too tired, too drained, and too caught up in the game to pay him any heed. He leaned back against the cement wall and stared at the dirty metal toilet and sink, both placed so low on the wall it cramped his six-foot, five-inch frame just trying to use them. His bed was a white metal rack attached to the wall, and even it was too short for his body length.

He leaned his elbows on his knees and rested his head in his hands. He hadn't intended to get anybody killed. He was just trying to protect himself. Damian had hired him a lawyer, who assured Trevor he could get him released. The lawyer told him it was a clear-cut case. Trevor had been processed through the system, but no charges had been formally filed. The police were still gathering evidence to present to the state attorney's office to determine what he would be charged with. Though he had no prior record, he would have to wait for his arraignment to see if bail would be granted. Meanwhile, he was stuck here in this hellhole. Every passing day was one day too long.

Damian had told him Olivia and Des were on their way. Trevor cursed Damian for calling her. There was no way he could keep his secret life from her anymore. At this point the cops weren't aware of the real reason he was in the hotel room, and they weren't digging too deeply into it. They were taking it as an affair gone badly. If this went to trial, it was sure to come out why he'd gone there and how he knew the victims. Things could only get worse from there.

Sighing deeply, he leaned back against the cement wall and closed his eyes. He thought about his very first client.

She was an older French woman who owned an international cosmetics company. She was a steady client of Damian's, but he was tied up, and he sent Trevor to meet with her. Trevor pulled up to the gated mansion and pressed the intercom to announce his arrival. A butler answered and buzzed him through. As the massive wrought-iron gates parted to allow him access to the driveway, Trevor whistled under his breath. The house was breathtaking, befitting a tour on the homes of the rich and famous. He continued around the circular drive, convinced he was looking at Windsor Castle. He parked the car in front of the mansion. As he opened the car door, a valet mysteriously appeared and asked for his keys. He tossed the keys to the uniformed driver and walked up the front steps to the gigantic wood-carved doors.

The door had opened as magically as the valet appeared, and a butler bade him entrance into the cavernous foyer. Marble floors spanned the expanse of the foyer. Famous works of art and antiques were mounted on walls and pedestals throughout. Though it was the middle of the day, the foyer was dark.

"This way, sir," the butler said stiffly and pointed in the direction of a doorway off to the right. Trevor followed him silently, still taking in the magnificence of the decor. They entered a huge library. Rich, carved, mahogany bookcases filled with books lined the walls. There was a marble fireplace with a lit fire glowing inside. Trevor thought this strange in the middle of spring; it wasn't even cool outside today. Oddly it did not seem to generate much heat. The butler excused himself and closed the doors behind him.

Trevor wandered over to the nearest bookcase and began to peruse some of the titles. Many were rare first-edition books. He picked up an Edgar Rice Burroughs first edition, *Tarzan*, and carefully opened the cover. It was in pristine condition. He delicately fingered the pages. He reflected on the Tarzan movies of his youth. Johnny Weissmuller had been his inspiration for joining the swimming team in high school. Trevor was an accomplished swimmer, but it was at basketball that he excelled.

"Do you like to read, young man?" a delicate feminine voice asked from a wing chair near the fireplace. The lilting French accent was charming. Trevor raised his eyes from the page. How did he miss seeing her there? She stared into the fireplace as though transfixed. He placed the book back on the shelf and walked over to face her.

"Yes, ma'am. I love to read. I especially like historical novels and ancient tales." He smiled down at her. She was a well-preserved woman. He wasn't certain of her age. She was very petite with a slim build. Her flawless, unwrinkled skin was the color of cocoa beans. Her long dark brown hair was coiffed in two French braids. The ends of the silky braids were intertwined and fell down the middle of her back. Her fingers were long and delicate. Even in the darkened room he could see her sea-green eyes. She was still a stunning woman. She wore a long sleeveless yellow floral dress. It had a high-neck mandarin col-

lar, exposing delicate shoulders. She seemed a very fragile creature. He wondered how well she could hold up during sex.
Since it was the reason he was here.

"Please sit down, young man. Tell me, what is your name?"
she asked as she indicated with a slim hand the wing chair opposite her.

"Trevor, ma'am," he replied, settling into the chair and finding it surprisingly comfortable.

"No, what is your real name?" she asked, arching one eyebrow slightly.

"My name is Trevor," he repeated.

"I see. Yes, this is your first time, isn't it? You have much to
learn, young man. I'm certain this is why Damian has sent you
here." She adjusted her position in the chair slightly. "First, please
call me Claudette. You make me feel so old when you call me
ma'am. I know I am old, but you should not remind me of this,
oui?"

"My apologies, Claudette," he replied, glancing down at his
watch. Damian told him he was to spend no more than an hour
here. It was all he would be paid for.

"Mistake number two," she said and looked at him sternly.

"I'm sorry," he fumbled again. *Maybe I'm not cut out for
this,* he thought. *I'm screwing up already, and I don't even
know how.* "Maybe I should not be here," he said and started
to rise from his chair.

"Sit down, my friend. You are young and inexperienced in
the venture you are about to undertake. If you are to be successful, you have much to learn. Patience is the first and fore-
most of the tools you will need," she said. She pushed a button
on the table, and in a few moments the butler appeared in the
doorway.

"Henri, please bring my friend a warmed cognac and a pot
of tea for me," she said to the butler. He nodded his head and
closed the door behind him.

"Never allow a woman to see you watching the clock. Nothing will spoil the mood faster than the thought you are in a rush or racing off to make love to someone else. It will only serve to remind her she is paying for your time," she said and paused to clear her throat. "Trevor." She paused thoughtfully. "The name does suit you," she concluded with a smile and then continued. "Today we will spend the afternoon talking. I am sure you are an accomplished lover, but I can see already you do not have an understanding of women. Not the kind of understanding you will need to command the money Damian does. If you are to become his partner, you must learn many things."

Intrigued, Trevor leaned back in his chair. Who did this old broad think she was talking to? He'd yet to receive a complaint from any of the women he'd been with. He prided himself on leaving them satisfied and wanting more. Still, Damian had sent him here, and he was curious to hear what she would say.

The butler returned and placed a tray with a small teapot, cup, and saucer on the table next to Claudette. He poured her a cup of tea and then came back with another small tray and set it on the table next to Trevor. The tray contained a chrome brandy warmer with a little votive candle in it. He poured a generous shot of Courvoisier Imperial in a Baccarat crystal snifter and lit the candle. Carefully he placed the snifter in the warmer. He looked questioningly at Claudette, who nodded her head, and then he departed the room. Trevor was making mental notes of all he was exposed to. The Courvoisier Imperial was something he'd never even heard of. The elegance of this whole atmosphere was astounding; he'd never witnessed this kind of sophistication firsthand before. It was certainly a lifestyle he could see himself getting used to.

"Now, dear. Let's talk about love. You see, to be successful in pleasing women, you must remember that women, for the most part, believe that sex and love are intertwined. I know women are very bold these days and want to put forth the image that sex is all about pleasure. But to truly be pleasured, a woman must feel loved, if only for the brief time you are with her. She does not have to love you, and you certainly do not have to love her, but she must feel for that brief span of time that you are in love with her body. In most cases, she will be the only naked woman in the room, so this should not be so hard to accomplish." She laughed delicately at her own wit.

Trevor picked up the warm cognac and took a sip. The first sip spun like liquid fire down his throat. His second sip was smooth, like liquid gold, and unlike any he'd ever tasted. A warm glow settled in the room as he listened to Claudette.

"Where do you kiss a woman to light the fire in her?" she asked and took a sip of tea. She watched him closely as his emotions flashed across his face. He did not like to be tested, but she could see that part of him wanted to be right when he responded.

"On her neck, behind her ear, her breasts, and her sweet spot," he answered slowly.

"Do you have any idea how many erogenous areas you have omitted?" she asked.

"No," he replied quietly. He had failed the first test, and it annoyed him.

"Lesson one, my dear. The inside of her wrist is a wonderful place for soft, feathery kisses. She need not be naked for you to do this. You begin to set the pace before the clothes are even removed. The next spot would be the inside of her upper arm. It will tingle and even tickle slightly, making her giggle, but she will enjoy it immensely. The key is to go slowly, build the fire one twig at a time. You need not pour starter fluid all over to develop a bonfire in the end. Stoke your fire slowly, and it will burn a very long time," she explained.

Trevor leaned back in his chair, snifter in hand, and listened aptly. Claudette gave him a lesson in pleasure, which astounded him. He spent three hours with her the first afternoon, and she insisted on paying him for his time. They would spend several more afternoons together just talking, laughing, and learning about one another. Sex was not a pressing issue for Claudette, and she so enjoyed his company, she hesitated to disrupt the bond growing between them just to satisfy a carnal need.

Each time he visited her, she would present him with a special gift. She showered him with gifts in addition to the money she paid him. She'd given him his first case of Molton Brown products and explained how important it was for him to keep up his body, not only with workouts, but also with moisturizer and toners to keep his skin supple. She brought in a professional valet and tailor to teach him how to coordinate his clothing and accessories. They explained the best cut of suit for his frame to achieve the look of class and elegance befitting a man of means. There was more to looking good than just spending ungodly amounts on designer labels. He learned quickly and enjoyed applying himself to his lessons. Claudette taught him not only about making love, but she applied a polish and a hint of class he never realized was missing until he met her.

Several weeks after their first afternoon meeting, Claudette decided it was time to move their relationship toward a more physical level. She'd grown quite fond of Trevor, and her desire for him increased with each visit. He was a handsome man, but it was more than appearance that drew her to him. She detected sensitivity in him, which would make him an outstanding lover.

He arrived late in the evening and was directed to the master suite. He knocked softly on her bedroom door. He'd been in this room before, but only once when she explained the nuances inherent in setting the right atmosphere for lovemaking. She told him this would not play a role so much in his business as it would in his personal life and for the woman he would eventually choose to share it with.

She called out softly for him to enter. He opened the door, and it took only a moment for his eyes to adjust to the muted lighting in the room. Illumination was provided by a few randomly placed, scented oil lamps. From the doorway he could see the glow from the fireplace in the adjoining sitting room. Claudette was not in the bedroom, so he moved toward the sitting room. The sitting room was a small enclosed area she often used for reading or meditating. It was sparsely decorated, with only two pale rose, upholstered, antique, fauteuil French highback chairs. A mahogany Pembrook table was placed between both chairs. On this night, a silver tray had been placed upon it, which held two fine crystal champagne flutes along with a silver bowl of freshly cut bite-size melon wedges cradled in ice. White linen napkins were folded and laid beside the tray. A short distance away, a fine linen cloth was wrapped around the mouth of a bottle of 1996 Dom Perignon as it chilled in an ice bucket.

Claudette was not in this room either. Puzzled, he turned back to the bedroom and saw her standing on the balcony across the room, watching him. She was wearing a long silver peignoir set. The peignoir and gown underneath were both sheer, and together they gave only the mildest illusion that the wearer was clothed. Sheer nylon sleeves were trimmed with lace. A lacework pattern of roses adorned the sheer bodice of the empire-wasted gown. High-heeled slippers exposed her perfectly manicured, small toes. Her dark, thick hair had been freed from its usual braided style and was left long and flowing across her shoulders. She was regally stunning.

Trevor's breath caught in his throat. In that brief moment, he glimpsed the young woman she had been a long time ago. He imagined her young, stylish, and gorgeous, with men fawning at her feet just to be graced with her favor. He smiled. "Good evening, gorgeous."

"You handsome devil, what am I to do with you?" she responded girlishly as she came toward him and into the bedroom.

As she moved from the balcony to the more lighted bedroom, Trevor was confronted by the sheerness of her gown. He could clearly see the outline of her feminine curves, her full breasts and dark nipples. The split at the high waist of the gown flowed open in A-line cut and exposed the neatly trimmed dark hair covering her sweet spot. He looked away, embarrassed. He had known this moment would come, but he never thought beyond the idea. He never anticipated the reality of being here with her like this. She was his mentor, his friend. He revered this woman and had so much respect and admiration for her. Now she stood naked before him and expected him to please her in all the ways she needed.

Claudette anticipated his response. She had not reached such an advanced age without understanding the psyche of men. If he were not embarrassed, she would have miscalculated, and that was a rarity. Tonight he would learn how to pleasure a woman to the fullest extent, and the next time he would need no instruction. She moved to his side and placed her hand on his cheek; slowly she turned his face back to hers. She studied his eyes for a moment before she smiled gently and then began to speak softly.

"Trevor, you came to me initially for a reason. We have enjoyed each other's company immensely for the past several weeks, but we both knew those conversations would lead us here."

His admiration for her did battle with his desire to please her and made him uncertain for the first time in his adult life. He'd never been with a woman over the age of forty-five, and he guessed Claudette was close to seventy, although she did not look it. "What do you want me to do?" he asked.

She determinedly took his hand and led him to the sitting room. "Sit down," she commanded, and he readily complied. "First, we must talk straight," she told him seriously. "Tonight you will make love to me only as I instruct you to. You will not race ahead thinking you know more than me about my body. Est-ce que vous comprenez?"

"Oui," he replied and smiled. She was like a little dictator tossing around orders. He tried to take his mind off the fact that she was naked and in his face.

"Second, in order to please a woman you must first understand all the secrets of her body. You must recognize every little nuance of her behavior. I will help you with all this, and I promise your heightened level of awareness will increase your pleasure as well. Êtes-vous disposé à écouter?"

"Oui, madame. I am listening," he answered softly and began to unbutton his shirt.

"Not yet, mon amour. Third, most important, c'est très important. I am not your mother, your grandmother, your great aunt, or cousin. I am a woman, like every other woman, who wants and desires to faire l'amour avec un monsieur beau. It sounds so much nicer en français. Anyway, providing this type of sexual passion is a task you have chosen to perform. Correct?"

In spite of himself, Trevor could begin to feel a stirring in his loins. How long was a man expected to have a beautiful, naked woman two inches from his face and not react? Claudette was still a very beautiful woman. "Okay, okay. I got it," he replied.

"Okay," she replied, and, still standing in front of him, she untied the lace string at the bodice of her gown. "First, you must undress me slowly."

Trevor began by removing the peignoir first. It was light and flimsy in his hands. He was methodical in his movements as he exposed one small slim shoulder and then the other. He rolled the sleeves down her arms and eased it passed her fingertips.

"Stop there," she ordered. "Now, tell me what you see."

"Huh?" he responded, not understanding the question.

She leaned over and whispered suggestively in his ear as her breasts brushed against his shoulder, "Tell me what you see. Talk to me."

Comprehension dawned, and he paused for a moment and then began the process of removing her sheer gown. His hands were gentle as he slid the thin strap of the gown off her shoulder. He peered closely at her shoulder and said, "I see a tiny scar on the tip of your collarbone. I wonder how you got it?" He planted a soft kiss on the spot and continued his inspection. He brushed her hair behind her shoulder and slid his hand behind her head, cupping her earlobe between two fingers, and kissed the nape of her neck. "I see you've had your ears pierced," he whispered and pulled the lobe of her ear into his mouth and nibbled on it gently.

Claudette breathed deeply and smiled. The muscles in the heart of her desire ached as they contracted in response to his touch. A familiar tingling sensation of anticipation filled her body. His touch was as light as a feather and teased her nerve endings as his hands continued their exploration.

With the palms of his hands he slid the gown down her arms until it fell to the floor, leaving her totally exposed and vulnerable to him. Tenderly he cupped both breasts with his hands and circled each nipple with his tongue.

"Don't get distracted. Keep talking," she urged as her knees grew weak and she knew she would not be able to support her own weight much longer.

"I cherish your breasts. And I want to . . . He lifted one breast to his mouth and closed his lips completely over the rigid peak and sucked.

"Oh, oh my!" Claudette exclaimed and couldn't stop the tiny orgasm that raced through her body and caused her to buckle at the waist. "You cheeky bastard, you're cheating. I told you about skipping ahead."

Trevor laughed aloud, picked her up gently, and carried her into the bedroom. "You're very petite, ma chère, light as a feather. Are you sure we should continue?" he murmured against the soft skin of her neck.

"Oui, keep talking," she replied.

He laid her down in the center of the king-size bed and then began to unbutton his shirt again. He stopped when he remembered the rules. "May I?" he asked, indicating the shirt.

"Oui," she agreed. She watched as he removed the shirt and undershirt as well. Trevor was an extraordinary specimen of manhood. His boyish good looks, broad shoulders, and muscular physique would have lesser women begging to climb into his bed. When he began to unbuckle his belt, she couldn't stop the escalated palpitations of her heart. It had been so long since . . . She closed her eyes and tried to focus on the task at hand. Tonight was about teaching him what he needed to know; it wasn't about her. She felt his breath on her face and the tip of his manhood rubbing against her belly. She opened her eyes to see him poised above her, staring intently. She also got a good look at what she was about to become intimately acquainted with, and a flurry of unrestrained French rushed off her tongue.

"Mon Dieu! Vous êtes si grand! Il est mon plaisir d'être avec vous!" she exclaimed and then breathed a deep, contented sigh.

"Are you okay?" he asked.

"Yes, why?" she demanded.

"You're breathing kind of heavy," he replied, concerned.

"I'm fine, get back to work," she scoffed and closed her eyes.

He smiled and resumed his exploration. He lay on his side and used his fingertips to explore the skin of her stomach. Her skin did not have the firmness and elasticity of a younger woman, but he was surprised by its smooth, satiny texture.

"Your skin is soft. I'm not sure what I thought it would feel like, but it is like the velvet on the petal of a rose." He laid his head on her ribcage and ran his hands along the length of her legs. "Your legs are strong, like a dancer's legs would be. You must have danced when you were younger," he mused as he slid his hand between her legs, slowly parting them. He moved between her legs for closer inspection. "The skin on the inside of your thighs reminds me of a newborn baby's skin, protected and silky smooth." He kissed the soft flesh of her inner thighs.

Emotion rushed to the surface as her mind and body did battle. Her mind begged for reason, and her body begged for satisfaction. She allowed him to roll her onto her stomach and continue his quest.

He rubbed his hands gently along the outline of her body and stopped at the rising mound at the top of her thighs. For a petite woman she had a nice round butt. He placed both palms on her surprisingly firm cheeks and massaged gently. Then he brushed aside her hair to whisper in her ear. "Your ass is still perfect," he said and planted a kiss at the base of her spine.

He rolled onto his back and pulled her into the crook of his arm so she was once again on her back. He placed his hand on the flat of her stomach and then moved it slowly down until his fingers slipped into the fine, curly hairs shielding her desire. "May I?" he asked quietly.

"Yes, but you must listen carefully to my instructions. It is important to focus on each task along the quest. At the end of the quest is the reward, but meeting each task sets the stage for a greater, more joyous reward," she explained quickly. Her body was on fire, and the ache was more than she could bear. But this part would be so important, he must get it right.

Trevor began to nibble on the delicate skin behind her ear. At the same time he slid his hand between her legs and cupped her treasure with his palm. His breath was warm in her ear as he whispered, "Here?"

"Oui. Now apply pressure here." She guided his hand a little lower and pressed the heel of his palm directly on the hidden and highly sensitive passion button. "Massage here lightly, rotating your palm slightly. Let me feel its heat." She gasped as she felt a rush of moisture between her thighs. "Now," she started, caught her breath, and started again, "now slowly insert your finger . . . ah, ah, yes." She struggled with rational thought as he expertly followed her directions. "Test the inner walls, ah, do you feel the passage will be easy, or is more lubrication necessary?" she asked breathlessly. "This must be your call, not hers," she cried and bit her lip to stifle a deep groan from bursting forth. "You must know instincti . . . instin . . . ahh . . . know instinctively when she is ready to accept you without pain," she gushed.

Trevor was dealing with his own growing ache while he followed her directions. Her instructions were driving him crazy, and he couldn't wait to delve deep into his instructor. All thoughts of her advanced age were long gone. His rock-hard dick only recognized the fact that there was a hot, juicy pleasure depot nearby it needed to dip into.

"Trevor, you . . . must . . . understand . . . the difference . . . between pressure . . . and pain. Pressure is good; pain is not always."

He decided she felt more than ready to accept him. His fingers were covered with her own natural lubricant. He rolled over and poised himself above her.

"Not yet, mon amour. Everything, you must learn everything." She opened her legs wide and guided his hand to her aching spot. "This is my treasure. You must dive into the sea to find the pearl and reward me for sharing my treasure with you."

He slipped his fingers back inside her to rewet them and then gently parted her flowery lips and exposed her pearl. He teased and nipped the tiny jewel with his tongue and lips alternately until she screamed for him to stop.

"Now, mon amour, now," she whimpered, exhausted.

He needed no other urging as he pushed his throbbing reward deep inside the warmth of her treasure. Fireworks exploded in his head as her muscles contracted around his shaft. He remained still for a few moments to allow her to adjust and then began slowly stroking in and out of her treasure. He could feel her squeezing and releasing him as she matched her movements to his. She was demanding and insatiable. He slipped his hand under her back to raise her hips higher and then hesitated.

"I will not break, silly," she admonished him. "If a woman cannot take what you give, she will let you know."

Permission granted, he picked up the pace a bit and increased his tempo. He wasn't certain how much longer he could hold off, and he wasn't sure she'd had enough.

As if she were reading his mind, she responded, "Remember, it is not so important what you are feeling—it is critical what *she* is feeling."

What!? His brain screamed as his body primed for an explosion. "How am I supposed to know?" he demanded.

"She . . . will . . . tell . . . you!" she shouted as a growl started at the base of her throat and forced its way out of her mouth in the form of an agonized scream.

Almost simultaneously, he felt a gush of hot fluid rush from her body and finally released his hold on a stream of his own. He groaned aloud as he collapsed on the bed beside her.

They lay there quietly for a few minutes before she raised herself up on her elbow and peered at him. "That was lesson one," she advised and then laughed delightfully at the shocked expression on his face.

A short time later, Claudette retrieved luxurious terry-cloth robes for each of them, and they returned to the sitting room where Trevor stoked the fire with wood, and they toasted each other with champagne. As she rested comfortably in her chair, a serious expression appeared on her face. "There is a very important matter you must take very seriously, as it relates to sharing your body with women."

He looked across at her quizzically and waited for her to continue. He valued her opinion, and he knew if she felt the issue was serious, he should pay attention.

"It is about protection. Tonight I am sure you were prepared for the activities of the evening, and you cleverly and very discreetly noticed I was prepared as well with the condoms placed conveniently within your reach on the nightstand. I compliment you on retrieving one without interrupting the flow of the act. However, you may feel a certain amount of trust in me; do not be so foolish as to place this much trust in other women, especially women of child-bearing age. You are a very handsome man, and there will be those women who wish to bear a miniature copy of you. You would not be the first man to fall prey to a 'pinhole' in a seemingly sealed condom. Always bring your own protection. The application of the condom should never disrupt the flow of the moment. For bold women, you may suggest they put it on for you; it will enhance the experience. For shy or inexperienced women, you should always handle this with finesse and sensitivity. Protect yourself and your future partners from any of those ugly diseases. They will appreciate you even more if your actions display concern for their well-being as well as their sexual satisfaction."

Trevor understood the importance of what she advised him and appreciated that she cared enough to bring it up. It was a delicate subject, and a reminder of his own responsibility in the sexual act did not hurt.

"Thank you, ma chère. I will be mindful of my responsibility in protecting myself and my clients," he said. He had been curious about the melon wedges on the tray and took this opportunity to change the subject. "Do the melons have a special meaning?" he asked.

"No, not at all. In fact we were supposed to have the melons and champagne before the lesson," she replied simply.

"But if we are setting a romantic tone, why would you have melons and not strawberries? Or, better yet, chocolate-covered strawberries?" he persisted.

"Well, my dear, it may not apply so much in our situation. But if you ever want to really impress a lady friend, you will try this. Bear with me as I must demonstrate. Strawberries can be bitter sometimes; chocolate makes the teeth not so pretty and leaves a chocolate smell in the mouth. We have not had any melon wedges yet, so this demonstration will work quite nicely. Kiss me," she instructed.

He rose from his chair and stood in front of her and gave her a brief kiss on the lips. He was surprised when she raised her eyebrows and looked disgusted.

"Mon Dieu! How do you expect to keep women calling you if you do not know how to kiss them avec passion?"

"Wait a minute, you didn't ask for all that," he countered and pulled her up from the chair and into his arms. He kissed her lightly at first and then coaxed her willing lips apart and slipped his tongue into her mouth. His tongue enticed hers in a brief but very sensual tête-à-tête.

As he began to pull away and end the kiss, she forgot this was a test and instinctively stood on tiptoes to follow his retreating tongue and extend the moment. Then she caught herself and realized how easily he'd swept her in and made her lose her head. He would be a dangerous lover, and women would pay dearly to be with him.

"Okay, much better," she agreed and then continued. "Tell me, what do I taste like?"

"Huh? Uh, champagne? Honestly, not much of anything. Sorry," he confessed.

"My point exactly. Now let us each have a melon wedge." She offered him the bowl and ate a few of them herself. "What does your mouth feel like now?" she asked.

"Well, actually, it feels refreshed and clean," he commented thoughtfully.

"Now kiss me again."

He repeated his performance, but this time their mouths tasted sweet and alluring.

"Wow!" he said playfully. "You really taste good."

She laughed and smiled warmly at him. His kiss had started those tingling sensations all over again. "Ready for lesson two?" she asked as she dropped her robe on the floor and sashayed naked back toward the bedroom.

"You're just trying to kill me," he protested weakly as he downed the last of the champagne and returned the glass to the table. He tossed his robe in the chair and then stretched and flexed his muscles. His body was already poised for the next challenge as he followed her lead.

Claudette enjoyed many young lovers over the years, but none after Trevor, who held a special place in her heart. She explained the rules of the service business: never give your true name, never be seen in public with a client, and never take a client for granted or make her feel cheapened by her need for his service. Women would have different needs and desires, which would drive them to call him, but they should never feel sullied by giving in to those desires.

Trevor spent a year as Claudette's lover before she fell ill and her health no longer permitted the sexual escapades she so enjoyed. Up until his arrest, he still visited her once a month to check on her. He would sit by her chair in the library and plant feathery kisses on her wrists. She would lean back in the chair, enjoying the sensations and reliving the memories.

A loud scuffle in the corridor brought him sharply back to the present and his dismal surroundings. He lay down on the cold metal cot and again pondered how he ended up in Cook County jail.

3

He'd been in the business for about eight months when he first met Paige. He immediately recognized something different in her. There was a sense of vulnerability about her that wasn't evident in the other women he was servicing.

She opened the hotel door and gazed up at the tall, handsome stranger in the hallway. Immediately she experienced second thoughts. What was she doing? Did she really call this man here to have sex with her?

"May I?" he asked in a deep voice as he arched an eyebrow in her direction. Conflicting emotions were doing battle in her head, and the uncertainty was etched on her face.

"I'm not sure what I was thinking when I asked you to come here," she began nervously. She stepped back and allowed him to enter the room. He walked through the doorway and glanced around. It was a standard no-frills hotel room: queen bed, end tables, dresser, and TV armoire. He noticed the curtains were drawn tightly, preventing any outside light from filtering in. The door automatically closed behind him.

He observed her nervously shifting eyes and wringing hands.

QUENCH MY THIRST / 39

She was an attractive woman. Slim of build, smooth tan complexion, and small waist. Her breasts were rising and falling quickly with her sharp, short breathing. He, too, began to wonder why she called him, but then he stopped himself. He never knew what drove women to call him. He just complied with all reasonable requests. After all, that's what they paid him for.

"I'll still pay you. But I've changed my mind," she explained haltingly.

"Are you sure?" he asked kindly. "We can go very slowly if that would make it more comfortable for you."

Paige finally looked up into his warm brown eyes. He was an extremely handsome man, and it had been a very long time since a man touched her in any way. She longed to feel his body next to hers, if just for a short while. "I don't want to sound stupid, but could we just get in the bed and be close for a while. If that's okay?" she asked timidly.

"Sure, whatever you want," he said, resisting the urge to check his watch.

"I—I've never done anything like this before. When do I pay you? Now?" she asked, reaching for her purse.

"You know what my fee is. My preference is for you to leave it on the table by the door in an envelope. I will collect it on my way in or out as I see fit. I prefer we not pass cash between us. It sullies the mood of our afternoon. If we are to do business together, there must be a modicum of trust between us. I should not feel it necessary to count the money while I am with you. It cheapens you, and it cheapens me. If you were ever to shortchange me, then simply do not call me again," he stated quietly.

"Okay, I'm sorry," she said, putting her purse back on the dresser.

"Since this is our first time together, I will need a little time to learn your preferences. Would you like my clothes on or off while I am in bed with you today?"

"Off, please, except for your . . ." she stammered, blushing profusely.

"I understand," he interrupted and began removing his shirt.

She felt like a voyeur watching him as he peeled off his shirt and sleeveless T-shirt he wore under it. She stared intently as he pulled it over his head to reveal a caramel six-pack and hairless rock-hard chest. His pectorals jumped as he raised his arms above his head, releasing the shirt. Small brown nipples capped each solid breast. She began to feel the familiar tingling sensation in her loins.

Trevor was used to women watching him undress and was proud of his physique. He worked hard to keep it this way. His hands moved to the belt buckle, and she continued to stare as he unbuckled his belt and then unzipped his pants.

Still feeling like a voyeur watching a strip show, Paige turned away. Embarrassed by the hunger, which must have been evident in her eyes, she busied herself with pulling back the spread and cover on the bed.

She looked up to see him standing next to the bed in his briefs. How long had it been since she had seen a man in this state of undress? Three years at least, she thought. His thighs were strong and muscled. Seeing the large bulge at his crotch, she got weak in the knees.

"Are you going to change?" he asked.

"Yes, I'll be right back," she said as she walked quickly into the bathroom and closed the door behind her. Her breathing was quick and shallow, and she was once again gripped with fear. It took her a few more minutes to gather her wits again as she leaned her hands on the edge of the sink and closed her eyes. "You can do this," she said quietly, picturing the handsome stranger waiting patiently for her in the other room. Uncertain of this step she was taking, but determined to go through with it, she nervously slipped out of her slacks and pulled her sweater over her head. She retrieved the thin nylon gown from the counter and pulled it down over her head. She chose this gown because the thick straps would conceal her brassiere underneath. It was thin but not sheer. She checked her reflection in the mirror and adjusted the prosthesis in the left breast cup. Taking a deep breath, she opened the door and returned to the bedroom.

He was in the bed leaning back against the headboard. If her granny-style gown surprised him, he gave no indication. He pulled back the top sheet so she could crawl in beside him. Tentatively she scooted closer to him in the bed until her skin touched his bare thigh. He reached out and pulled her into the crook of his arm. Slowly, testing the feel of him, she nestled her head in the little niche of his shoulder and placed her hand on his chest. She found it firm yet baby smooth. She raked her fingers lightly across his chest, enjoying the sensation under her fingers. She sighed deeply as she snuggled in closer to him. She breathed in his scent, clean with a subtle hint of cologne.

He glanced over her head at the clock on the end table. He'd been here thirty minutes already. Usually by this time he was deep between a woman's thighs, and she was screaming like a banshee. At this pace he knew there wouldn't be any of that today.

"Is this okay?" he asked.

"This is perfect," she mused.

Tentatively his fingers began caressing her back. His hand lightly brushed across the fastening of her brassiere. He felt her immediately stiffen in his arms.

"I'm sorry," he said, realizing something was not quite right here. He assumed she was a virgin and thought it might have been the reason for her strange behavior. But why was she wearing a bra? He moved his hand back up to her shoulder.

"I guess you think I'm weird or something?" she said sadly, slipping back into her shell.

"No, I think you're frightened—very beautiful, by the way,

but very frightened. Do you want to tell me why?" he asked
with concern. He wondered if perhaps she'd been raped. He
couldn't put his finger on the cause of her fear.

"I'm not beautiful," she said adamantly. "Not anymore."
Tears welled up in her eyes.

He felt the wetness from her tears as they fell onto his chest.
She didn't even look at him during the exchange. He lifted her
off his chest so she was sitting up and facing him. "What do
you mean?" he asked softly.

"I haven't been beautiful since the surgery, since they took
my breast," she blurted out and began to cry.

He wasn't prepared for that admission. A rape victim, a virgin—he could handle that. He'd handled it before. But this was
different. This woman was beyond fragile, and what he did
now would affect her psyche for years to come. "You're still a
beautiful woman. You are more than the sum total of your
breasts," he said as he pulled her back onto his shoulder.

"Jamal didn't think so. He left me because he couldn't deal
with it," she said angrily.

Once again Trevor found himself in the position of having
to fix some other man's screw up. He placed his hand under her
chin and raised her face to his. Tenderly he kissed her. Her lips
were salty from her tears. She responded slowly to his kiss. It
had been so long. He deepened the kiss, flicking her lips with
his tongue. She opened her mouth to accept his probing tongue.
She was growing moist as her body responded to him. Normally
he would have reached across to caress her breast, but without
staring he wasn't sure which one was missing. He didn't want
to make her uncomfortable so he placed his free hand on her
flat stomach instead. Sliding her hand down his stomach, she
felt the top of his briefs; unable to stop herself, she placed her
hand against his organ through the cotton briefs. It was not erect.
Disappointed, she pushed away from him.

"I don't excite you either," she accused.

"Yes, you do. But you don't want this right now. And I don't think it would be a good idea to rush into this. I only have a little time left with you today," he explained.

"But how come you're not . . ." she asked. Jamal had always gotten an erection from kissing her, and he'd stopped getting an erection after the surgery.

"Because I'm not fifteen, and this is what adults call control. Don't worry, I won't disappoint you," he said easily. He smiled as he climbed out of the bed. She sat there looking forlorn and lost. He leaned back over the bed and kissed her again. "Next time," he said. He collected his clothes and walked into the bathroom. She climbed out of bed and hastily retrieved his fee from her purse and put it on the corner of the dresser. Today she did not have an envelope; next time she would be prepared. Next time, she thought. Yes, she'd ventured this far; there would be a next time.

He emerged from the bathroom and headed for the door. Smoothly collecting his fee, he shoved the cash into his pocket. Turning at the door, he looked back at her. "Call me when you're ready," he said.

"What's your name? Can I know your name?" she called to him.

"My name is Steve," Trevor replied and closed the door behind him.

4

Sister Jenkins had a standing appointment on the third Wednesday of every month. Trevor rang her doorbell at eleven o'clock at night, and he was on time as usual. Denise never allowed him in through the front door. He was required to drive his car around to the back of the house and enter through the kitchen door. She was undoubtedly afraid her neighbors might see him and begin to ask questions. He could hear her heels clicking on the steps as she made her way down the short narrow stairwell leading to the door. She opened the door and retreated into the kitchen to allow him to enter the house. This night she was dressed in a long white satin gown. A lone strap crossed over her left shoulder. Her right shoulder was bare. The dress dipped daringly across her large, firm bosom. Nipping in across her flat stomach, it flared out again at her hips. A thigh-high split in the right side revealed a peek at her thick thighs.

The lady spares no expense on her clothing, he thought as he started up the steps into the kitchen. He started to turn toward the bedroom in the back of the house where he usually spent his time with her, but she grabbed his hand and pulled him toward the front of the house. Puzzled, he followed her lead.

The drapes were drawn in the living room. Dozens of candles were lit along the fireplace mantel and strewn around the end and coffee tables. The strong aroma of vanilla musk filled the air. He set his bag down on the floor and looked at Denise. In the flickering light of the candles she did not look half bad, more feminine than usual.

She pointed to the grand piano in the far corner of the room. He raised his eyebrow at her quizzically. Surely she did not think he was going to make love to her on top of that piano. Women had the wildest imaginations sometimes. He would have to put this as delicately as he could. She was a very large woman, and the weight of the two of them on top of that piano could be a disaster waiting to happen.

"Honey, I am not Richard Gere, and you are not Julia Roberts. If we get on top of that piano, the legs will break like Pixy Stix," he cautioned.

"No, they won't. That's a good strong piano, and I want you to make love to me just like they did in the movie," she said sternly.

"It's up to you," Trevor replied and turned away from her. Quietly he began unbuttoning his shirt, silently praying the piano would take the strain, but there was no way in hell he was picking up her big ass and putting her on top of it.

"Wait!" Denise said, moving around to stand in front of him. She placed her hands over his to stop his progress. Pulling him over to the piano seat, she started to finish unbuttoning his shirt. She began planting wet kisses on his neck as she worked his shirt free of his pants. Diligently working on her fantasy, she unbuckled his belt and eased her hand inside his trousers.

Trevor could feel his manhood stiffening in response to her eager touch. He would give her what she was paying for. He placed his hands on her waist. The gown was satiny and slippery to his touch. He worked methodically, running his hands up and down her sides from hip to just under her armpits; delicately raking his fingertips along her skin through the flowing fabric.

Denise was growing hot and eager, her breathing quick and shallow as his lips fastened onto her neck. His breath was hot and moist in her ear as he sucked her earlobe. Pulling away from him, she feverishly pushed his trousers down off his hips. She gazed longingly at his rigid member jutting forward against the thin fabric of his silk briefs.

Trevor began nipping softly at her collarbone as he slipped the strap off her shoulder. His lips followed the line of the falling gown as it slipped lower on her bosom. The rigid tips of her large breasts held the soft fabric in place, not allowing it to fall. With each heaving breath the fabric rose and fell but stayed in place, covering her breasts. Deftly he cupped his hands under her arms and then inserted his hands in the sides of the gown and pushed it down off her breasts. Her breasts were like giant orbs of firm brown flesh. She stood naked to the waist before him. He cupped one breast in both hands and brought it to his mouth, teasing her nipple with his tongue.

Denise could feel the liquid moisture dripping between her thighs. If he touched her there, she knew she would be unable to contain the scream, which was burgeoning in her throat.

Determined to give her as much of her fantasy as he could, Trevor pushed back the piano seat and moved Denise to stand in front of him at the piano. The cover was closed over the ivory keys.

She could feel the cold rigid wood against her butt cheeks as Trevor slipped his hand into the side split of her gown. Expertly he found the wet throbbing bulb and stroked it lightly. Denise's orgasmic scream pierced his ear as her breathing became more ragged and she went limp against his chest. Continuing to stroke her clitoris, Trevor slipped out of his boxers.

Standing on tiptoe, she tried to move away from his insistent fingers, unwittingly easing herself up onto the piano-key cover.

She gazed hungrily at him and reached out to touch his erect penis.

He gently removed her hand from his shaft and placed a condom in it.

"Dress me," he said huskily, latching onto her heaving breast with his mouth.

Feeling the wet juices beginning to run down her legs, Denise clumsily took the condom from his hand and unwrapped it. Fighting the weakness in her knees, she slid the condom onto the tip of his penis and began the process of unrolling it up the length of his shaft. She'd never done this before and would never have imagined how exciting it was to watch the silken skin disappear inside the latex casing, knowing full well the length of it would soon be disappearing inside her.

Trevor moved the piano seat closer to the piano and instructed Denise to raise one leg onto the stool. With the stool as leverage he was able to ease her buttocks into a seated position on the piano keys and enter her from a standing position.

Ignoring the discomfort of her position on the piano, she relished the feel of him inside her. Wrapping her free leg around his waist, she accepted the pain of the unyielding wood against her back as she pushed forward, driving him deeper inside. His hands clasped firmly onto her buttocks, holding her aloft while he rhythmically stroked in and out of her body.

He admired her strength. He knew she was uncomfortable, but she was taking every inch he had to offer. She was as strong as a bull. She was a large woman, but her skin was taut and firm. Her stomach was flat, her hips wide, and she possessed firm, round buttocks. Nothing on Denise jiggled; daily workouts made sure of this.

Feeling her orgasm again, he eased her down off the piano and led her down the hallway to the back bedroom they always used. Denise followed silently behind him. She stopped just inside the doorway and looked at him as he stood next to the bed waiting for her. His shirt was completely unbuttoned, and he was naked from the waist down except for a fresh condom, which she'd never even seen him put on. Such a handsome specimen of African-American manhood, and he was waiting for her. She smiled at the thought. *He's waiting to make love to me again.*

Trevor studied the play of emotions on her face. Denise was a walking, breathing contradiction. She wanted a man as a permanent fixture in her life, yet she couldn't yield the inevitable control over her life she assumed having one would take. If she gave herself a break, she would make a fine wife and mother. But she was too hard on herself and those around her. So she paid for the fantasy instead. He held out his hand to her. "Come on, sweetheart," he said and invited her to join him.

She smiled demurely and started toward him. Her large breasts swayed naturally with the sexy roll of her wide, rounded hips. As she started across the room, her gaze fell upon a framed picture on the opposite wall. She looked from the picture to the man who waited at her bedside, and her fantasy came alive. He was home; her man was home.

She pressed her breasts against his bare chest and laid her face on his shoulder. She breathed deeply of the essence of him and was warmed by his scent.

He nestled his face in her long, thick hair and cupped her jaw in the palm of his hand, lightly running his tongue along the outline of her ear. With his other hand he caressed her large buttocks and pressed the length of his manhood against her belly. Small asses might be cute to look at, but he liked Denise's ass. It was large, sturdy, and made a great cushion in the bed. When he pounded her deeply, her buoyant ass gave her a boost right back up against his dick. The throbbing in his dick got harder just thinking about the ride he was about to take.

Without further delay he got into the bed and pulled her onto it with him. He eased into the comfort of her soft, rounded curves. Her body enveloped his, and he rested comfortably on her double-D-cup breasts before pushing deeply inside her hidden passion.

Denise emitted a deeply satisfied sigh as she matched her movements to his. She rocked him back and forth, using the strength of her stomach muscles and buttocks to create a rolling sensation. She preferred the missionary position because it allowed her to watch her partner's expressions. She'd practiced and perfected her own special hip roll for maximum pleasure.

Trevor let her take control because that's what she paid him for, and he enjoyed the feeling of free-falling into her deep sea whenever she hit the perfect wave. He massaged one of her breasts and brought it to his lips, covering the large brown nipple with his mouth. His tongue encircled the sensitive button tip sensuously, licking and sucking alternately.

Denise's breathing quickened, and her heart beat faster. His warm, wet tongue on her nipple was creating a raging storm in her body, and she knew an explosion was near. Her legs tightened around his thighs, and she gripped his ass cheeks with her long nails.

He felt the change in her body and immediately picked up the pace. He pumped faster, longer, and deeper inside her body until her rumbling moan signaled her climax had been reached. This signaled him to release his own cum deep inside his protective sheath.

Five minutes later he was back in the living room collecting his clothes off the floor. He checked his watch. Fifteen minutes over. He would have to be more careful next time. Clients weren't allowed extra time unless they planned it in advance and paid for it. He wasn't too worried about Denise, though. Usually she didn't even keep him the full ninety minutes anyway. He dressed quickly and headed out the kitchen to the side door. His envelope was waiting on the side table as always. He stuffed it into his pocket and closed the door behind him.

* * *

Denise lay in the queen-size bed staring at the ceiling above her. The ceiling fan was still and the room eerily quiet after his departure. She stared vacantly at the white blades of the fan with the gold-accented tips, the tiny ball chain dangling beneath. She switched her focus to the E.C. Wright framed print on the far bedroom wall—the handsome Black Union soldier leaning down from his horse to plant a kiss on the upturned mouth of his black wife as he prepared to journey to war. Denise had loved this picture from the moment she'd first seen it. She was deeply touched by the handsome ultramasculine soldier heading off to war, stopping for a tender moment to say good-bye to his wife.

The perfect man, the man she'd never found. The embodiment of what she wanted was only a figment of someone else's imagination. She'd often felt she was born in the wrong century. Not that she would have wanted to have been born a slave, but certainly in the after years she could have seen herself as the mistress of the plantation. Resplendent in the glorious gowns of the period with a manor-style home decorated with the finest artwork and collectibles. Yes, she could even see herself being waited on by servants. Even the idea of black servants did not disturb her dream; after all, she would be a good mistress to her help.

She shifted her position in the bed again and thought about the stunning specimen of a man who had just left her. She could picture him in the soldier's uniform sitting upright on the horse, his sword holstered and his rifle at the ready, his strong steed dancing lightly beneath him as he used the strong muscles of his thighs to control the snuffling beast. There she was beside him in her fabulous pink gown, cinched at the waist and puffing out over the crinoline underneath. Her hair would be swept up in a French chignon, with little wisps escaping, creating a subtle softness to her face. She saw it all in her mind's eye with a matte finish; painted with an artist's brush. This was what she desired most but gave up looking for many years ago.

She rolled off the bed and walked to the bedroom door. Turning back into the room, she looked longingly at the print once more. Brushing an errant tear from her cheek, she closed the door and headed down the hallway toward her bathroom.

5

Naomi sat at the kitchen table reading the local entertainment newspaper Greg had picked up at a free newsstand on their last trip into town. Greg always liked to see what was happening around town. She flipped it to the personals section out of curiosity and began perusing some of the ads. While reading the *Women Seeking Men* section, her attention was drawn to an ad that read *Handy Men, Inc—Specialists in cobweb removal, pipe cleaning, lubrication, and rejuvenation of unused facilities. We promise discreet, quick, responsive resolution to your in-home woes. Call now: 312-555-HMAN.* She naively thought the ad was misplaced in the personals section. Shaking her head and sighing deeply, she closed the paper and got up to make a pot of coffee.

Naomi was meeting Ida, her best friend, for lunch at the mall later in the afternoon. In the meantime, there was housework that needed to be done. The ad kept popping into her head as she thought of a few minor repairs around the house that Greg had not had a chance to take care of. An hour later she returned to the kitchen and cut the ad out of the paper and stuck it into her pocket. A handyman might just do the trick, she thought. It would take some of the stress off Greg and give him more time to relax when he was home from work.

Ida was waiting for her at the Nordstrom entrance to the Woodfield Mall. They exchanged a greeting hug and proceeded to the housewares department. Ida was redoing her master bath and had enlisted Naomi's assistance with the decorating. An hour and a half later, they were both loaded down with new towels, facecloths, and matching accessories.

They made their way across the mall to the Rainforest Café for lunch. Their lunch discussion centered on Ida's twins, who were in first grade this year and were spending a full day away from her. She said she found it so freeing to have the little ones out of her hair for several blissful hours every day. So her first project was to redecorate all the bathrooms in the house.

Naomi mentioned she wanted to get some work done around the house as well and pulled the ad from her pocketbook to show Ida and ask her what she thought.

"I found this in the paper this morning. I was hoping to get some work done around the house. Do you think I should call them?" she asked.

Ida took the ad and looked it over carefully. A small frown puckered her brow.

"Where did you get this?" she asked.

"From the newspaper," Naomi replied innocently.

"It reads a little strange. What paper was it? What section of the paper?" Ida asked, turning the paper over in her hand and perusing the reverse side of the ad. It didn't look like the *Chicago Sun-Times* to her, and there was half a naked woman on the back.

"That paper you get free on the street in those newsstand boxes on the corner. Greg picked it up. I think they misplaced it in the personals section. I almost didn't see it. I don't know how they expect to drum up business that way," she replied.

Ida burst out laughing. Naomi, not sure what the joke was, became embarrassed.

"What's so funny?" she asked.

"Oh, Lucy. I love you," Ida replied between her tears of laughter.

Naomi knew when Ida called her Lucy it meant she'd done something dumb. Ida loved Lucille Ball, and while Naomi tried not to become offended by the nickname, she always inadvertently found out she'd made a huge gaff when Ida called her Lucy.

"What did I do this time?" Naomi asked, exasperated.

"Honey, you found this in the personals. Now I won't even ask what you were doing reading the personals, but . . . here, read it again," Ida said and attempted to hand the little cutout back to Naomi.

"I read it already. I don't know what you're talking about," she said, pushing the paper back at Ida.

"I'll bet this was in the section of women looking for men, am I right?" Ida asked.

"Yes, I think it was," Naomi replied quietly.

"Okay, look here where it says 'pipe cleaning, lubrication, and rejuvenation of unused facilities'." Ida pointed to the lines in the ad.

"All right," Naomi said and looked up, puzzled.

"'Discreet, quick, responsive resolution to your in-home woes'?" Ida continued.

"Okay, what am I missing?" Naomi asked.

"How regularly does Greg clean your pipes?" Ida asked seriously.

"Jeez, I don't think he's touched them in years," Naomi replied with equal seriousness. She couldn't remember the last time Greg went up on the roof to clean the gutters.

"Naomi, you clearly do not understand what I am talking

about. So let me be blunt. When was the last time you and Greg had sex?" Ida asked boldly.

Naomi flushed a deep red. How did they get to the topic of sex, especially between her and Greg? It was not a topic she liked to discuss, even with Ida.

"Ugh, last week. Why? What does that have to do with anything?" she whispered, highly agitated by where this conversation was going.

"This is a sex ad, Naomi. This type of handyman services your sexual pipes and needs—nothing else. Do you understand now?" Ida said slowly for effect.

"Oh!" Naomi said, clutching her hand to her chest. With her other hand she snatched the ad back and crumpled it up. "How could I be so stupid?"

"You're not stupid. You just haven't been exposed to things like this. So you don't see it for what it really is. You're just too innocent. Sad to say," Ida counseled.

Naomi stared down at her plate for a long time and said nothing. Slowly she picked up her napkin and dabbed at the corners of her eyes. Ida was shocked to see her so upset over something so silly.

"Is there something you want to talk about? Is everything okay at home?" Ida asked.

"Yes, it's fine. I just feel really dumb right now," Naomi lied. She couldn't get over the fact that she felt drawn to that ad. Was it a subliminal message? Had she really been looking for something more than housecleaning when she'd cut out the ad?

"I'm sorry. I didn't mean to make fun of you, really I didn't. You were just too sheltered as a kid, I swear. I bet Greg was your first?"

"Actually, he wasn't." Naomi smiled, a little proud of the fact she'd experienced sex with more than one man.

"Well, he must have been the best. 'Cause you married him," Ida said pointedly.

Naomi just smiled again. "Of course," she replied as she regained her composure. She wouldn't discuss her dismal sex life with even her best friend. She wouldn't shame her husband that way. She loved him, and it was all that mattered.

"Let's get out of here. I've got to be home by two thirty to pick up the kids," Ida said, gathering her packages and purse.

Naomi nonchalantly knocked the little crumpled ball of paper off the table and onto the floor as she reached for her purse. While picking her own packages off the floor, she scooped up the little ball and dropped it inside her shopping bag, hoping Ida didn't notice.

Naomi put on her Johnny Gill CD while she did her housework. Her hair tied up in a scarf, wearing gym shorts and a tank top, she danced around the living room, imagining herself at a club, shaking and gyrating to the music. She dusted the end tables and rearranged the magazines on the coffee table. As she reached for the vacuum, she heard Johnny singing the red-dress song. She stopped and closed her eyes. Allowing her body to sway with the music, she saw herself in a sexy red dress and Johnny singing to her and running his hands along her body. She twirled around the room like a jazz dancer, creating a romantic scene in her mind. By the time the song was over, she was hot and horny.

Greg was upstairs in the office working. She took off her scarf and fluffed her short curls. She smiled as she imagined herself accosting Greg at his desk. Skipping up the stairs, she headed for his office. A quick glance revealed him intent on his computer screen. She entered his office, walked up to him, and kissed him on the mouth. She pushed his chair away from the desk and climbed into his lap.

"What's this all about?" he asked, laughing. He reached over and clicked off the screen he'd been looking at.

"What are you doing?" she asked, nibbling on his neck.

"Browsing. Nothing particular," he replied.

"Do you think there is something else you might want to do?" she asked.

"Hmmm, maybe there is," he said, joining in the mood. He assisted her off his lap and slipped out of his sweats and briefs. His thickened rod was already firm and ready for action.

She dropped her shorts and panties and pushed him back down in the chair. Eagerly, she climbed onto his lap and inserted his rod inside her body. Smiling, she adjusted her position while he grabbed hold of her buttocks to keep her from falling. She wrapped her arms around his neck and started moving back and forth on his groin. He nibbled her neck while she moved. Still engrossed in her own fantasy, she started to rock deeper and more aggressively. Working steadily, she was enjoying the feel of his body inside hers.

Suddenly his fingers tightened on her buttocks. And he let out a loud, howling groan. She raised her head from his neck and looked at the wall on the other side of the room. With a blank expression on her face, she kept her face averted. If he looked at her she would not be able to hide her disappointment. This was not how her fantasy was supposed to end. She wasn't even worked up yet.

"I'm sorry, baby. You hit that spot again," he said sorrowfully. He knew she hadn't climaxed. It embarrassed him that he could not hold off his ejaculation. "Maybe I should see the doctor and get some of those pills," he offered.

Naomi climbed down from his lap and collected her shorts off the floor. "You're too young to need Viagra, Greg," she replied. As she turned to leave, he reached out and grabbed her hand.

"I love you, honey," he said. The naked emotion in his eyes implored her to understand.

"I know, Greg. I love you, too," she said and walked out the door. "Damn Johnny Gill," she muttered to herself as she walked into the bathroom. She locked the door and turned on the water in the shower stall. After she removed her shirt and bra, she stepped into the stall under the jet stream of hot water. The water rained down over her head and body. Her nerves were on edge, and the usually relaxing spray was not providing relief. She loved Greg, but his lack of control had become more and more frustrating. She tried not to think about sex too often, but then there were days like today when her body wanted it and she couldn't resist the temptation to seduce her husband.

"I should have known better," she grumbled and removed the mesh sponge from the shower rack and poured a generous amount of scented gel onto the surface. Rubbing it across her skin, she worked up a good lather and began to wash. Her strokes across her body were angry and hard as if to wash away the desires of the flesh. She scrubbed her arms and legs vigorously. As she stepped under the spray to wash away the suds, she caught sight of her naked reflection through the glass doors. She stared at the reflection as if it wasn't her own image. The woman in the mirror stared back at her for a moment and then began to move the soapy mesh sponge across her breasts. She stared vacantly at Naomi as she continued to lather her body in slow, sensuous circles. The trail of suds covered her breasts and continued down her midsection toward her navel and then disappeared between her legs. As the mesh sponge passed over her sensitive clitoris, it sent a message to her brain. It said *Touch me again.* Naomi heard the sharp intake of her own breath as the message registered loud and clear. Suddenly the mysterious woman was gone, and she stared at her own image in the mirror. She dropped the sponge and used her hand to massage the raw ache between her legs. Her eyes closed as she leaned against the shower wall and applied more pressure. The muscles of her abdomen contracted as she bent forward in response to the tiny orgasms passing through her groin. The shower spray pelted her hunched shoulders. She continued to massage her clit firmly but still hadn't reached a good climax. Her body ached painfully with unfulfilled desire, and she couldn't wrap her mind around a decent sexy thought or vision. She just wanted to come, to give it all up in a blazing climax. To let her body flush away all its pent-up feelings in one amazing rush. It wasn't happening. She was rubbing herself raw, and nothing was happening. Desperate, she snatched the goosenecked showerhead down from the wall. Changing the jet spray to pulse, she used one hand to expose her clitoris and the other to point the shower spray directly on it. Her body jerked violently in response to the rapid stream of water pellets pounding her tender and raw clit. She cried aloud as the force of her orgasm shoved her back against the shower wall. She snatched her facecloth off the towel rack and thrust it in her mouth, muffling her moaning cries as she continued to direct the stream at her exposed and tender clit until the pain became unbearable. She leaned weakly against the cold tiles of the shower as anger suffused her body. She was angry at him for forcing her to punish her body this way and angry at herself for being so mentally weak. She was saddened by the knowledge that her only sexual release was found at the end of a showerhead. She turned off the water and returned the showerhead to its holder on the wall. Drained and emotionally distraught, she sat down on the shower seat and rested her head in her hands. Her pubic area was inflamed, and she couldn't cross her legs without pain. She didn't think she could take much more of this. As a young woman, she felt she needed more than Greg could give her. *Tomorrow*, she thought, *tomorrow I make the call.*

Naomi waited until Greg left for work the following morning. She stood by the living room window and watched his car drive off down the street. She walked back to her bedroom and retrieved the tiny piece of paper from the inside zipper pocket of her purse. She sat down on the side of the bed and wondered if it was too early to call. Slowly she picked up the receiver and punched in the numbers. After the third ring, a man answered.

"Handy Men, Inc," he said.

"I'd like to make an appointment," she said nervously. Her palms were beginning to sweat, and she rubbed her free hand along her thigh.

"What day of the week?" he asked.

"Uh, I didn't . . ." she said. She realized she hadn't thought this out very well.

"First time?" he asked.

"Yes."

"This is what you do. You figure out what day or days of the week are best for you. Pick a time, preferably after five. Plan for an hour and a half. Secure a location, and call us back. By the way, the fee for the service is five hundred dollars. Call us back when you're ready," he said and hung up.

"Five hundred dollars," she repeated aloud. "Five hundred dollars?" The man on the phone had been very pleasant. His voice was nice, but five hundred dollars was a lot of money. How could she justify spending so much money at one time in her own mind? She also didn't think about where she would meet this man. Apparently it was up to her to secure a room, because she wasn't stupid enough to have him come to her house. More money, she thought. She groaned as she got up from the bed. She would have to think about this some more.

6

It was lunchtime, and Marissa collected her lunch bag from under her desk and made her way to the employee cafeteria. After heating her Tupperware container of leftovers, she joined a few of her coworkers at one of the tables. The women were deeply engrossed in a sexual conversation. Margie and Thelma, two other phone reps, were discussing different positions and which they liked best. Marissa listened but did not want to get involved in this particular topic. She was surprised to learn these women actually seemed to like sex. Marissa didn't care for it and couldn't imagine going out of her way to get a man's attention.

"Marissa, you haven't said anything yet. We need a tiebreaker vote. What's your favorite position—missionary or doggy style?" Margie asked suggestively. Thelma turned to Marissa to await her answer.

She kept her head bowed toward her plate. She didn't care for Margie putting her on the spot that way. Now they were waiting for her to say something. Without looking up, she mumbled, "Sex is overrated."

"Overrated?" Thelma asked, laughing. "Girl, what are you talking about?"

"I just don't think it's all you are making it out to be. It's all about the man anyway," she mumbled and shoved some food into her mouth so it gave her an excuse not to say any more.

Margie and Thelma exchanged quizzical looks. They knew Marissa was married, and she did seem like a timid creature, but this was the new millennium, and women were in control of their sexuality.

"Marissa, sex is not all about what a man wants anymore. Don't you read books or magazines even? Women have been getting their groove on for years now," Thelma said.

The panicked look on Marissa's face caused Margie to interject quickly. "Look, nobody's gonna tell your husband anything. This is a woman thing, girl. You get to have your needs satisfied, too. There are some men out there who don't care about their woman's satisfaction, but you have to tell him what pleases you and what you want."

Marissa realized she'd opened Pandora's box with her comments, and it was too late to pretend she hadn't said them. Maybe these women could give her some advice on how to make sex better with Toby. He always complained she was boring in bed and she should be grateful he even had sex with her. If she were better at it, then maybe he would be nicer to her.

"My husband says as long as I please him and make him happy, then I should be happy. I am supposed to get my pleasure from his enjoyment," she explained.

"No, no, and no," Thelma said emphatically. "He tells you that so you won't want to enjoy it. It's a control thing. He probably isn't all that good. And forgive me for saying so, but if you really got your world rocked, it would be all over for him. 'Cause obviously he can't take you there."

"Sex is a good thing, girl. It's fun for the man and the woman," Margie chimed in. "Have you ever looked at another man and thought what it might be like to climb on top of him and . . ." She shoved her hand in her mouth and pretended she was biting it as she twirled her head around and growled for effect.

Thelma reached over and nearly shoved Margie off her chair. "Stop it! You'll end up scaring the kid. I'm going to bring you a magazine tomorrow, and I want you to read some of the stories in it. Then we can talk some more. I gotta get back to work. To-morrow," she said as she put her containers back inside her lunch bag and pointed at Marissa.

Marissa nodded her head in agreement. She was curious about the sexual pleasures these women spoke of. Her mother never spoke of sex with her, and she had been a virgin when she met Toby. All she knew she learned from Toby. He told her what pleased him but never asked what she wanted. She didn't know he was supposed to.

The following day Thelma dropped a couple of magazines on Marissa's desk. One was a magazine of romance stories, an-other was a magazine of erotic tales, and the third was a *Playgirl* magazine. Marissa quickly shoved them in the top drawer of her desk. Between calls she would peer inside the drawer but couldn't see very much. She waited eagerly for her first break. Slipping the *Playgirl* into her purse, she headed for the seclusion of the ladies' room. She breathed a deep sigh of relief to find the restroom empty. She walked quickly to the last stall and slipped inside. Stealthily, though no one could see her, she removed the magazine from her purse. Seated on the toilet she quietly flipped through the pages. She was afraid at first to look at the naked men in the pictures. Toby was the only man she'd ever seen naked. These men were handsome and boldly displaying their genitals. Her fingers lightly touched the images of their bodies on the page. As she continued to slowly peruse the pages, she began to feel an unfamiliar tingling between her thighs. Embarrassed and alarmed by the sensations, she closed the magazine firmly and put it back in her purse. She glanced at her watch. She was late.

It seemed an interminable amount of time between her first break and lunch. Finally the clock showed twelve thirty. She added the other two magazines to the one in her purse, collected her lunch, and headed for the cafeteria.

Thelma and Margie were waiting for her at the table. She greeted them both and sat down. "Well?" Margie asked. She couldn't wait to hear what Marissa thought.

Marissa felt the heat rise in her cheeks. "I didn't get to look at them all. I was busy this morning," she explained as she pulled the magazines from her purse and put them on the table.

Thelma reached across the table and picked up the magazine of erotic tales. She flipped through a couple of pages to a particularly hot story and set it in front of Marissa. "Read this page," she said.

Marissa put down her sandwich and began reading at the top of the page. It was a scene of a man and woman in a hot tub. The scene was very detailed and descriptive, from the moment their bathing suits came off in the hot tub to the moment the woman screamed in ecstasy at the end. Marissa squirmed in her seat. Why was her body reacting this way? Her mind wandered to the photos of naked men. She imagined them in this story. She couldn't stop the images from crowding her mind. Her body ached in places it never ached before. Agitated, she closed the magazine.

"What's wrong?" Margie asked. She was disturbed by the look on Marissa's face. This was all in fun, an attempt to show her what she was missing. Instead she looked sad and unhappy.

"Nothing," Marissa replied and shoved her uneaten sandwich back into her lunch bag. Her appetite was gone. She was smart enough to know this story excited her. Just like the woman in the hot tub who craved fulfillment, her body wanted something, too. Her body was talking to her. "Can I keep these a little while longer?" she asked.

"Sure," Thelma replied. "I've read them a hundred times. As

a matter of fact, why don't you keep them? I get new ones every month anyway."

"Thanks," Marissa said as she put them back in her purse and collected her lunch bag. She returned the magazines to her desk drawer. There was no way she could take them home.

Over the next several days, Marissa spent her lunch hours alone in the seclusion of her car. She read the romantic ones with mild sensual stories and she read the more graphic erotic tales. She finally realized Toby was a selfish lover. He did not care for her pleasure at all. Marissa wanted to experience the reckless abandon the women in these stories experienced. She wanted someone to take her to the heights of passion, and she did not want it to be Toby.

Two months later, Marissa sat nervously in a hotel room and waited for a perfect stranger to show up. She was dressed seductively in a filmy black negligee. To prepare for the evening, she'd taken a leisurely bath and perfumed her body in all the secret places she'd been reading about. Scented candles were placed strategically around the room. There was an open bottle of wine on the dresser. She'd already drunk one glass to settle her nerves.

Toby was out of town on business. He'd checked in earlier in the evening and told her he was going out with a few clients. She forwarded the house phone calls to her cell phone just in case, but she doubted he would call again tonight. It would never occur to him she might leave the house. The LCD on the clock showed 9:29. A soft knock sounded at the door.

Her hands began to shake. She rose from the bed and clenched and unclenched her fists to stop the shaking. She peered through the peephole in the door. There was a man on the other side, but the magnifying glass distorted his image. She took a deep breath and opened the door.

Oh, my, she thought as her heartbeat accelerated with excitement. He was better looking than the men in those magazines, and so tall. He was wearing an open-collared, white silk, button-down shirt, tan trousers, and brown shoes.

"Hi," she said breathlessly and allowed him to enter the room. Trevor surveyed the candles, wine, and filmy negligee. There was a small white envelope on the corner of the dresser. She was obviously ready for the evening. "Hello," he replied. "This is a very romantic setting. Is that what you want? Romance?"

"Yes," she answered and looked away, embarrassed by her desires. She tried to forget she was paying him to be here. Was she supposed to say more? Would she have to tell him what to do? All these questions were filtering through her mind, and she wasn't paying attention to him.

He walked up behind her and slipped his arm around her waist. He lifted her hair from the back of her neck and kissed her nape softly. She smelled good. Slowly he turned her in his arms and brought his mouth down upon hers.

Marissa fought the desire to faint. His mouth was so sweet, and he tasted so good. She eagerly inserted her tongue into his mouth. This oral exploration was new to her. The sensations running up and down her spine were new. She welcomed all feelings.

Trevor's hand lightly cupped her breast through the negligee. Her nipples were erect and craving for attention from his lips. He did not deprive them or her of the glorious sensation of his mouth on their rigid peaks.

Marissa lost herself in her desire for fulfillment. The fact that this man was not her husband didn't matter. Toby never touched her like this. He never turned her body to liquid fire like this man. At this moment, she was all that mattered. What she wanted and was getting right now. She raised her arms as he slowly undressed her by pulling the negligee above her head. With her arms raised in the air, he kissed the firm skin of the inside of her upper arm. Lightly he ran his tongue along the smooth, baby-soft skin.

Marissa's body buckled at the strange sensation. She stood naked before him, but he did not allow her time to dwell on this. His tongue continued down the length of her arm to her wrist. He planted a few soft, feathery kisses there and then more on her fingers. Gently he pulled her fingers into his mouth and sucked them. His mouth was warm and wet. He bent down and scooped her up in his arms and carried her to the bed.

She lay supine in the middle of the bed and watched him as he undressed. His body was gorgeous, and she never thought she would find a man's body attractive. When he slipped out of his boxers, a nervous fluttering of doubt crept back into her mind. She was about to allow this stranger uninhibited access to her body, a body only her husband had touched before.

Trevor joined her on the bed and leaned on one elbow as he placed his hand on her rib cage. He could feel she was tense and nervous. Her eyes were like giant saucers of indecision. His fingers lightly drew circles around her belly button and moved upward toward her heaving breasts.

She fought the insane desire to giggle as he tickled her belly button. Her special place was tingling, and she could feel his naked stick on her leg. *He's going to put that in me,* she thought wildly. *He's going to put that in me. Toby's gonna be so mad.*

He kissed her ear and pulled the soft, fleshy lobe into his mouth. At the same time his hand slid down into the soft, curly hairs protecting her vulva. Expertly parting her nether lips, he brushed the tiny protrusion.

Marissa's body jerked violently at the strange sensation created by his fingers. Instantly she felt unidentifiable moisture between her legs and jumped off the bed.

"Hey," Trevor called to her as she darted away. "You okay?"

"Gotta pee," she mumbled and closed the bathroom door.

She sat down quickly on the toilet to relieve herself, but nothing came out. She rubbed herself with her fingers and they were wet; she smelled her fingers, and they did not smell like pee. *Hmmm*, she thought. *What is this*? Gingerly she slipped and rubbed the same spot he had and got that strange feeling again. Suddenly she remembered the book said something like this was supposed to happen when her body was getting ready for the man to enter her. Or maybe she had just had an orgasm? Had she come that fast? She didn't know. She never had this happen with Toby. He always complained she was too dry. He was always spitting on her so he could shove his thing inside.

Trevor meanwhile was ready to get on with the process. He hadn't planned to be here all day. "Hey, sweetheart, are you coming back to bed?"

She took a deep breath and opened the door sheepishly. She didn't want to appear as naive as she knew she must appear right now. Slowly she climbed back into the bed next to him and lay on her back with her eyes closed. His man stick was rubbing on her thigh again.

"Sweetheart, this is not an execution. I'm here because you called me, remember? Open your eyes," he commanded softly as he began to nibble on her ear again.

She opened her eyes and stared at the ceiling, afraid to look at him. He took her hand and placed it on his stiffening rod. "Look at me," he whispered.

Her eyes moved down to her hand as she opened and closed her fist tentatively around his pulsating dick. She felt his hand move toward her special place again, and she was once again getting tingly and wet. Her grip tightened nervously around his manhood.

He delicately extricated himself from her death grip and positioned himself between her legs. He pushed gently at first, expecting resistance, but her pussy was so slick with her own juice he slipped right in at full mast.

"Oh, my, oh, my," she breathed as her body was suddenly filled with a thick, pulsing fullness.

He began slowly at first, trying to get her to follow a rhythm, but she couldn't, wouldn't, or didn't know how. Finally he placed his hands on her ass and guided the movements of her hips.

"Oh, my, oh, my," she kept murmuring over and over. Her body was screaming, and she couldn't contain all the feelings racing through her. She was hot and flushed. He felt so good. His man stick felt so good sliding in and out of her special place. She couldn't think straight.

He knelt on the bed and pulled her hips up to his thighs. His pace quickened as this position allowed him to pleasure her with long, deep strokes. It was time to wrap things up here. He moistened his fingers and flicked her throbbing clit, at the same time continuing to ply her with deep, fast stroking.

Marissa thrashed wildly in the bed. Her head was about to explode, and she couldn't bear the feelings rushing through her body. "Oh, my god, oh, my god! Sweet Jesus!" she screamed as heat flushed from the top of her head and gushed out of her special place like a wave crashing ashore. She continued to whimper softly as her body collapsed deep into the mattress.

Trevor, who'd timed his own release with hers, smiled to himself. He doubted she'd even realized he'd come. She was a noisy little heifer. He exited the bed as quickly as he could and took a quick shower.

Marissa had a true sexual awakening that afternoon. As she lay reposed in the middle of the bed, exhausted, drained, and thoroughly fucked, tears flowed from her eyes—tears of joy, tears of wonderment, and finally tears of satisfaction. As she watched him walk out the door, she knew she wanted more. She made a decision: she *would* have more of him.

Two hours later Marissa was home cooking dinner when Toby arrived in an unexpectedly cheerful mood. He swooped into the kitchen and grabbed her around the waist. Then he planted a firm kiss right on her astonished open lips. He waved a piece of paper in front of her face and danced a little jig around the kitchen. "I've got great news, Mo," he said.

Stunned by this new Toby, she weighed her words before she spoke, not wanting to break the spell of this moment. "You look so happy, honey. What's the news?"

"First, I got that promotion I been wanting for two years. They finally saw the light and gave me what I deserve. 'Bout damn time, too. And secondly, I get to go to New York for four weeks of training," he said and continued his gleeful dance.

"New York?" she queried. Her mind tried to digest the information. Number one, Toby would be out of her hair for a month. Yippee, hooray for the break. Two, he was sure to get mugged, lost, or possibly end up dead on some New York City street. His dumb country ass had never been out of Bumblefuck, Illinois. She could never even get him to take her into Chicago. He claimed he hated big cities, and now he was happy to go to New York.

"Yeah, New York, baby! We're staying at one of them big hotels in Manhattan. Can you imagine? Me, in New York? Woo-wee! I'm gonna have a good time."

There was only one question left to ask, and she knew he would expect her to ask it. If she didn't, he would get suspicious. With as much feigned sincerity as she could muster, she asked, "Can I go, too? Not for the whole time. I mean, I know we can't afford that, but maybe I could join you for a weekend or something?"

Toby stopped dancing long enough to take a cold, hard look at his wife. Ain't no way in hell he was dragging her along on this trip. His boss even told him it was okay to make plans for her to come up on the weekends, and they would pay for it. But she wasn't about to spoil his escape. He'd been hearing from some of the other guys about all the sweet pussy he could find in New York, and some of it free if you was willing to pay the cost of dinner. Shee-it! He'd been saving up for just this little vacation away from her whiny ass. He tried his best to look disappointed when he replied, "I'm sorry, babe. I did ask about you, 'cause I know you ain't been nowhere neither. But they said not this time, 'cause it was training and all. I gotta really concentrate and learn the job."

She breathed a silent sigh of relief before replying. "I understand, Toby. I want you to do well at this new job. I'm so happy for you. Just be careful in New York, okay?" She gave him a quick hug and then returned to cooking dinner.

A satisfied gleam crossed his face as he headed toward the bedroom. He knew she wouldn't complain; she never did. He was going to the Big Apple for a good time without her.

As Marissa stirred the pasta sauce, her mind drifted back to earlier in the day. Steve was a wonderful lover, and now she knew how an orgasm really felt. His hands were magic, and she was getting moist just thinking about those hands roaming all over her body. Toby turned on the shower in the bathroom, and his off-key baritone could be heard all the way to the kitchen. She'd gone to Chicago all by herself today, and it wasn't nearly as bad as Toby wanted her to believe. She giggled with guilty pleasure. She wondered how many times she could see Steve in the next four weeks.

7

The black stretch limo pulled up to the corner of North Avenue and North Wells Street at two o'clock on a Saturday morning. Trevor emerged from the shadows and climbed in the open door. As usual, Nina was seated in the far corner of the darkened limo. This time she was wearing a shiny spandex dress, which was pulled taut across the tops of her thighs. Her breasts were half exposed over the top of her strapless dress. A Prince song blared from the ten speakers and two subwoofers inside the car. The song was as wild as the noise was deafening.

Trevor could tell she wore no underwear as she delicately fingered her clit and watched him through the burnt-orange spectacles. The smoke-black partition between the driver and the rest of the car remained shut. He felt the car pulling away from the curb as it began its circuit around the city. She's already gotten this party started, he thought, as he began unzipping his jeans. He usually wore something light and easy to get out of, but this was a last-minute job, and he did not have time to be too picky about what to wear. He donned a sleeveless tank and black jeans with loafers.

Nina maintained her position in the corner of the limo, watching him undress through half-closed lids. She removed her hand from her private parts and sensually swirled her tongue around the tips of her fingers.

Trevor's manhood was straining against his briefs in anticipation. He'd barely taken the time to sheath his organ when she sprang like a cat from her corner and pounced on him. Climbing into his lap, she eagerly guided his stiff rod inside her body. Sucking in a deep breath, she adjusted her position and wrapped her arms around his neck. He grabbed her bare buttocks with both hands, stretched his long legs out across the floor of the limo, and relaxed into the seat, allowing her to take control of her pleasure. Nina rocked and gyrated against him for what seemed like eons before she finally reached orgasm. Still wanting more, she pulled the top of her dress down to her waist, exposing her breasts, and thrust one directly in his face, rubbing her nipple across his lips. He obliged, sucking on the peaked tip until she screamed in ecstasy. Pushing away from him, she raised her body off his rigid staff. The condom was wet and dripping with her body juices. She eyed him hungrily and dove down on him. Taking half the shaft in her mouth, she looked up at him as she licked and sucked her own body juices off the condom.

Trevor leaned back, enjoying the sensation of her mouth on his organ. She was in rare form tonight. Probably on something, he thought. She wasn't usually so aggressive, and she looked a little wild. She knelt in the middle of the limo and wiggled out of her dress completely and then tossed it into the corner. Turning her back on him, she presented him with her beautiful behind as she leaned facedown on the opposite seat. Her long black hair cascaded down her back. He knew from past experience with her that she wanted it doggy style. Easing off his seat, he crawled up behind her, reached his arm around her waist, and placed his hand on her mound, lifting her body to his kneeling height. With his other hand he guided his rigid shaft between her thighs. Pushing his full length inside, he heard her sharp cry of pleasure. Rocking and stroking her at the same time, he drove her to several frenzied orgasms before relieving himself.

He lifted her body up onto the seat cushion, where she curled up in a fetal position. He covered her naked body with a blanket from the console. Disposing of the condom in a plastic bag, he quickly put his underwear and jeans back on. He sat silently in the corner of the limo for an additional five minutes. She never spoke with him. It was always the driver who called and made all the arrangements. He was a dick for hire, and her behavior made it crystal clear it was all she required of him. The car stopped, and the glass partition silently rolled down halfway. The driver passed a white envelope to Trevor, and the partition closed again. He climbed out of the car on the corner of North Wells and North Avenue where he'd been picked up and walked toward his parked car.

He climbed into the driver's side and tossed the envelope on the seat. With a slight turn of the key, the Jaguar roared to life. He eased out of his parking space and headed home. Thirty minutes later he pulled into the driveway and hit the remote to open the garage. He was tired—more drained than physically tired. He was growing weary of the performances, of the countless women. He was tired of coming home to an empty house. The first two years had been exciting and fun. He'd put away a lot of money. But ever since Olivia came back into his life, he'd started to view his sideline differently. He was embarrassed by what he did. Not when he was doing it, but the thought of her finding out worried him.

He'd run into her unexpectedly at a café in New Jersey two years ago. It was late in the afternoon, so there were just a few patrons at the outside tables. The conference he was attending had broken for lunch, and he had decided to pass on the buffet offered at the hotel. He'd gone in search of a good deli sand-wich.

As he approached the café, he noticed an attractive young woman engrossed in a magazine while she ate her lunch. Some-thing about her struck him as familiar, but he couldn't see her face hidden beneath a curtain of dark shoulder-length hair. He made his way closer to the table for a better look, and he couldn't believe his luck.

"Olivia?" he asked.

She looked up, and a smile broadened her face as she arose from the table and stepped immediately into his welcoming embrace.

"Trevor, how are you?" she asked, clearly delighted to see him.

"I'm great, even better now that I've seen you. It's been ages. I almost wasn't sure it was you. How long has it been?" Trevor asked.

"Wow, I guess about four or five years. Jeez, you haven't changed a bit, except to get even better looking," she teased. "Have you been working out, because you didn't have all this the last time I saw you," she said as she squeezed his biceps playfully.

"A brother's got to do what a brother's got to do. You know the honeys don't like skimpy men," he replied, flexing as he pulled over a chair and they sat down.

"So true. Tell me what's going on? What are you doing here? I thought you had moved to Chicago or some other big city," she asked.

"I'm here for a conference at the Hyatt off Route Eighteen. I just was trying to get out and see a little of the old neighbor-hood while we were on a break. I'm living in Chicago, but I swear I can't get used to the cold."

"I know what you mean. I've had to do three too many

Chicago conferences in December, and I dread it each time. How long are you in town?" she asked.

"Through the end of the week. Can you spare some time for dinner with an old friend? Maybe we can catch up. By the way, I was sorry to hear about Eric. I thought he was a real stand-up guy. I could see that he made you happy," he said.

"Thanks, yes, he did make me very happy. I think we made each other happy. But onto a happier subject: you and I definitely have to catch up. Take my number, and give me a call when you know what night you're free." She tore a small piece of paper from the napkin and wrote down her office and home numbers. She checked her watch and gathered up her lunch items.

"Darn, I hate to rush off, but I have to get back to work," she said reluctantly as they both stood up to leave. "By the way, have you settled down yet?" she asked.

"Not yet," he replied.

Olivia stood on her tiptoes and kissed him on the cheek. "I have to run. Call me," she said and waved as she headed back to her office.

As he'd watched her leave, a rush of good memories flooded back. There was no one like Olivia Cane. She was smart, beautiful, sexy, and she used to be the one person in the world he could count on. She was also the woman he loved more than any other in the world and knew he couldn't have.

Two years older than he was, she always treated him like he was her younger brother. He had lived a few houses down the street from her when they were small children. She was the youngest in her family, so she pretended Trevor was her little brother, so she could be the big sister. That was easy until he turned twelve and shot up to six feet tall and towered over her. She still tried to be the bossy older sister in spite of the height difference. They went through grade school and high school together and experienced plenty of misadventures along the way. He was always getting into one scrape or another, and she had been the one to get him out of trouble more often than not. In high school he had discovered the power his good looks had over the girls and developed into a regular Lothario. Olivia had been his willing decoy on more than one occasion to scare off girls he had no interest in. They shared stories of their first loves and teenage heartbreaks.

Throughout their college years they remained close. She stayed close to home and attended Rutgers University, while he'd gone to Duke University in North Carolina on an athletic scholarship. They remained connected by letters and holiday visits. She wrote more often than he did, but every now and then he would send a brief note in reply. After college both had been busy focusing on their careers and saw each other less and less often. Then he had accepted a job in Atlanta and moved farther away. He stayed there two years before he moved to his current Chicago location. After the terrible accident in which Eric was fatally injured, Olivia withdrew from many of her friends and social activities. Contact with him had been a casualty of her withdrawal.

They'd gone out to dinner while he was in New Jersey that week, and ever since then he and Olivia had spent countless hours on long-distance phone calls. She'd even spent a week with him at his home. They'd had a great time catching up. At the time she was unattached and suffering from her own sexual drought. It was an issue he certainly could have handled for her, but he was afraid to scare her off by moving their friendship in a new direction. So instead he'd introduced her to his best friend, Damian. A man he knew could cure her sexual woes and the only other person he truly trusted.

The night he introduced them he could see there was an instant and mutual physical attraction. However, they didn't hook up. He never knew why, but he'd been immensely grateful they hadn't. He wasn't sure he could take the thought of her being intimate with his best friend.

Whenever he saw something he thought she would like he'd impulsively send it to her. Price had no bearing if he wanted her to have it. On a few occasions she'd asked how he could afford such expensive presents, but he never explained where the money came from. There were times he was tempted to confess and share his secret life with her. But he couldn't bear to hear the disappointment in her voice or see her look at him differently. He knew she would try to convince him to give it all up. He wasn't ready; not yet.

When she and her new love, Desmond, moved in together a few months ago, it created a void in his life. He no longer felt comfortable calling her at one in the morning just to talk. Over the last year and a half, she'd become his rock. She'd grounded him and kept him sane. Now she was keeping Desmond sane. He did not want to intrude on their relationship.

He had an opportunity to meet Desmond when they'd flown out to Chicago for business and stopped in to see him several months ago. He thought Des was a good guy, and he was happy to see Olivia in love again. They didn't need to know about his other life, his other source of income. He much preferred for her to think he was a successful sales manager, and, truthfully, he was. His job paid him a very good salary, and it afforded him many nice creature comforts. But the service business provided him with luxuries beyond his wildest dreams.

Closing the garage door, he walked into the house and up the stairs to his bedroom. He threw the two envelopes from today on the bed and walked into the bathroom. Stripping off his clothes, he tossed them into the hamper and turned on the shower full blast. When the water was hot, he stepped in and scrubbed his body clean with Molton Brown shower gel. Fifteen minutes later he emerged, dried off, and put on a T-shirt and gym shorts. He left the bedroom and went down to the kitchen and grabbed a beer from the fridge. Twisting off the top, he tossed it on the counter and took a long, refreshing drink. Belching out loud, he wandered into his family room and turned on the plasma-screen television in the family room. He put his beer on the table and picked up the remote control and began scanning through the channels.

His mind drifted back to earlier in the day. Claudette and one hot, horny movie star. Nina paid him well for his discretion and silence. It was generally a thousand dollars for barely thirty minutes of his time. He'd gone to see Claudette earlier to check on her. He always felt relaxed and at ease in her presence. Her home was a serene haven for him, away from the wild and crazy Ninas of the world.

Claudette, his mentor, still liked to buy him gifts. He always assumed it made her feel more like he was her lover than her hired hand. She continued to shower him with gifts even after the sex was no longer a part of their relationship. His bedroom closet housed an armoire full of Coogie sweaters and Armani shirts, compliments of her. She bought him expensive colognes and showed him what liquors his bar should be stocked with for guests. She explained the importance of paying attention to the smallest details when it came to women and pampering them. Claudette enjoyed introducing Trevor to the finer things in life, and she held a special place in his heart. Even though she was no longer a client, he liked to consider himself her lover still. He was in awe of her and always would be.

The business was Damian's idea initially. As required by their firm, Damian and Trevor both attended very high-profile social gatherings. Some time during the evening Damian hooked up with one of the wealthy widows there, and he ended up spending the night with her. When he was departing the following morning and she handed him five hundred dollars for his time, he was immediately offended. She convinced him it was pocket change to her, and she merely wanted to give him a gift because he made her feel special. It was a lark at first, and he didn't mind spending a few hours with a very fit older woman. She treated him very well. After a month or so she suggested she might know a few other women who would be willing to pay for his services. He was intrigued by the idea and the possibility of a lucrative sideline.

Soon there were too many women for him to handle on his own and confessed to Trevor what he'd been doing. Trevor, too, balked at the idea at first. After all, prostitution was illegal. It took Damian a month to convince him to give it a try. Damian began by passing a few clients to Trevor. The first time Trevor brought in two thousand cash dollars in one week, he knew Damian had stumbled on a gold mine. The two of them sat down and formulated a business plan, detailing how they would seek out new clients, use discreet advertising, and how they would conduct their business. Trevor maintained his list of special clients, while Damian maintained his own. They swapped clients only on the rare occasion one of them was too booked for the week. Only certain clients could be swapped. There were to be no public appearances with the women or anything that might be misconstrued as a date. If they suspected any woman was getting involved beyond the sex aspect, she was immediately removed from the client list. They would both maintain their regular jobs and would mainly work the business in their off hours. Occasional special requests for afternoon delight could be accommodated, but it was not the norm.

Trevor was the more business minded of the two. Damian was the go-getter and motivating force, but Trevor handled the promotions, investments, and client list. It was this client list he'd been updating and sending to Olivia on disk.

They thought they knew all the pitfalls, and avoided them strategically, but they didn't plan for the inevitable burnout Trevor was experiencing now. After all, who would have thought two strapping, handsome young men would get tired of getting paid big money to have sex with women? He picked up the beer from the table and finished the rest in one long gulp. Leaning back on the arm of the sofa, he closed his eyes and went to sleep.

8

She arched her back and spread her legs, ready to accept him. He pressed his organ against the tight opening. He did not want to hurt her. She was tight and dry. He reached over to the side of the bed and grabbed the tiny bottle of lubricant he carried with him. Generously lubricating the condom and her vagina, he tried to enter her again.

Her nerves were fragile, and she was tense. Paige tried to relax. She wanted him so badly. But she was nervous and couldn't relax. She felt him probing at her, and she tried to open her legs wider to permit his entry. It wasn't happening. Her muscles were squeezed too tightly.

Trevor pulled away from her and sat up in the bed. He knew to continue would be too traumatic for her. She would definitely feel pain if he forced himself inside.

"Sweetheart, you have to relax. I can't do this with you so tense," he said.

"I know, I'm sorry," she replied, lip quivering.

"Now, don't cry. We can do this. You have to trust me," he said coaxingly.

"I do, I do trust you."

He leaned back against the headboard and pulled her into the crook of his arm. He'd been watching her more closely this time. He could tell the left breast cup was filled with an unnatural substance. If this was going to work, if he was going to give her what she wanted, she was going to have to trust him completely. Gently he kissed the top of her head. He didn't have all day to spend with her; he needed to get started. He was already getting limp again. He reached down for the hem of her gown and gathered it in his hands. Slowly he moved the gown up her legs to the top of her thighs. Straddling her legs, he leaned down and planted a soft kiss on the tip of the triangular patch of curly hair.

She sighed deeply and closed her eyes. Willingly she gave him free access to her body. His tongue made light circular motions on her abdomen as he moved upward toward her navel. He was surprised to find a navel ring and pulled it teasingly into his mouth. Playfully he tongued the ring. Hearing her sighing contently, he continued his path up her body. The gown was now rolled up under her breasts. He pulled her to a seated position and began to raise it up over her head.

Panic set in for a moment, and she resisted the removal of the gown. She hadn't allowed anyone but the doctors to see her in this state of undress. She tensed again.

He felt her body tensing again; swiftly he moved in and claimed her mouth in a deep, erotic kiss, gently but firmly flicking his tongue inside her mouth, teasing her until she relaxed back into the mattress. He eased the gown over her head. The pink lacy bra was the only remaining barrier. He could clearly tell now which cup held the prosthetic. Taking a deep, silent breath, he lay down beside her; pulling her into his arms, he expertly unhooked the back clasp on the bra.

Her mind raced back to the present as she grabbed the bra to stop it from falling away and sat up. She couldn't let him see her. He wouldn't want her once he did, she was certain. Just like Jamal. The dream would end.

Tenderly he put his hands over hers. Looking deeply into her eyes, silently he implored her to trust him. He easily pried open her grasp on the bra and watched it fall away. Catching the silicone prosthetic in his hand, he leaned over and placed it on the nightstand. He shifted his attention back to her. Fear and apprehension gazed back at him from her gorgeous blue eyes. Her remaining breast was beautiful. He concentrated on that one, latching on to the brown nipple with his lips and playing with it until it was erect and rigid. He felt his manhood rising again. She gasped pleasurably at the feel of his warm, wet mouth on her breast. He laid her back gently against the pillows. He could not ignore the scar on the left side of her chest. He would cause her further emotional harm if he tried to pretend it wasn't there.

He rose above her and gazed down at her. It was a strange sight, the one breast and the flat chest on the other side. As it was strange and ethereally beautiful, his heart filled with compassion for her. He leaned down and placed a series of soft butterfly kisses on the scarred area before claiming her mouth once again with his.

When his lips touched the scar, she felt her heart swell. Her body was already responding to his touch. She was wet and eager to fulfill the rest of her dream. He rose above her, and she opened her legs eagerly to receive him. He inserted a finger first to see if she was relaxed enough. Assured she was, he began pushing against the entrance to her sweetness again.

Her mind was ready this time. She arched her back, eager to take all of him. After minimal resistance he was able to slip beyond the entrance. He was large, larger than she expected, and much larger than Jamal. She clasped her hand over her mouth to muffle the scream as he pushed farther inside. She felt her muscles contracting around his engorged rod. He paused for a moment to allow her a chance to adjust to his size. When she nodded her head in agreement, he began slowly stroking in and out.

His hands caressed the soft firm flesh of her thigh as he nuzzled his face in her neck. Her small body fit perfectly in his arms, but he knew she couldn't hold his large frame comfortably for long. He rolled onto his back and pulled her astride his hips. With his hands placed firmly on her thighs, he allowed her to find her own pleasure. He watched as she became less self-conscious and gained confidence in her ability to please him.

She savored the fullness of his manhood inside her as she closed her eyes and moved slowly up and down against his groin. Low groans of pleasure mixed with mild discomfort rolled off her lips. Although his large size at times caused slight pain, she was overwhelmed by the pleasure of their union and adjusted her pace and position to accommodate him. Emboldened by the smile he gave her, she leaned on his chest and circled his nipples with her tongue. Her fingers caressed the firm, sculpted muscles of his chest and abs. He was perfect and gorgeous. More importantly, she was making love to him. She closed her eyes as heat spread through her body. She pushed herself up into a sitting position again and paused momentarily to get her breath.

He recognized an intensity of feeling building in her body as her muscles tensed and her posture became more rigid and taut. He could feel a climax was near. He separated the lips of her vulva, exposing the bulging pink orb, and tweaked it fast and lightly with his fingertips.

Her body arched violently, and she screamed aloud as a fierce orgasm gripped her body. Her sweet honey flushed down his staff like hot molten lava.

He felt the heat from her honey on his dick, and his excitement grew. He deftly lifted her from his hips and laid her on her side and then spooned up against her small round ass. He put his hand between her thighs, opening them slightly, and then slipped easily into her heat once again from the rear. His arm cradled her body tight against his as he continued to pleasure her. Her small breast was cupped in one palm, and his other hand was pressed flat against her stomach. This position allowed him to feel every movement and orgasmic ripple flowing through her body. When he felt her body tensing again for the next wave, he pressed his hand on her groin and pulled her tight and deep against his shaft. He released his cum simultaneously with her final orgasm.

Although weak and exhausted after their session, Paige realized she'd never experienced such sexual pleasure or fulfillment. Sated and happier than she'd been in a very long time, she snuggled down under the covers after he exited the bed.

On his way out, he bent over to plant a good-bye kiss on her lips. "You're a very beautiful, sensual woman. Don't let anyone tell you you're not," he said softly.

She whispered, "Thank you," for more than just his words— for all this night meant to her. It had been special in ways he could never imagine.

He turned and headed for the door. He paused at the little stand and looked at the envelope waiting for him. Ignoring it, he smiled to himself and thought *This one's on me* and closed the door behind him.

9

Trevor pushed through the door at the gym on West Pryor Avenue. The heat and musty odor of sweat welcomed him. The gym was slightly dark because of the bad lighting, but it wasn't enough to deter the men who gathered here every Tuesday night to run the floor and hone their shooting skills. The squeaky squealing of leather on wood, along with the pounding steps of the antelopelike sprinters running up and down the court, made conversation almost impossible. Conversation wasn't necessary because these men let their bodies do the talking.

Trevor tossed his gym bag on the floor and pulled off his sweatpants. Pulling his basketball sneakers from the bag, he slipped off his running shoes and put them on. Several men walked by and greeted him. After he was done he stood up and stretched for a few minutes. He checked out the men gathered here, looking for his partners. On Tuesdays after eight they ran five-on-five teams. He only saw three of his team members. Damian was missing. He pulled his basketball from his bag and wandered off to one of the side baskets to practice his shot. He wasn't in a mood for talking tonight.

He knew it was a mistake not charging for his services tonight, and Damian would give him hell if he found out. What bothered him more than Damian's wrath was the fact that he hadn't felt right about taking the money. It wasn't because he pitied the girl—she'd been through a rough time for sure, but she was still a very beautiful woman. Once he'd gotten her to relax, he'd actually enjoyed making love to her. That was what bothered him. For the past three years he was able to keep his emotions out of it, but recently he had allowed two women to tap into his emotions. He knew this was dangerous. Maybe it was time for him to stop. God knew he'd accumulated more than enough money, and he was tired of being alone. He longed for the kind of relationship Olivia and Desmond shared. He wanted someone to come home to and to build a future with. Lately he'd started to wonder how he would ever explain his lifestyle to a woman and expect her to accept it. The longer he stayed in the game, the less likely it would be for him to find her.

He dribbled the ball for a few moments, made a few quick steps to his left and right, faking out his invisible opponent, and then jumped out for a soft fadeaway shot. He watched his shot as it arched toward the basket. Seconds before it would have swished through the rim, it was snatched out of the air as Damian swooped in and grabbed it.

"Goaltending, man," Trevor said as Damian laughed and dribbled away and then elevated to release his own sweet jump shot.

"Caught you sleeping again," Damian said, retrieving the ball and walking up to Trevor. They clasped hands in greeting. "So, what's up, dog? Ain't heard nothing from you in a while. Everything all right?"

"Yeah, everything is cool," he replied. Damian had known him for too long and could easily pick up on his moods. He didn't want to get into it with him yet. He changed the subject.

"You ready to run tonight, 'cause I feel like kicking some major ass up in here."

"You know I'm always ready," Damian replied as they headed back to the bleachers to wait their turn on the court.

Two hours later they were sitting in a bar talking over a couple of beers. Damian reminded him of a corporate party they had to attend the following month at the Knickerbocker Hotel. Every year their firm hosted a huge fund-raising dinner for the United Negro College Fund. All the who's-who in the corporate world would be there. It was fifteen hundred dollars a plate, and their firm insisted they go, as well as some of the board members. The company had no qualms letting the world know two of its top sales executives were black. It would be a black-tie affair, and Damian, social butterfly that he was, was looking forward to it. Trevor wasn't as eager, but he knew it would be unprofessional for him to miss out on the major networking opportunities the evening would present.

"What's on your mind?" Damian asked, looking directly at Trevor.

"What are you talking about?" Trevor replied evasively. He signaled to the waitress to bring another round of drinks.

"Don't play me, man. Something is bothering you. I'm gonna find out anyway, so you might as well tell me now."

"I've been thinking of getting out of the game," Trevor replied and looked across at Damian for his reaction.

"What happened?" Damian asked. Assessing Trevor's mood, he leaned back in the booth.

"Nothing. I just ain't feeling it like I used to," Trevor countered.

"What's to feel? It's big money for fucking women who are willing to pay big money to be fucked," Damian said bluntly, not convinced something hadn't happened to throw Trevor. "What's the problem?"

"I don't need the money anymore," Trevor replied. "Some

of these women," he started and then hesitated. "I feel sorry for them," he finished.

"You feel sorry for them?" Damian asked incredulously. "They pay good money for the best dick some of them have ever had or will ever have in their lives. Shit! You're doing them a favor. Some of these women couldn't get it any other way," he said.

Trevor looked across the bar at the football game on the television mounted on the wall and did not reply. He knew Damian would not get it. To him it was purely a business. People's feelings and emotions were not part of the equation. He was sure Damian would have experienced no qualms about taking the girl's money this afternoon. To be honest, he doubted Damian would even have given her a second visit.

"You getting soft, man?" Damian asked.

"No! I'm just reevaluating my life. And I'm not thrilled anymore with this part of it," he answered.

Damian looked at him. The boy was soft when it came to women. He always had been. When it was a man issue, street fight, bar fight—and they'd had their share—he could have no better man beside him than Tré. He'd had his back on many occasions when Damian's mouth had gotten him more than he could handle. But with women he was different. He knew the excitement of the game would wear off sooner or later. Still, he could see Tré was sitting on the fence. He wasn't sure whether Tré really wanted to give it up or if he was just having a bad day. Suddenly Damian had an idea. He scribbled an address on a piece of paper and shoved it across the table.

"I want you to take my two o'clock tomorrow. It's at the Omni Hotel downtown," Damian said.

"I'll be working, man," Trevor replied.

"Take a late lunch. It won't take long, I assure you. She never uses the full time," Damian said.

Trevor thought of the freebie he gave today. It would make

up for the missed money. He wasn't certain, though. This was Damian's client.

"Is she open to a swap, man. Some women aren't. You know this," Trevor said.

"Some women get too comfortable with one man and need a reminder this is a business. I think this one is getting too comfortable with me, and you showing up will bring her a taste of her own reality. If she objects, then don't push it. Tell her she can reschedule with me when I have time," Damian explained.

"All right, I'll do it," he said and stood up. He tossed a few bills on the table, and they both left the bar. Damian watched Trevor as he walked up the street to his car. Trevor was not going to be very happy with him after tomorrow. But it was necessary; she was a necessary evil.

Agnes paced around the hotel room while she waited for him to show up. She hated waiting for anyone, and he was supposed to be there at two. Agitated, she glanced at her watch again. It was one fifty-nine. A knock sounded at the hotel door. She opened the door to see a total stranger standing there. Too peeved to even attempt pleasantries, she asked, "Who are you?"

"I'm Steve. Mike had an emergency and couldn't make it," he replied. His gaze took in her crisp white silk shirt and expensive business suit.

Sucking in her breath audibly with annoyance, she snapped, "He should have called."

"It came up at the last minute, and he called me. If you prefer to reschedule with Mike, I can leave," Trevor offered. Her attitude was a definite turnoff, and he would be glad to skip this appointment.

Her fixed stare traveled from his head to his feet before she turned away and tossed over her shoulder, "You'll do." He was extremely handsome, and she was salivating at the thought of handling him, but she wasn't about to let it show. She walked away from the door and removed her jacket and hung it in the closet.

Trevor stepped into the room and closed the door behind him. He walked over to the chair in the corner and began removing his shirt and kicked off his shoes. Agnes unbuttoned her blouse and paused to glance at Trevor, who was unbuckling his belt.

"Do you think you could speed it up a little? I have a meeting at four, and time is money," she said.

He paused for a moment to look at her. *What a bitch*, he thought. *Small wonder she had to pay someone to fuck her.* This was Damian's regular client, so he declined to comment. He continued to remove his trousers at the same pace. He knew she was trying to push his buttons and take control, but he wasn't interested in playing her game. Now completely naked, he looked across the room to see her clad in a black Victoria's Secret brassiere and garter set—thigh-high black stockings attached to little black silk straps hanging from the garter. She wore no panties. If he concentrated on her from the neck down, it could be good.

Agnes watched him from the corner of her eye as he stood there like a caramel Mandingo warrior. His muscles were rippling in all the right places. Her feminine juices started flowing, and tingling sensations of anticipation played havoc between her hot and musty thighs. She could see he was well endowed and had no doubt he would be a fun ride, but she was determined to make this as difficult for him as she could. Mike always gave her trouble, but she'd gotten used to battling him. This guy was fresh meat, and she intended to break him.

"How do you want it?" he asked coolly, moving toward the bed. Might as well find out what she had in mind before he got started.

"I want it hard," she said snidely, looking directly at his semierect organ. *What an asshole*, she thought. "For as long as you can keep it hard," she continued.

Trevor had taken about all he could stand of her nasty attitude. He was out of patience with her, and having sex with this woman was definitely not going to be fun, no matter how rocking her body was—and he admitted to himself she did have an awesome body.

"Look, lady, I've never been with you before. So I'm merely trying to gauge your preferences. Do you want it on the bed, the floor, or the fucking dresser? Let me know." His tone clearly indicated he had taken enough of her nonsense.

Deciding not to agitate him any further because he might decide to leave, she climbed into the bed and waited for him to join her. It had been a month since she had been laid, and she wasn't waiting another month for Mike to give her another appointment. His fees were bordering on the ridiculous as it was. If he hadn't been so damn good, she would have stopped calling him a long time ago. But this man was an unknown. He was an enticing specimen, and she was anxious to get this on and see what he could do. Perhaps she was pushing him too hard.

Trevor slipped into bed with her. She relaxed back into the pillows as he placed his hand between her legs and inserted two fingers inside her. She was juicy wet already. Obviously, demeaning men was a huge turn-on for her. He was glad he would not have to work getting her ready. He slipped on a condom and rolled over on top of her. Forcefully he parted her legs with his knee and thrust himself inside her.

Agnes bit her lip as he pushed and ground deeper inside her body. Forcing herself to remain quiet, she refused to allow him to think he was controlling her. She matched his aggressive grinding by rolling and arching her hips, matching his strong rhythms stroke for stroke.

Trevor did not want to be excited by this woman, but her aggressive bucking was undeniably increasing his excitement. Her breasts were firm orbs nearly flowing over the cups of her brassiere. He pushed aside the cup and exposed her breast. His lips latched onto the brown nipple, and he sucked hard. Pulling the tip between his teeth, he bit her lightly.

Agnes gasped involuntarily at the sharp pain he inflicted on her breast. Shock and awe were overridden by the cascading waves of orgasm the bite generated. She could feel the juices escaping her body.

Trevor continued to work his magic on her body. He could feel her excited responses to his aggressiveness. *So she likes it rough*, he thought. He reached around and grabbed her buttocks in his hands; he stroked deeply into her, at the same time firmly squeezing her butt cheeks. Little cries of pleasure escaped her lips.

Agnes berated herself silently for allowing him to see her pleasurable responses. Her body was betraying her, and he'd taken control. She didn't relinquish control in anything. He was still rock hard and grinding away. She wasn't certain how many more times she could stand to climax or how much longer he would continue before he came.

Trevor wasn't even close to climaxing; control was something he had learned early on, and he could go for a very long time. He raised his body up into a kneeling position, wrapped his arms under her thighs. Lifting her buttocks off the bed, he pulled her body flat against his groin and pounded her fast and furiously.

Agnes began growling like a hungry lioness. He was good; he was damn good, she thought between moans of pleasure. But she also realized he was in control and not she. He was wearing her out, and she couldn't allow this. If she came now, she would lose her mind. Her innate meanness reared its ugly head so she could regain control. She pushed her hands against his chest and said, "Stop!"

"What?" he asked incredulously, stopping in the middle of a downward stroke. He wasn't even breathing deeply.

"That's enough. I've had enough," she said, pushing him off her and rolling away.

Trevor looked down at his rigid penis. *No, she didn't,* he thought. She purposely left me with a dick hard as Chinese algebra. Calmly he climbed out of bed and proceeded to the bathroom. He stood there staring in the mirror and took a few deep breaths to control his anger. He had no intention of letting her think she had gotten to him. He discarded the used condom in the toilet and washed quickly with a washcloth. He returned to the bedroom, walked past the bed without saying a word, and began to dress. His envelope was lying on the dresser. He paused to look back at her. His expression was actually one of pity. He didn't understand how someone could be so spiteful and mean. He collected the envelope and proceeded to the door.

"Steve," she called softly from her position on the bed. He turned to look back at her. "Its about my pleasure, not yours," she said smugly.

"Apparently not, because you're not getting half the pleasure you could be," he replied confidently and walked out the door.

He looked at his watch as he walked down the hall toward the hotel elevator. It was two forty-five. It had seemed longer. He pulled his cell phone from his pocket and called Damian. Trevor stepped inside the empty elevator and pushed the button for the lobby. Damian answered as though he was expecting the call.

"What's up?" he asked.

"What the fuck was that?" Trevor demanded angrily.

"A wake-up call," Damian replied smoothly.

"Wake-up call? What the hell are you talking about?" Trevor spat.

"I told you before, this is a *business*. You need to remember that. I knew she was the perfect one to remind you. She's all about the business," Damian explained.

"Business? She's a fucking psycho, and I wouldn't fuck that bitch again with somebody else's dick," Trevor continued, his anger unabated.

"Look, man, I'm sorry. I'm used to dealing with her silly shit. This isn't all fun and games. Did you open the envelope?" he asked.

"No, why?" Trevor asked as he stepped off the elevator and into the lobby. He walked out the door onto Michigan Avenue and looked for his car. After getting into the driver's seat, he pulled the envelope from his pocket. He counted roughly a thousand dollars. "What's up with this, man?" he asked. He had only spent half the usual time with her.

"She's a royal bitch who likes to dominate men. It makes her feel powerful. So I charge her twice the rate for half the time. Obviously she can afford it because she keeps calling," Damian explained.

"You know what, man? There's taking care of business, and there's getting used. I ain't up for this shit. So you can keep that one for yourself. I'll pass. I don't care what she pays," Trevor said seriously.

"That's cool. But just remember what I said. This is business, man. Keep your head on straight," Damian cautioned.

"Yeah, I got it. I'm out," Trevor replied and disconnected. He shoved the cell back in his pocket and pulled away from the curb. He meant what he said. He didn't care how much he got paid. Women like her tried to take your self-respect and your balls; his weren't for sale.

Agnes grabbed her shoe off the floor and threw it at the closed door. Her vagina was aching and throbbing, and it was her own fault. He had brought her this close to a final climax, and she had stopped the show. It was all about control. She was most angry because she knew he was right. She couldn't allow herself that reckless, abandoned type of orgasm during which you forget who you were, where you were, and your purpose in life. She'd heard about them, even read about them. But she wasn't giving that much power to anyone. Steve nearly pushed her over the edge, which was why she stopped him. *Damn Mike for sending him*, she thought, as she rolled over in the bed and pressed the palm of her hand over her throbbing vagina. She was not only aching but also sore from his onslaught. The kind of soreness that made you smile because you knew you'd been thoroughly screwed.

She'd been having enough trouble with Mike lately, but felt she could still control him. He understood it was all business. This man seemed to think it was about pleasure, and he was wrong. Pleasure had nothing to do with it. It was about satisfying Mother Nature's urges and relieving tension, working out the stress and nothing else. This is what she convinced herself of, what she truly believed. She would make sure Mike never sent him back; he was too dangerous.

10

Olivia and Des walked down the cold, dank halls of the prison to the visiting area. Olivia clasped Desmond's hand for dear life. She had never been in a prison before. Never thought it was someplace she would ever have to go in life. She couldn't believe Trevor was locked up in here. Questions kept flashing through her mind: scenarios on how this could have happened. It had to be a mistake. He wouldn't kill anybody. She was positive they had the wrong man.

They were shown to a waiting area, and in a few moments Trevor appeared. He was unshaven and dressed in a prison jumpsuit. At six foot five, he towered over most of the guards. Even the bulky prison garb could not disguise the muscles and inherent strength underneath. But the guards had weapons. Olivia watched as he entered the room and then turned away as tears pooled in her eyes. She wiped her cheeks and looked back just as he was taking his seat opposite them on the other side of the glass. Trevor looked sad and ashamed. Ashamed because he was the reason Olivia was in a place like this. He picked up the phone on his side of the glass. Des handed Olivia the phone on their side.

"I'm sorry, Livi," Trevor said. "You should never be in a place like this. I don't want you to come back."

"I love you," she said, trying her best to smile, "and there's no place in the world I would rather be than here for you. We're gonna fight this Trev. We'll get you out of here, I promise."

"It was an accident. I didn't kill him. I swear I didn't," he said emphatically.

"I believe you," she replied. She noticed the cuts and bruises on his knuckles and blue-tinged bruise on his cheek. It was apparent he had been in a fight.

"Let me talk to him for a minute?" Desmond asked, reaching for the phone.

"I love you," Olivia repeated and handed the phone to Des. She sat back in her chair and allowed them to speak for a few minutes. Her eyes wandered around the stark room. This was a dreadful place. Her purse had been confiscated and searched when they entered the facility. They even searched her person. She felt violated by the inspection but knew it was a necessary precaution for the prison. He'd told her not to come back, but she knew nothing would keep her away from helping him in any way she could.

Desmond tapped her on the leg, and her focus returned to the present. Trevor was standing on his side of the partition. The phones had been re-placed in their cradles. Their time was up. She blew him a kiss and allowed Desmond to lead her out of the visiting area.

They walked all the way out of the facility in silence. Both were deep in thought. As soon as they breathed the clean, fresh air outside, Olivia broke her silence. "What did he say?" she asked.

"He said Damian had gotten him a really good attorney, and as soon as he is arraigned, they will ask for bail," he replied.

"Do you think they'll give him bail?" she asked, not at all certain bail would be set if the charge was murder.

"He has a clean record, so it is possible. But it may be a pretty steep bail. Question is, will he have the money to post it?" he stated. "The arraignment is tomorrow, so we'll know more then. He wants us to bring him a suit for the arraignment, and he said we should stay in his house while we're here. Damian has the keys."

"Okay, I'll call Damian and have him meet us there. Then we can talk to him and find out what the hell is going on here," she said, her righteous anger brewing. This was pure craziness, and someone had better explain this to her.

An hour later, they pulled into the driveway of Trevor's house in Forest Glen. Damian's Mercedes E500 was already parked in the driveway. He opened the door and greeted Olivia with a warm embrace. He shook Desmond's hand as they were introduced. He showed them into the family room and then offered them a drink.

Seated on the leather sectional in the family room, Olivia couldn't wait to launch into a barrage of questions. Damian looked in Desmond's direction. His look clearly questioned how much he should tell her. Desmond reached for her hand and began to speak.

"Livi, the newspapers are reporting this as a love triangle. But that's not what really happened. Trevor was not having an affair with this woman. She was a business client of his," he explained.

"Okay, so what's so bad about that? Obviously there is more to this story, and neither one of you wants to spit it out. I never thought Trevor would get involved with a married woman anyway," she replied. Desmond and Damian exchanged looks, which infuriated her. Why were they keeping something from her? "Why was he in a hotel room with this woman?" she asked.

"She had been beaten up by her husband, and he was trying to help her hide for a few days," Damian supplied.

"Okay, I'm still not getting the bad part of this. It sounds like he was doing a good thing," she said, irritated.

"Honey," Desmond interjected, "do you have any idea how Trevor makes his money?"

"He is a salesman, the top regional salesman for your firm. Right, Damian?" she said and flashed Damian an accusatory look.

"Yes, that's true. But Trevor and I have a separate business we work on the side for extra money, and she was one of those clients. I hate to be the one to tell you, Olivia, especially since I'm the one who got Tré started doing this, and I know he's not going to forgive me for telling you," Damian replied and then hesitated. He looked over at Desmond, who nodded his head in silent agreement. She needed to be told. "We provide sexual service to a select clientele of women. Generally, the women are very affluent, and it is all very discreet."

Olivia couldn't comprehend what she'd just heard. She sat silently with a puzzled look on her face. Her brain rejected the thought that her baby brother was screwing women for money. With as much money as he made as a regional sales director, why in the world would he need to do this? She leaned back in her seat and said nothing. Thoughts began crowding in on her brain. She replayed Damian's words in her head: *sexual service.* Suddenly she remembered what Trevor's sister had said: "His sinful ways, that demon, Damian." Her righteous anger resurfaced, and she rose from her seat. Slowly she walked over to stand in front of Damian.

"This is your fault! You made him do this. Trevor would never have thought of something like this by himself. I know he wouldn't. You started this!" she screamed at him.

"Livi." Desmond rose from his seat and reached for her hand. She snatched it away and faced Damian again.

"This is your fault! All of this is your fault. Money! That's all it's about with you. Money! Look what you've done to him," she continued. Tears began streaming down her cheeks. Desmond grabbed her from behind, and she swung wildly out at Damian. Her hand missed his face by inches. She could barely breathe. He was the devil. Just like Edith Calhoun said he was. He had corrupted Trevor, corrupted him for money.

Desmond tried to calm her down. "Livi, Trevor's a grown man. He knew what he was doing. You can't blame Damian for that."

"Don't you understand? Trevor never cared this much about money. He had more than enough from his job. Why? I don't understand why he had to sell his body for money! A prostitute, that's all he was. A high-paid prostitute!" She pushed away from Desmond and ran from the room. Her footsteps resounded on the wooden stairs as she raced up to her room.

Desmond started to go after her and thought better of it. It was best to give her some time to absorb what she'd been told. He knew her disappointment and disillusionment with Trevor was at the root of her anger toward Damian. When she came to terms with the situation, she would understand it was not his fault. Everyone had to make choices, and this was a choice Trevor made. He sat back down on the sofa opposite Damian.

"Tell me everything," he said.

Upstairs on the bed, Olivia continued to cry. The pain in her heart was unbearable. She wanted this all to be a bad dream, but she knew it wasn't. She'd always looked out for Trevor; ever since he was the little boy down the street who loved to follow her around. How had she let him down? When had she not been there for him? He could have told her what he was thinking, and she could have talked him out of it. Or even after he started doing it, he could have come to her. Come to her and what? Confessed? She knew she put her on a pedestal. Had she become so unreachable he didn't feel he could confide in her anymore? How long had he been doing this?

She thought back to her last visit. He had wined and dined

her and Desmond as though money was no expense. She thought further back to the week she'd spent here with him before she met Desmond. She remembered how Damian told him he needed to hit the gym. Told him he couldn't afford to get flabby. She'd asked him how he made so much money and to let her in on his secret. He'd gotten angry and told her she couldn't do what he did. Her mind flashed back to the scene in the kitchen the night she mentioned that Nadia told her she needed to get a handyman, and Trevor got really rattled. Then he offered Olivia the services of his buddy, Damian; his prostitute buddy. She cringed when she realized he'd been screwing women for money even then. Almost two years ago.

She rolled over onto her back and stared at the ceiling. Brusquely she wiped the tears from her cheeks. Crying wasn't going to solve anything. She remembered the late-night phone calls before Desmond moved in. She could tell he wasn't happy, although he wouldn't explain why. He kept saying he wanted to change some things in his life but never said what. He talked about moving out of Chicago. She wished she'd pressed him harder for answers. Wished she'd realized he was calling on her for help but didn't know how to ask. He was probably too ashamed to admit what he was doing.

When Eric died, she thought, *that's when I withdrew from the world and everyone in it.* A chill enveloped her body, and she wrapped her arms around herself to ward off the memories. She and her late fiancé, Eric, met in college and had been together for only four years before his death. They were kindred spirits with the uncanny habit of finishing each other's sentences and thoughts. They unleashed their adventurous spirits, traveling often to the Caribbean, Mexico, and Europe, and they spent most of their nonworking hours together.

It all changed seven years ago when Eric took an early morning jog and never came home. He'd been struck by a drunk driver. The driver of the SUV claimed he'd swerved to avoid hitting a deer. Instead he swerved onto the jogging path and hit Eric, tossing him two hundred feet into the brush. It amazed the first responders that he was still alive when they arrived. He'd suffered massive internal injuries. She was devastated by the loss of her best friend and partner when he succumbed to his injuries a week later.

Eric had been everything to her. The very air she breathed was different without him, and when she lost him nothing mattered anymore. She couldn't face her well-meaning friends. Everything and everyone reminded her of a special time spent with Eric. It was during this mourning period that she'd lost contact with Trevor.

By the time she'd decided it was okay to move on and reclaim her life, almost five years had passed. Then she bumped into Trevor purely by accident during a lunch break. They were so happy to have found one another again. Based upon the time frame Damian mentioned, Trevor would already have been involved in their business, and there was no way he would have shared his secret with her. Especially after she had been gone so long.

She sat up on the side of the bed. Resolutely she walked into the bathroom and washed her face. It wasn't anybody's fault. *We all let Trevor down*, she thought. *Now we have to save him.* She wrung out the facecloth and folded it over the towel rack on the wall. Looking at her face one last time in the mirror, she turned and made her way back downstairs to the family room.

11

Trevor walked slowly back to his cell. The guard followed on his heels to ensure he would not try anything crazy. Trevor scoffed at the very idea of acting out. He'd seen what happened to inmates who got a little overzealous in their agitation, frustration, or just plain lunacy. He wasn't looking for that type of beat down. The bars of his cell loomed ahead. He stepped inside and backed away from the entrance. The guard locked the cell behind him.

After the guard moved away, Trevor walked back up to the bars of his cell. Unconsciously he placed his hands on the cold steel bars. He laid his head against the bars for a second. Deep in thought, he was startled when his vision focused on his bruised hands gripping the steel bars. In his mind's eye he saw all the prison movies he had ever watched in which the criminals leaned against their cells bars with their hands poking through, craving for the freedom outside the tiny cell. He hadn't seen himself in their shoes until he saw his own fists grasping the bars. The vision disturbed him, and he snatched his hands off the bars as if they were hot coals and backed up quickly until the sink hit the backs of his knees.

Olivia's face flashed across his mind. She was beautiful as always. But he saw the fear she couldn't hide in the depths of her eyes. He knew what she had been put through just to get into the room to see him, and he knew she would do it over and over again just to be there for him. He would deal with whatever came his way because he put himself in this position, but it was unfair to ask her to go through this with him. It was the main reason he had not wanted Damian to call her. Soon she would find out what he had been doing for the last few years, and she would never look at him the same again. It was a thought he could not bear, to have become such a disappointment to her. He unleashed a stream of expletives and pounded his fist on the wall. The need to release the pent-up fury forced him to the floor. He did two hundred crunches and an equal number of push-ups. Still unable to get Olivia's tear-stained face out of his mind, he paced back and forth in the cell from wall to wall for twenty minutes. Finally he lay down on the cot and covered his eyes with his forearm. Nothing was worth this nightmare he was trapped smack in the middle of.

He tried to focus on something positive, and his mind drifted to Paige. The last time he'd seen her was nearly eight months ago. He'd been with her only two more times after the night they'd successfully made love for the first time. He smiled when he realized he considered it making love and not just sex. He wasn't in love with Paige, but there was something about her he was attracted to. Once she got passed being self-conscious of her mastectomy scar, she was a very sensual and giving lover. He looked forward to her calls. The last time had been very special, almost as if they both knew it would be the last time they would be together.

She'd given him her home address this time. He assumed she was tired of paying for hotel rooms. When he arrived she was seductively dressed in a navy-blue tank top and matching boy shorts. A light jasmine musk scent wafted through the room from the incense cones she had been burning. He kissed her lightly on the lips as he entered the apartment. She presented him with a glass of wine. He smiled and took a sip; it had a very deep, rich flavor. He nodded to her in appreciation and inquired if it was okay to look around.

She smiled in return and nodded her assent. She watched him closely as he wandered around the room looking at her family photos and souvenirs. She'd realized she was falling for him the last time they were together. But she was levelheaded enough to know it would be a very unwise decision on her part to attempt to pursue anything more than what they had. She debated for a long time whether or not to call him again and finally decided she would see him one more time to say goodbye. He'd given her a measure of confidence she never thought she would have again, and for that she was grateful. It was time to let him go. She needed to let the fantasy go and move on with her life.

He was so handsome in his tan sweater and brown slacks. She tried to capture a picture of his face in her mind, a mental snapshot she could keep forever. Lately she had begun to notice men watching her on the streets. Admiring whistles were coming her way. Had men always been doing that, or had her newfound confidence suddenly attracted them again? It really didn't matter; she felt good about herself again.

"Steve," she called to gain his attention. He was standing in front of the fireplace, staring at a picture of her as a little girl.

"Yes," he said and turned back in her direction. He drank the last bit of wine from his glass and walked over to the sofa.

He waited for her to say more, but she said nothing. She watched him as he glanced down and picked up the romance novel from the end table. It would be nice for one night to pretend he was her man and he'd just gotten home from work.

He looked at the front cover of the lusty romance novel and quickly perused the back cover. He smiled as he laid it back down on the table. She walked up to him with the wine bottle in hand and refilled his glass and hers. As a rule, Trevor did not drink when he was working, but he, too, had a feeling tonight was going to be special.

He took another drink and then placed the wineglass on the table and pulled her into his arms. With her body pressed close against his, he cupped her chin in his hand and claimed her mouth with his. The intoxicating sweetness of her mouth combined with the rich wine flavor on their tongues stirred his loins. He felt his body growing in desire to mate with her once again.

Paige allowed her hands to explore the bulge straining against the zipper of his slacks. Gently she rubbed her hand up and down its length. She continued to return his kisses with equal and growing passion as she unbuckled his belt and then unzipped his pants. Sliding her small hands into the elastic sides of his boxers, she pushed his pants down off his hips.

Trevor was still standing in the middle of the room, pleased by her newfound confidence and sexual aggressiveness. He stepped out of his pants and boxers and tried to concentrate on removing her tank top. He managed to slip it over her head and cupped her breast in his hand as he leaned down and brought the rigid button to his mouth. With his free hand he clasped the back of her head, allowing her silky hair to flow through his fingers.

Paige concentrated on the silky-smooth, rigid organ in her hands. She lightly stroked the smooth flesh, feeling it pulse and jerk in response to her touch. She nibbled on the small brown nipples of his chest, pulling one and then the other into her mouth and lightly flicking them with her tongue. Tonight she intended to do all she ever dreamed of doing with him.

Trevor breathed in sharply in response to her inquiring touch. He was used to creating the sensations women responded to, but this night he welcomed her touch. He closed his eyes as she sucked on his nipples and caressed his manhood in her tiny hands. Slipping into a world of sensations, it took him a minute to realize she had dropped to her knees. He felt her grasp on his manhood become suddenly firmer. His eyes flew open just as she put her mouth on the tip of his penis.

"No!" he cried out and attempted to push her away. She didn't have to do this. It wasn't necessary, he thought. Startled, she looked up at him, with unmasked hurt at his rejection shining brightly in her eyes. "Paige, you don't have to," he whispered and caressed the back of her neck with his strong fingers.

"I want to," she replied huskily. She could see he wanted it as much as she wanted to please him. She looked up at him with determination in her eyes and repeated, "I want to."

She swirled her tongue around the tip of his organ before pulling it into the warm, wet cavity of her mouth. His sharp intake of breath assured her he enjoyed it as much as she hoped he would. She worked slowly and steadily, sending pleasurable sensations along the length of his shaft for several minutes.

Finally he pulled her up to her feet and kissed her passionately. She could feel the urgency in his desire as he left her gasping for breath. He swiftly picked her up and laid her on the sofa. He pulled her to the edge of the sofa, slipped off her shorts, and then buried his face in her stomach. The rules of his game were discarded as he nibbled softly at her navel ring. His lips and mouth were making wet circles on her belly. Her breathing quickened. His tongue left a trail of fire from her navel down to the small protruding bulb of her sweet spot. With his hands placed firmly on her buttocks he brought the tiny bulb to his mouth and began lightly flicking it with his tongue. Alternately flicking and sucking on the ultrasensitive jewel, he felt her body convulse in his hands.

Paige arched her back in reaction to his mouth on her sweet spot. She had not anticipated he would do this but was eternally grateful for the pleasure he was giving her. She reached down, grabbed his head, and pulled his face up to her mouth. She kissed him with all the unleashed passion exploding in her body.

He stood up and lifted her to her feet. Effortlessly he carried her into her bedroom where he continued his intimate exploration of her body and pleasure zones.

His exploration began at her toes as he sucked each small digit, careful not to leave any one untended. Then slowly his tongue made a soft, wet trail up the inside of her calf to her knee and soon the inside of her soft, silky thighs. He burrowed his tongue deep inside her heat and enjoyed the natural essences of her body.

Paige, energized by her lover's eagerness to please, felt a strong desire to reciprocate. She pushed him away and teasingly forced him onto his back. She wasted no time in straddling his chest and placed her honey maker squarely on his face so he could resume his tasty exploration. She leaned forward on his belly and engulfed his bulging dick with her mouth.

He groaned an appreciative response as they savored the essence of their desire for one another with mutual oral stimulation. As their stimulation increased, so did the fever pitch of their lovemaking. She was ready for more than his tongue. She wanted the connection she could get only through the deep penetration of his body melding into hers.

He recognized her burning need as well as his own as he once more shifted position. He quickly opened a condom and started to put it on, when she stopped him.

"You don't have to," she whispered. "It's okay. I'm on the pill."

He paused only momentarily before kissing her gently and putting on the condom. "This is for both of us. We can't take chances. You can't take chances. Not with me or anyone else," he said as he kissed her again. He sat upright and pulled her onto his lap. Gently he eased her hips down on his thick and voracious staff.

With her eyes closed tight and her arms wrapped around his

neck, she exhaled deeply to relax her taut muscles as they expanded to accept his abundance. She felt his hands on her buttocks as he lifted and eased her back down in rhythm. She adjusted quickly to the movements and circled her legs around his waist as she took over the rhythmic pumping. Her breaths came in quick, short bursts as he hit her pleasure spot again and again. Faster and faster she pumped as he supported her back with his hands. Her body shook and her head flew back in reckless abandon as she cried louder with each cresting orgasm.

He urged her to continue finding her own release as he whispered huskily in her ear, "Come on, baby. Fuck me."

Her hands on his shoulders became vise grips as she slowed her pace and began to rock back and forth, grinding her honey as deep as she could into the curly hairs of his groin. She swallowed every inch of his sizable manhood with her womanly essence. A final strong surge of pleasure, and emotion rushed through her body. It left her weak and breathing heavily as she leaned on his shoulders for support.

"Not yet, baby, not yet," he whispered. He placed both hands on her back and pulled her away from his chest into a reclining position. He leaned forward and captured her ripe and rigid nipple with his mouth, suckling with an urgency that was almost painful. Mindful of her scar, he pressed his lips against the rippled flesh and circled it with his tongue. His attention soon returned to her mouth as her pulled her into his strong embrace and took her breath away with a passionate kiss.

He deftly rolled her under him and made love to her as though their lives depended on their mutual sexual satisfaction. His climactic release was accompanied by a loud, animalistic groan she'd never heard before.

As they both lay in her bed, sated and spent from exertion, Paige sat up, with her elbow leaning on the bed, and looked at him curiously. She couldn't stop the giggle that burst from her lips. "What was that?" she asked.

"Hey," he said in protest, "I don't complain about your primal screams, so be nice."

She laughed delightedly and nestled her head in the crook between his shoulder and collarbone. He enjoyed the feel of her in his arms and relaxed his guard. He wrapped his arm around her shoulder and covered them with a blanket. For the first time he did not leave immediately after sex; instead he closed his eyes and fell asleep.

Two hours later he awakened to unfamiliar surroundings. As his eyes adjusted to the darkened room, he remembered where he was. Paige was sleeping peacefully at his side. He took advantage of her unconscious state to allow his eyes to roam freely over her sleeping figure. Her dark curly hair was tousled and fell endearingly across her forehead. She slept lying on her side, facing him. Her features were soft and relaxed in sleep, her breathing soft and rhythmic, her smooth olive-toned skin marred only by the rippled scar on the left side of her chest. He pursed his lips as he watched her stretch kittenlike in her sleep. She was beautiful, and no matter how often he told her this, he knew the scar still made her very self-conscious.

When he'd once asked why she hadn't gotten plastic surgery to restore the breast, she'd told him she didn't have money to pay for the reconstructive surgery. Her insurance declined to pay for what they considered cosmetic surgery. He thought then as now what an injustice the whole situation was. She'd told him not to worry. She'd gotten used to it, and when it bothered her too much she remembered to be grateful she was still alive.

He quietly climbed out of the bed and returned to the living room, where he dressed and made sure all the incense flames were extinguished. He stopped at the table by the doorway where she'd left the envelope for him. He hesitated for a moment or two, not sure he wanted to take her money, and knowing if he didn't, he would be sending a message he wasn't sure he wanted to send. No matter how he felt at this moment, she was not his lover, nor his woman. She was someone who paid him for his services. He had already dropped enough barriers tonight. It would be best for both of them if he did not come back.

Firm in his resolve, but saddened by the reality of the situation, he picked up his envelope from the table. At the same time he noticed her incoming mail. He took a pen from the cup holder and quickly copied her name and address onto his envelope and shoved it into his pocket. He'd figure out what to do with it later. He closed the door behind him as he left.

Paige lay in her bed and listened to his movements in the living room. She'd felt a sudden coldness when he'd gotten out of the bed. She'd pretended to remain asleep and eased herself into the warm spot left by his body when he went into the living room. So much had happened tonight, and she hoped he didn't regret spending the extra time with her. She knew she was in love with him, and she also knew it was wrong to feel this way. Her common sense told her it was because he had given back her sexual confidence, her femininity. She supposed she was grateful, but it felt like so much more. He told her she was beautiful, and because he didn't pretend her scar didn't exist, she finally believed him. But she also knew her need for his services was over, and she knew from the way he made love to every part of her body tonight he knew it, too.

She didn't get out of bed. She couldn't make herself get up because she did not want to have to say good-bye to him. The front door closed softly, and she knew he was gone. She rolled out of the bed and padded quickly to stand by the front window. Tears brimmed in her eyes and fell noiselessly down her cheeks as she watched him walk down the front path and stand for a moment, looking up at the building before he got into his car. Her lips quivered with the painful emotion filling her heart, and as she bit softly on her lower lip she tasted the saltiness of her tears. She stayed by the window until his car pulled off down the street and she could no longer see the taillights in the darkness. Then she kissed her fingertips and transferred the kiss to the cold windowpane. She whispered, "Good-bye," and brushed her hands across her wet cheeks and returned to her bedroom.

Trevor wanted to find a way to get Paige the reconstructive surgery she needed, but he also knew he could not afford to pay for it. It would take all the money he'd saved to pay for everything out of pocket. He knew who would have that kind of money and not bat an eyelash about spending it. He decided the next time he saw her he would suggest it to her.

A month later he was sitting in the back of the limo watching Nina. There was an unusual excitement about her tonight, and it was not an artificial, substance-induced high. She was in a very good mood because there was Oscar buzz about her possible nomination for best supporting actress. She hadn't jumped him the minute he got into the limo as she usually did. This time she offered him a glass of champagne, which he gladly accepted. He knew what he wanted to propose tonight and was waiting for the right moment.

Nina was dressed in a beautiful designer evening gown. She'd kicked off her shoes and was eagerly glancing out the window as the limo drove down Michigan Avenue. She had instructed the driver to find all the theaters that were currently showing her movie so she could ride by and see the throngs of people lined up waiting to see it, to see her. She was like a kid at her first time at the world's fair. With her face pressed up against the window, she was able to see out, but no one could see in.

He'd taken some time over the last month to read up a little on Nina. Most importantly, he'd checked out Nina's special causes. He discovered she was a big supporter of the Breast

Cancer Foundation. The article stated she'd lost a favorite aunt to breast cancer five years earlier. This was the aunt who'd raised her after her mother passed away when she was five. Nina was placed in foster care after the death of her mother, Yvonne, from a drug overdose. The division of children's services had been unable to locate a relative to take her in until her aunt Nettie flew in from St. Louis to advise she would take the child home with her. The authorities were so eager to have one less case to deal with, they were all too happy to pass Nina onto Nettie. They never bothered to check to see if Nettie was a blood relative. She wasn't. Nettie had been an old childhood friend of Yvonne's. When Nina's mom became pregnant, she'd made Nettie her baby's godmother. It wasn't done in church or with witnesses. It was as simple as two teenage girls swearing they would take care of one another and their children forever.

A year after Nina was born, Yvonne had moved to Chicago's south side with her drug-dealer boyfriend. He was arrested and jailed shortly after the move, and she was left alone in a strange city with a baby and no money. It wasn't long before her recreational drug use became an uncontrollable habit. She did many unsavory things to support her habit. In her lucid moments she knew she wasn't doing right by her little girl, but Nina was the only good thing in her life.

Yvonne, embittered by her experiences with men, made sure Nina knew from an early age that there was nothing a man would do for you except get you in trouble and leave you to fend for yourself. She advised her to steer as far away from them as she could. When Nina began inquiring at the age of five why Yvonne had so many men coming to visit, she told her it was to help pay the bills. She'd shut Nina up in her bedroom and service the men in the living room. Sometimes she'd get enough to pay the rent and feed them and other times just enough for another high.

Two weeks before she died she wrote a letter to Nettie, asking her to come and get Nina. She said she couldn't handle her anymore, and she wanted her to have a better life. She addressed it to her "sister, Nettie." This was the letter Nettie showed up with to collect Nina after Yvonne died.

A twenty-three-year-old Nettie bundled Nina up and took her back to St Louis, where she raised her as her own. Nettie never married and devoted her life to providing the best her meager salary could provide for Nina. Nina's musical and acting talent surfaced early, and Nettie took her to all the agencies and talent scouts in the area for years, hopeful she would get discovered. Finally, when Nina was ten, she landed a role in a local musical. It was all uphill from there. A major musical agent was in the audience and heard this little kid with a big voice and signed her right away. Nettie and Nina moved to New York and stayed there until Nettie was diagnosed with breast cancer at the age of thirty-six. She died two years later, and Nina was once again on her own at the age of twenty-one. Nina had since become a big proponent for early detection and self-testing.

Trevor watched and wondered how he could introduce the topic without sounding self-serving. Truthfully, he had nothing to gain. This wasn't about him or even someone who was a permanent part of his life. Still, it was touchy asking one client to help another. He contemplated whether he should bring it up before or after they got it on tonight.

Nina finally turned her attention back to Trevor. "What's on your mind?" she asked as she eased back into the plush leather of the seat.

He was surprised to hear her address him directly. He smiled in response to her question. This was the opening he needed. "I was just thinking about your work with the Breast Cancer Foundation," he replied.

"Why is that?" she asked, her eyes narrowing speculatively. She'd known him for more than a year now and had never bothered to have a conversation with him. What interest could he have with the foundation?

"I met someone recently, a very young woman who ended up having a radical mastectomy. I was surprised to learn her insurance would not pay for reconstructive surgery," he replied. He wanted to keep the conversation casual to see if it would pique her interest.

"How young?" she asked and refilled her glass with champagne.

"I'm not sure, but I would guess her age to be mid to late twenties," he replied and drained his glass.

"That is young. She's probably about my age then. Some insurance companies are very good with taking care of the reconstructive surgery, and some have not yet realized its importance," she said as she gathered her gown in her arms and slid onto the limo floor. She crawled toward him until she positioned herself between his legs. "Is she important to you?" she asked, looking up at him as she leaned her arms on his thighs to pull herself up to a kneeling position. The length of the gown impeded her movement.

"No, not in the way you mean," he replied. "I think the loss of her breast has done great damage to her self-image, and I know these days there has to be something that can be done to help her. But I would imagine the surgery must be very expensive," he finished. He could see her mood was changing, and he wanted to finish this conversation before she got sidetracked.

"Is she a client of yours?" she asked and begun to unzip the side of her gown.

"No," he lied, "just someone I met in passing. Someone who left an impression, you might say."

She looked up at him. He was a handsome devil. A stud well worth the money she'd been paying him. He never disappointed her, and he upheld his part of their discreet relationship. There was never a hint of their meetings in the tabloids. He knew how to stay under the radar, and she appreciated it. She could tell this woman was important to him, whether he was willing to admit it or not. He'd never asked her for anything other than his fee. She could assign someone in her organization to check into this for her. Discreetly, of course, she would see what could be done for this woman.

"Leave her name and number with Charles. I'll see what we can do," she said.

Trevor breathed a sigh of relief and started to offer her his thanks. She put up her hand to stop him from speaking. "No more talking," she said. She allowed the gown to fall down to her waist, revealing her small firm breasts. Her breasts were cradled and lifted by a tight-fitting bustier. She leaned forward and offered them to him. "See what you can do with these," she said in a sultry voice.

He reached down and grasped her waist with both hands and hoisted her out of her gown into his lap. All thoughts of Paige left his mind as he kissed the small rising mounds of Nina's perky breasts, one after the other. Underneath her gown she wore only a black lace bustier and a red thong with black lace trim. Her golden skin gleamed in the moonlight streaming through the limousine window. Tonight she wanted to be adored and recognized for her accomplishments as a movie star.

Sensitive to her celebratory mood, he eased her off his lap and laid her on the seat. He moved to the other side of the car and hit a button in the side panel of the door. The seat opposite automatically extended into the middle of the floor and opened outward into a full-length bed. Two huge fluffy pillows folded into the bed from side panels just beyond the rear doors. He returned to her side and transferred her from the seat to the bed.

Nina waited patiently for him to undress and join her on the bed. She rose up on her knees and began an impromptu striptease. First she pulled apart the strings of the bustier and slowly began undoing the front closure hooks. Her hips gyrated as she swayed to the smooth jazz music filtering through the speakers inside the limo. With each hook she loosened, more and more of her silken flesh was exposed. She removed the clips from her hair and shook her head to loosen it from the tight bun she'd worn early in the evening. Her long black curly hair cascaded down across her shoulders.

Trevor leaned against the pillows and watched her tantalizing movements with an appreciative smile. In the dark interior of the car, his gently sloping brown eyes took on a distinctly smoky appearance. He knew she wanted something different this evening and dug deep into his repertoire.

Nina was only halfway through her hooks when he reached across the bed and tugged her closer until the hooks were within his grasp. She knelt between his legs as he finished unhooking her bustier one hook at a time. Between the unlatching of each hook he would stop for an intimate inspection of her body. Softly he began describing everything he saw on her body.

"You work out a lot," he said as he ran his hand lightly across her taut abdominal muscles. He opened the last hook and pushed aside the bustier. He ran his tongue under the soft full curve of her breasts and paused to inspect a small black tattooed rose on her left breast. "A black rose?" he queried.

"Death is never far away," she replied with chilling ease.

He placed his hands around her waist and pulled her against his bare chest. Removing the bustier completely, he nipped the tender flesh behind her ear and blew warm breath into her ear.

"But life is good," he countered and eased her onto her back amidst the pillows on the bed.

Nina sank into the comfort of the fluffy pillows and raised her arms above her head. A thin black lace string rode high across her hip bone, and a tiny red triangular patch of silk covered her treasure.

He turned her onto her stomach and continued his inspection. Her small back and shoulders were muscular and strong in a feminine sort of way. He ran his hands along her hip bones and noticed another tattoo on the back of her right hip. It was a dagger with a drop of blood falling from its sharp point.

"Another omen of death?" he asked as he planted a kiss in the small of her back.

"Tomorrow is not promised," she answered and rolled over onto her back and spread her legs. Her manicured fingers disappeared into the red triangle, and she moaned aloud before she continued. "That's why I like being with you, Steve. When you fuck me, I forget all about yesterday, last week, and last year." In an uncommon moment of vulnerability, tears pooled in her eyes, and she smiled wryly. "I forget about the liars, the cheats, and the evil people who only want to hurt me and take away my joy." She slipped her hand between his legs, tickling the sensitive area between his scrotum and anus. Tenderly she wrapped her fist around his stiff organ and gently tugged it toward her aching sweet spot. "Nothing else matters when you're fucking me," she whispered.

When she rubbed the tip of his dick against the satiny-smooth fabric of her thong, he needed no other urging. He slid the thong off her hips and exposed her completely hairless treasure. He pressed his lips to the baby-smooth skin before slipping his finger inside her mysterious depths. Her moist warmth welcomed him. He silenced her moans with a deep passionate kiss, at the same time easing a condom on his thick and rigid dick.

"Nothing matters when I do this?" he asked as he delved deep inside her treasure and ground his hips against hers.

She exhaled aloud as he entered her secret garden, and she submitted to the overwhelming feeling of fulfillment he provided. Her hips rose up to meet his with each downward stroke. Their rhythmic rocking increased in tempo as her quest for orgasmic pleasure took over.

"Nothing matters," she replied and gasped as an orgasm sent

tremors up her spine. "You make me forget everything. I'm in this moment with you, and I don't care if there's nothing beyond this moment. Fuck me, Steve, so I can forget everything and everyone," she begged and wrapped her strong legs around his waist, pulling him deeper.

He pumped faster and faster, pushing her to the brink of orgasm several times and each time pulling back before she crested the wave. Deliberately, he created a tempest of unbridled, unreleased passion inside her. He raised her legs over his forearms and stroked fast and furiously until he could feel her essence spilling over his dick. He could tell she was about to come and pulled his dick out quickly and laid her back onto the bed.

Nina's breath caught audibly in the middle of her throat when his dick left a vacuum inside her as she was about to climax. Her mouth flew open, and she gasped for air; her clit was throbbing and ready to burst. Suddenly his lips closed over her engorged clit and sucked. She screamed and clawed wildly as a giant orgasm rocked her body. Her mind went numb, and her pent-up dam of love juices burst forth. She collapsed, exhausted, on the bed and shuddered involuntarily several times as she relived the moment in her mind.

"I am alive every second I am with you," she murmured softly before turning her back to him. "Tomorrow is not promised," she whispered as she curled up into the fetal position and once again retreated into her own world.

He covered her with the blanket and prepared for his departure. He knocked on the partition, and Charles opened the window and handed him an envelope. He gave him Paige's information and sat back in his seat for a few more minutes until the car rolled to a stop. He alighted from the limo and walked to his car.

Paige was sitting in her living room when the phone rang. She set the book she was reading on the table and rose from her seat to answer the phone. An unfamiliar voice greeted her and asked if she was Paige Martin. She confirmed she was, and they told her she had been selected for a free consultation with one of the renowned plastic surgeons in the Chicago area. She inquired where they had gotten her name, and they told her it was a random selection process. She fit the criteria for a new breast reconstructive procedure they were doing. She was under no obligation, but they would greatly appreciate it if she would at least come in for the consultation.

She was very leery and did not want to get her hopes up. There had to be some costs involved. Still, on the off chance there wasn't or the deductible was minimal, she didn't want to pass up the opportunity to find out what could, if anything, be done. She agreed and set up an appointment for the following week. She replaced the receiver and wandered to the living room window and looked out. It was a beautiful Chicago fall day, she had a date tonight, and now maybe, just maybe, something else good was on the horizon for her.

12

Trevor stood outside the hotel door waiting for his new client to answer his knock. There was no audible sound coming from the other side of the door. Perhaps she'd changed her mind. He turned away from the door and headed toward the elevators across the hall. As he waited for the elevator, he heard the sound of the latch being removed from the door behind him.

Naomi opened the door and scanned the hallway. There was a very tall, very handsome man standing at the elevator. Her eyes traveled farther down the hallway, and she saw no one else. She looked again at the stranger at the elevator. He was now moving in her direction.

"Naomi?" he asked and smiled down at her. He briefly took in her attire: gray wool slacks with a formfitting, pale pink sweater. She had a very nice figure. She was a medium-sized woman, thick where it counted. Her hair was cut in a short feathered bob that suited her heart-shaped face. Deep, sexy dimples dented the sides of her cheeks. Her unblemished skin was the color of finely ground cinnamon, and her eyes were almost black with long thick lashes.

"Steve?" she inquired in return, with a slight lifting of her right eyebrow. Naomi was very nervous but doing her best not to appear so. She wanted to appear to be the sophisticated kind of woman who did this all the time.

Trevor remembered the first time she had called and how nervous she had sounded. He could tell she had been disappointed at the fee, and he did not think she would call back. He tried not to think of what had prompted such a gorgeous woman to call them. She could have found any number of men willing to bang her for free. From his position in the hallway, he could see a white envelope on the corner of the dresser. He surmised correctly that too much conversation would turn this situation sour real quick. She had made the choice to be here; he didn't want to give her time to second-guess her decision.

At the same time, Naomi was doing exactly what he thought she was. She was starting to think about Greg and how wrong it was for her to be here seeking sexual satisfaction from a total stranger. Hesitantly she stepped back into the doorway and allowed him to enter the room. The longer he stood in the hallway, the more opportunity there was for someone to see him. Naomi moved to stand in front of the dresser and face the mirror. Her reflection stared back at her. There was an unmistakable sadness in her eyes. Also reflected in the upper right corner of the mirror was the image of him removing his shirt. A rippling six-pack and well-formed pectorals were exposed. She felt like she was staring at a perfectly formed male model. Her body throbbed in anticipation. *This isn't right,* she thought, as her body begged for sexual release.

Trevor watched the play of emotions on her face. Guilt was written on her forehead like a scarlet A. As much as he didn't want to, he was going to give her the opportunity to send him away. He walked up behind her and slipped his hands under her sweater. Slowly he slid them up her rib cage until he cupped both breasts in his hands. He massaged them gently.

A sharp gasp slipped through her lips when his hands touched her bare waist. When his fingers began caressing her breasts, tingling sensations started between her thighs. She held her breath and closed her eyes. Still, her mind screamed this was wrong.

Trevor noticed her hands tightly gripping the edge of the dresser and the huge diamond engagement ring and wedding band. He removed his hands from under her sweater and turned her to face him. He leaned in and claimed her mouth with his. Her lips parted under the gentle pressure of his. His tongue explored the sweet corners of her mouth. He pulled her lower lip into his mouth and sucked it firmly and then stood up and away from her.

The throbbing between her thighs was unbearable. She had never been kissed before with such expertise. It wasn't the passion of his kiss, it was the sensual coaxing of a man who clearly knew how to kiss a woman.

"Yes or no?" he asked as he looked into her eyes and saw the raw desire reflected there. He left the decision to continue up to her.

Naomi looked up at him. This was something her body needed desperately. She pushed all thoughts of Greg from her mind. Sadly she realized she hadn't thought of Greg at all while Steve's tongue was in her mouth.

"Yes," she said slowly.

Trevor reached over and pulled her hands free from the dresser. In one easy motion he pulled her sweater over her head, at the same time clicking off the light on the dresser. The room was plunged into darkness. Only a smidgen of light peeked through the thick hotel drapes. As much as he would enjoy watching himself with her, he knew she would be much less inhibited in the dark. Slowly he guided her to the bed. He sat on the edge of the bed and pulled her close until she was standing between his legs.

She stood rigidly, unsure of what to do next. The darkened

room made her less self-conscious but did not take away from the clandestine mood. She was intently aware of his hands as they slowly unbuckled the belt on her pants. The room was deathly quiet, and the only sound she heard was her own rapid breathing. His lips explored the curve of her neck as he unbuttoned her pants. She didn't know which sensation was more overwhelming—his mouth on her neck or the gentle insistence of his hands as he slid her pants down over her hips. Her pants dropped to the floor with a soft whoosh. Meanwhile his lips blazed a trail from her earlobe to her chin as he hooked his thumbs in the elastic band of her panties and eased them down to her knees.

She didn't want to stand there with her panties around her knees and her pants at her feet, although he seemed more preoccupied with undoing the snap on her brassiere, so she leaned on his shoulder and stepped out of them.

His lips were continuing their southern venture, and his tongue snaked inside the top ridge of her lace cup bra, teasing the soft flesh of her breast. Trevor's movements were slow and methodical. He didn't want to move fast and overwhelm her, so he took his time and plotted his course. The thin straps of her bra were next on his list.

When his tongue touched the highly sensitive bud of her nipple, she gasped aloud. She'd never even felt him remove the bra; suddenly she was completely exposed and his warm lips were sucking and teasing her nipples. Her raw nerves were on edge, and her body was responding to his touch of its own accord. Small whimpers of pleasure escaped her lips.

His eyes took in the tempting vision before him: full firm breasts, slim waist, and wide hips. Excited by the promise of things to come, his manhood responded accordingly. He stood up and placed his hands on her waist, and then he lifted her onto the bed as if she were no heavier than a feather. It seemed only seconds later he was in bed beside her. When his bare skin touched hers, she resisted the urge to bolt. Instead she moved over into the middle of the bed and parted her legs.

Trevor hesitated only momentarily before heeding the call of nature and easing himself between her legs. Once he entered her sweetness, her whole body relaxed and gave in to the pleasure of the moment.

Naomi thought she was mentally prepared to be business-like and nonchalant about her sexual adventure, but once his rigid manhood became one with her aching, deprived woman-hood, all rational thoughts fled. Her hips rolled gently in response to his slow and deliberate penetration. She subconsciously found herself counting the minutes in her mind until he would come and she would be unfulfilled again. But he kept stroking and stroking. Then he rolled her up onto his belly and with strong forceful hip movements he stroked some more. He flipped her onto her back once more while staying deep inside her body, and with soul-penetrating, mind-bending strokes of passion, he invaded her body and took over her mind.

Ripples of orgasms sent shock waves through her body. She bucked and moaned uncontrollably with uninhibited wantonness. Her own voice echoed in her mind as it repeated *It's so hard; it's so damn hard*. It felt so good she didn't want him to stop.

As he increased his tempo, she stayed with him. It didn't take him long to realize she wasn't there for lovemaking. She was with him because she needed to get fucked, and he was happy to oblige. He turned her onto her stomach and lifted her hips into position. He'd wanted to grind up against her perfect ass ever since he saw her standing in the doorway. The way she filled out those gray slacks was a prelude to the fine ass inside. He hadn't been disappointed. Her ass was as silky smooth and unblemished as the rest of her.

Naomi voiced no objection when he turned her over doggy style. Her hands gripped the sheets, and she buried her face in the pillow as he buried his dick in her sweet spot again and again. Her muffled cries of pleasure were barely contained as she took every deep satisfying inch he gave her and then some.

He alternately squeezed and rubbed the round firmness of her ass cheeks as he pounded against them with fast, intense strokes. When her essence gushed from her sweetness and washed over his hands, he knew she didn't have much left to give. Still he had more for her. He pulled out of her and coaxed her to the edge of the bed. He stood next to the bed and pulled her hips to the edge. With her legs draped over his forearms and her hips elevated off the bed, he continued his tactical assault on her aching, throbbing passion.

Finally she couldn't take anymore. She'd come more in those ninety minutes than she had in the last several years, and it became quite clear that Steve was willing to make this a marathon. She weakly admitted she'd had enough and told him, "I'm done. I'm done."

He smiled devilishly at her and finally let go of his own flow of hot, sticky juice. He eased her limp body back into the middle of the bed and exited to the bathroom to dispose of the condom and take a quick shower. He was energized by his afternoon with Naomi. It wasn't too often he got a workout like that one with such a willing and sexually uninhibited partner. Once he'd gotten past her initial hesitation, she'd given up all she had to the moment. He dressed quickly and gave her a quick spontaneous kiss on her dimpled cheek on his way out the door. He'd be quite happy to spend more time with her.

Naomi sat on the edge of the bed, biting her lip as she watched the door close behind him. He'd satisfied every physical desire she had, even a few she hadn't known about. As she sat there, naked except for a sheet, on a strange bed in an empty hotel room, the enormity of the betrayal she committed was closing in on her. While she finally had achieved and immensely enjoyed the sensation of a real vaginal orgasm more times than she could count, she felt empty inside.

Sex for the sake of sex wasn't all it was cracked up to be. He'd done what she had paid him for. He'd fucked her every way but Sunday. Yet she found it wasn't all she really wanted. After all was said and done, she missed the emotional connection with the man who was invading her body. As expert as he was, she knew there was no personal feeling attached to his touch. He wouldn't look at her two hours later and smile as he remembered their lovemaking or wink at her with a promise of repeating the afternoon.

As inept as Greg was in bed, she knew beyond a shadow of a doubt how much he loved her. He would do anything in the world to make her happy. She simply failed to communicate how important sexual gratification was to her. Instead she sought it in the arms of a total stranger. Yes, she'd had her orgasms, which she had thought were so important a few days ago, but she had betrayed the man who loved and trusted her. That betrayal was going to haunt her for a very long time.

She rose from the bed and walked into the bathroom to shower. She left the hotel room physically satisfied but emotionally bereft and more confused than ever.

Marissa removed the book from the shelf and opened the secret compartment. She pulled off the rubber band and counted the thick wad of money. There was five thousand dollars in one hundred dollar bills. She counted the money she had picked up at her mother's—eight hundred dollars. She counted out three one-hundred-dollar bills and added them to the roll. She put the rubber band back on and returned the wad to the secret compartment. She looked at the five hundred dollars still in her hand and frowned.

There should be more money saved. She should have at least eight thousand dollars by now. Instead she had been spending her money on him. She couldn't help herself. She was addicted to the way he made her feel.

Sex with Toby had become even more unpleasant now because she knew what it could be like. She had disliked sex with Toby before, but she hated it when he touched her now. Forwarding the house calls to her cell phone had been sheer genius, but she'd almost gotten caught two weeks ago when she forgot to stop the forward service as soon as she walked in the house. She was cooking dinner when her cell phone rang in her purse at the same time she heard the garage door open. In a panic she looked at the clock and realized it could be Toby calling. She quickly ran to the phone and breathed a sigh of relief when she saw it was her mother's number. She answered and breathlessly told her to hold on. Then she picked up the house phone and dialed her stop-forward code. She returned to speaking with her mother as Toby walked in the kitchen door.

He eyed her suspiciously, and she immediately told her mother she was in the middle of cooking dinner and would call her back later. She made sure to say this loud enough for Toby to hear. Then she deliberately laid the phone on the counter because she knew he would check the last incoming call as soon as her back was turned.

Returning her concentration to the money in hand, she walked down the hallway to her bedroom. She opened her purse and slipped the money into her pocket calendar between the cardboard and the blue plastic cover. Tomorrow she was meeting him again at a hotel in town. She was taking a half day at work again. These short days were beginning to impact her sales, and she wasn't earning as much in bonus rewards as she used to.

Marissa had given serious thought to taking the money she had and leaving Toby now. She had hoped to meet a goal of ten thousand, but it did not look like it would happen. She wanted to see more of Steve, and she didn't want to sneak around to do it. Maybe if he realized she was free and available, he would admit he cared for her as well. She was sure he had to feel some-thing for her. He was so sweet, tender, and considerate. Yes, she was sure he was just keeping his feelings under control because he knew she was married and probably thought he could never have her.

She would tell him tomorrow. She was leaving Toby so she could be with him all the time. She smiled when she thought of him and giggled aloud when she reminisced on the magic feel-ings his fingers created. She blushed and felt herself growing moist just thinking about his naked body. A quick glance at her watch let her know she had at least two hours before Toby came home. "Oh, Steve," she murmured as she pictured his fine, rock-hard body in her mind. Remembering his touch, she slipped her hand inside her panties and began stroking herself. She groaned aloud in pleasure as she mimicked his touch on her special place. With her bed so nearby she could not resist the temptation to play a little longer. A quick trip to her closet and a hidden shoe box provided her with a small tube of lubricating solution and a ten-inch silicone vibrator. Her money had not been spent only on afternoons with Steve but on a few of the sex toys and sexy lingerie items she'd been reading about in her new stash of magazines. Awash with excitement of the guilty pleasure she was about to enjoy, she giggled as she stripped quickly out of her clothes and climbed onto the bed. Com-pletely naked and positioned in the middle of the bed between two pillows, she inserted the magic bullet into the center of the vibrator and turned on the switch. The thick silicone dick purred to life in her hands. She wet it slightly with her tongue and closed her eyes. Suddenly he was there with her; as she tickled the tips of her nipples with the pulsating organ, he was there licking and biting their rigid peaks. His short curly hair brushed her chin as she clutched his strong shoulders and pushed him lower in the bed. "Here, Steve, here, I want you to kiss me here," she whispered urgently as she moved the vibrator down between her legs. With her knees raised high, she opened her legs and lightly rubbed the purring dick against her clit. "Oh, Steve, oh, yes, Steve!" she cried as she visualized his mouth on her sweet spot. An animal-like scream escaped her lips as a violent orgasm overtook her body. "Yes, my sweetheart, yes. I taste good, don't I?" she cooed to her imaginary lover as she inserted her fingers into her own wetness and placed them against her lips. She licked her own sweet juice from her fingertips like it was cake batter dripping off a spatula. "Now fuck me, Steve," she commanded as she lifted her buttocks off the bed and slipped a pillow under her hips. She continued to give instructions to her imaginary lover. "Fuck me good and hard," she said as she placed a generous amount of lubrication on the shaft of the vibrator and pressed it against her sweetness. "Oh, you are so big," she moaned and pressed the rounded tip inside. A sharp intake of breath followed as her body welcomed her silicone friend. Slowly her imaginary friend stroked in and out of her pulsing love canal. She quickly adjusted to the size and girth of her new friend and pushed it as far as she could inside her body. Her hips pumped up and down in rhythm with her hands as she used her own special two-fisted insertion technique. Her fingers grew slippery and wet from her own natural lubrication. Orgasm after orgasm rocked her body as she continued to talk to Steve. "Fuck me harder and faster, you know you like it," she cried as he stroked faster and faster until a final strong orgasm rippled through her body from head to toe, and she released her hold on the vibrator. She lay quietly for a few moments until her breathing slowed down.

She opened her eyes and saw the lower half of the vibrator protruding from between her legs. He was gone. Steve had turned back into the lifeless purple silicone toy sticking out of her special place. A tear rolled out of the corner of her eye. "I love you, Steve. I love you so much," she whispered.

She gingerly removed the vibrator and proceeded to the

bathroom, where she washed it and returned it to its secret hiding place. She took a quick shower and cleaned up the bed. For a moment she considered her lustful behavior and wondered what kind of woman she was turning into. The magazines said there was nothing wrong with being sensual and sexually adventurous. It just had taken her a very long time to realize how much sensuality lay buried inside her. Tomorrow she was going to tell Steve everything. Tomorrow he would know how much she loved him.

At three o'clock the following afternoon, Marissa was waiting anxiously inside her hotel room for Steve to arrive. She checked her hair and makeup in the mirror several times. As soon as she had left work she had headed for the salon to get her nails done, a pedicure, and waxing done. She arrived at the hotel at one thirty and had run a bath and taken a leisurely soak until two fifteen. She had then put on her newest purchase from Neiman Marcus lingerie and perfumed her body.

Two fifty-nine on the dot, there was a knock at the door. Marissa gleefully rushed to open the door. She reached for his hand and pulled Steve into the room and wrapped her arms around his neck and kissed him eagerly.

Trevor responded to the passion in her kiss, but he did not like the urgency he could sense in her. She called him more frequently than any of his other clients, and he was beginning to feel a little leery about servicing her any longer. When she called for the appointment today, he'd decided to give it one more time to see if he was still getting those same vibes. He unwrapped her arms from his neck and stepped back to look at her. She wasn't a bad-looking woman, a little plain perhaps. She had a decent figure with a little meat on her bones. Not overly voluptuous or heavily burdened on the back end. She did not carry herself as someone who had an unlimited supply of money to spend on pleasure. Yet she had called him every other week for six weeks. While he didn't mind the money, he began to feel she was getting too attached to him. He smiled at her and began to pull his T-shirt over his head.

Marissa sat on the edge of the bed anxiously. She watched avidly as he undressed for her. She'd been reading about the pleasures of oral sex and wondered if she could get him to do it to her. The sight of his manhood turned her on like she never would have thought possible. She scooted back on the bed to allow him room to crawl in beside her.

Trevor climbed into bed beside Marissa and lay down to rest his head on the pillow. He closed his eyes momentarily, taking mental stock of what he was supposed to be doing. He was tired of this and never more so than at this moment. He would give her what she was paying for today, but this was the last time for her or anybody else. Enough was enough. He breathed deeply and turned on his side to face her.

Marissa watched him as he lay there with his eyes closed. Her eyes traveled the length of his exquisite body, the smooth, hairless chest; the rippling muscles of his abdomen; and the curly dark patch of pubic hair surrounding his sizable manhood. She licked her lips in anticipation. Her body was already feeling feverish. She returned her focus to his face to find him looking at her. She smiled.

Sliding her body close to his, she ran her fingers along his chest. Inching slowly downward she placed the flat of her hand on his solid six-pack. She smiled in her wondrous exploration. Tentatively she touched the curly patch of pubic hair and began running her fingers across it. She took his organ in her hand and closed her fist around it. It was soft and silken to the touch. She marveled at the way it seemed to respond to her touch and grow larger in her grasp.

Trevor watched her playing with his body like she had never seen one before. He knew this was not the case because she was wearing a wedding band. So she definitely had been with a man before. But she touched him like it was all a new experience for her, and she responded to him like a woman just learning the joys of sex. He didn't allow his mind to dwell on it too long. What happened in her bedroom at home wasn't his problem.

Marissa sat up in the bed and removed her filmy green teddy. She lay back down, spread her legs, and began to touch her private parts. She looked over at him, silently imploring him to know what she wanted.

Trevor sheathed his erect organ and watched Marissa fingering her clit. Her tongue was licking the corners of her mouth while she grew more excited. She wasn't waiting for him today. She was taking charge of the situation. He started to roll over on top of her, and she stopped him by putting her hand against his chest. Puzzled, he looked at her.

She pointed to her pulsing vulva and licked her lips in an exaggerated fashion. He hesitated. She couldn't mean what he thought she did. She removed her wet fingers from her sweet spot, licked them, and placed them against his lips. Without a doubt he knew she wanted him to go down on her. He wasn't feeling it. His mind raced to come up with an excuse that would not kill the mood.

"Steve?" She sighed and lifted her buttocks off the bed, raising her mound for his touch.

"Do you have any dental dams? You know there's an extra fee for that?" he asked softly as he placed his hand on her mound and began stroking her.

"Extra?" she replied breathlessly. His hand was like a heat-seeking missile on her crotch. The very heat in the palm of his hand was making her wetter. Waves of orgasms were causing her body to buck uncontrollably. "Dental what?" she gasped.

"Dental dam," he replied, biting her neck softly while rubbing her nipples in his fingers. Marissa continued to gasp and moan. He was certain she would soon forget her desire for oral sex. He moved his mouth to the tip of a nipple and began pulling the erect peak into his mouth, sucking on it aggressively.

Marissa's cries of pleasure grew louder as her body ached for fulfillment. Trevor rolled her over on top of him and pulled her to a sitting position. He looked at her and nodded in the direction of his jutting organ. Marissa poised her body above his hips as he guided his member into the wet recess of her body. Her sharp cries of discomfort were momentary as she adjusted to the feel of him deep inside her body. She bit her lower lip in agitation as she tried to move her body back and forth on the engorged rod filling her. Her breathing was ragged as she sat nearly motionless on him.

He sensed her inability to move properly and grasped her buttocks and then raised his hips, lifting her up and down, creating the stroking sensation for her. He released his grasp on her buttocks and grasped her breasts in both hands. Gently he pushed her backward into a reclining position.

Alarmed that his organ would snap off from the awkward position, Marissa flailed wildly as she tried to grab his hands and gain an upright position again. While he appeared no worse for the wear she could feel his stiffness pressing against the inner regions of her belly.

Trevor pulled her to an upright position again and swiftly shifted her position so she was lying under him. He nuzzled her neck softly and began slowly stroking in and out of her sweet spot.

Marissa, relieved to be on the bottom once again, relaxed into the lovemaking rhythm she'd gotten used to with him. Wrapping her arms around his neck, she opened herself up and enjoyed the rest of the ride.

When they were done, Trevor wasted no time hopping into the shower and preparing to leave. Marissa stood in front of the door to stop him before he departed. This was the moment Trevor was hoping to avoid.

"Steve, can I talk to you for a few minutes?" she asked and looked imploringly up into his eyes.

"Sure, Marissa. What's up?" he asked casually as he shoved the envelope from the table in his pants pocket.

"I want . . . I would like to . . ." she stammered. Damn, she cursed silently, why couldn't she get out what she wanted to say?

"Yes, Marissa? I have to go soon. Is there something on your mind?" he asked, reminding her at the same time he was on the clock.

"I want to take you out to dinner. On me, of course," she sputtered.

"Thanks, but that's not necessary," he replied more casually than he felt. He knew this was where she was headed all along, and he didn't want this confrontation.

"But I want to. I want to have a date with you, a whole night. Dinner, movies—you know, the whole thing," she said excitedly. She could feel him rejecting her, and it hurt. Couldn't he see how much she loved him?

He did not want to hurt her feelings, and he could tell she was getting upset. Gently he said, "Marissa, there is something you need to understand. This," he waved his arms around the room for effect, "is not who I am. This is only something I do."

"Then I want to know the other you," she said petulantly. The idea of staying with Toby was making her desperate.

"I'm sorry, Marissa. I don't do that. It's not a good idea. You're married," he replied and turned toward the door.

"I'm leaving Toby. I made up my mind a long time ago, and now I'm ready to do it. I have saved almost ten thousand dollars; we can run away together," she insisted.

Trevor felt chills running through his body. Her desperation was a bad sign. *Oh, God,* he thought, *get me out of here.* "If you want to leave your husband, that's up to you, and it is not any concern of mine. I cannot and will not see you again. You have to understand and accept that. This is the last time you'll see me, Marissa," he said adamantly and walked out the door. He pulled the door closed behind him and strode quickly to the elevator. Once inside he leaned on the back wall and ran his hand roughly over his face. "Shit!" he said aloud. He should not have met with her today. He should have ended it when she called for the appointment. He knew today was a mistake, and he couldn't shake the bad feeling it gave him.

Marissa stared at the closed door. She was trembling. He loved her, she knew in her heart he did. He was just afraid, afraid of Toby like she was. She had to go after him. She raced to the closet and pulled on her jeans and T-shirt. Quickly slipping on her sneakers, she grabbed the card key off the dresser and raced into the hallway. She grabbed the first elevator and rode it down to the lobby. He was nowhere in sight. She burst onto the street just in time to see a cream-colored Jaguar XJ8 pulling out of the parking garage. It turned away from the hotel, but only after she recognized the profile of the driver. It was Steve. She made a mental note of his license plate and went back into the hotel.

Trevor drove straight home from the hotel. His hands were shaking on the steering wheel. "I should have quit this non-sense a long time ago," he admonished aloud. He parked the car in the driveway and collected his mail from the mailbox. Not stopping to sort through the envelopes in his hand, he headed for the front door. He entered the house and tossed the mail on the end table in the vestibule and headed straight to the living room. A fully stocked built-in bar awaited him, and he wasted no time in grabbing a crystal highball glass from the shelf and pouring a generous amount of Old Kentucky bourbon in it. The shock of the fiery liquid was exactly what he needed as he took a huge swig. He formed a large O shape with his mouth and expelled a loud breath of air. Then he refilled his glass and carried it up to his bedroom.

His answering machine showed two messages waiting for him. He ignored them momentarily in lieu of taking another shower to wash away the feeling of dread overtaking him. His master shower was directly behind an oversize Jacuzzi tub. It was a sunken open stall behind the tile wall at the rear of the tub. The shower had two separate shower stations. A brick glass wall in the back of the shower provided natural illumination. He stepped down into the shower and turned the corner and then activated the gold-plated jets. They sputtered to life, and steam quickly filled the bathroom. He stayed an extralong time in the shower, trying to wash away the afternoon with Marissa. Lathering completely, he washed from his hair all the way down to his toes and back again. Finally he emerged from the shower. He dried at length and then stood before the full-length mirror and took stock of himself. He wasn't sure he knew the person staring back at him anymore. Why had he allowed himself to get so caught up in this game? Yeah, no doubt the money was good, and it wasn't at all hard-earned, in reality. For the most part he'd had some fun, but he'd known for a while now it wasn't as much fun as it was in the beginning.

He hung his towel on the rack and proceeded into his bedroom closet where he retrieved a pair of sweats and a T-shirt to put on. There were undeniably some fond memories associated with the service, but they were few. He thought first about Paige and then Naomi, two very beautiful women. Then there was Nina, who was like a caged animal. He was never sure what to expect from her. Agnes—he shuddered at the very thought of her. And then there was Denise, big, bold, and sassy, but who still did not have the confidence to let her guard down and open herself up to a real relationship. So she played it safe with him.

Seated on the side of his bed, he hit the PLAY button on his answering machine. The first voice surprised him. It was Cynthia, his ex-girlfriend. She was going to be in town in two weeks for a conference and hoped they could get together one night for dinner. For old time's sake, she'd said. He frowned at the thought of seeing her again. He had dated Cynthia for three years while they were carving out their prospective business careers, and, granted, he was a bit of a player at the time. In fact, he'd started dabbling in his second business during her out-of-town trips. Still, when he pressed her to seriously consider a life of commitment and children, he was hurt by the ease at which she cast him aside and moved on. He had covered his disappointment pretty well with the usual male bravado and then delved more deeply into the service business in his free time. Maybe he needed those women as much as they needed him, but differently. It could have been the distraction of not having to reflect on the emptiness of his own life or the thrill of living a lifestyle he'd only dreamed of, funded by the ladies. The only person who sensed there was something wrong under the surface was the second voice on his answering machine.

"Hey, big guy. Just wanted to say hi. Sorry I missed you. I love you," Olivia's voice floated through the air. He stared at the machine and hit the PLAY button again. He listened to her message two more times before he turned and left the bedroom.

13

Trevor pulled up to the Knickerbocker Hotel and left the engine running as he stepped out onto the pavement. A uniformed valet handed him the receipt for his car, and he turned to retrieve his tuxedo jacket from the backseat. He took a moment to check out the other arriving guests as he put the jacket on and closed the rear door. A veritable who's-who from the Chicago area, decked out in diamonds and furs, were queuing at the door.

As Trevor waited his turn to pass through the hotel doors, Marissa stood in the shadows of a doorway down the street. She sighed at the sight of him. He was more handsome than she remembered. It had been three weeks since their last encounter. When she had read about the fund-raising event in the paper, she somehow knew he would be here. Although she did anticipate he would be escorting some rich and beautiful woman, she was pleased and heartened to see he arrived alone. It gave her hope. A foolish hope rooted in her belief that someday they would be together. In an attempt to ward off the chill in the air, she pulled the collar of her wool coat close under her chin. She stayed in her hiding spot until he disappeared inside the building and then she turned and walked back to her car.

Damian surveyed the room. Dressed in an Italian-cut, black, three-button tuxedo made from merino faille wool with double satin besom pockets, he cut a dashing figure. The moss-green vest, matching bow tie, and pocket square served to bring out the green in his hazel eyes. The Crystal Ballroom at the Knickerbocker Hotel was filled with the local movers and shakers of the corporate world. Quite a few dignitaries from across the country were in attendance as well. The sheer gold-accented opulence of the room bespoke of the importance of the evening. Enormous crystal chandeliers hung from the arched ceiling above. Each table was covered with a white linen tablecloth and adorned with a four-foot-high floral centerpiece.

He took a sip of his Bombay Sapphire martini and noticed a group of associates he hadn't seen since the last big social event. He wandered over to join in the conversation. After greeting the familiar faces and being introduced to a few new people, he joined in the usual political debates. At affairs like this one in support of the United Negro College Fund, the issue of affirmative action was always a hot topic. Damian was in the midst of expressing his opinion when his eyes fell on a stunning woman walking between the tables on the far side of the ballroom. He paused only briefly and then continued to make his point. A mental note was taken of a midnight-blue gown and long wavy brown hair, and a mental task was assigned to follow up and seek her out at a later time. Damian's mind worked like an expensive day planner.

Trevor joined the group. He was similarly attired in a black tuxedo but chose a spread collar shirt with a graphite-gray silk tie and matching vest. He'd spent the last forty minutes or so networking and making a few new contacts. He was eager for the dinner to be served so he could make his excuses and leave.

Both were oblivious to the stares of the women across the room; the men were a hot topic of conversation. Fine, black, financially sound, eligible bachelors were a rarity. Damian and Trevor were chocolate and caramel twin towers of male perfection. Their clothing alone let women know these brothers had class and money. Damian had a smooth milk-chocolate complexion, perfectly aligned pearly white teeth, and hypnotizing hazel bedroom eyes. He was six feet four inches of rock-solid muscle carrying a very trim two hundred and forty pounds. Trevor was an inch taller and every bit as handsome, with deep brown eyes, sloping lids, and long lashes. Caramel in complexion with chiseled features and neatly trimmed mustache, he was a walking, breathing fantasy.

Trevor and Damian stepped away from the group to converse privately. Trevor asked Damian what his plans were for after the affair. There was always an after-party somewhere for a select few, and Damian always had the hook-up.

"I've got a room upstairs, and I plan on finding a sweet honey up in here to share it with me," Damian said, smoothly checking out the crop of women in the room.

"Damn, don't you ever take a break?" Trevor asked.

"I'm thirty-five years old, and I ain't thinking about a break," Damian said, surveying the crowd once again. "Ah-ha! There she is," he said and indicated the woman in the blue gown. "The honey in the dark blue with the long hair."

"Have you seen her face yet?" Trevor asked.

Damian darted a quick look at him. "No, have you?" he asked. He couldn't imagine that anyone with a figure as fine as that wouldn't have a face to match. He took in the shape of her curvy hips and long legs. She was at least five feet eleven, and her dress dipped daringly in the back, exposing smooth, pecan-colored skin. "But you know, now that you mention it, I swear I've seen that ass before." Damian laughed.

"Well, you would know better than me," Trevor replied and

shook his head. "It looks like she's talking to Chantel from the corporate office. Why don't you go on over and ask for an intro? I'm hungry, so I'm going to find our table. We should be sitting down soon."

Damian made his way across the room toward the group of women. The closer he got, the more certain he was he recognized this woman's figure. He stepped up to the group. Deliberately ignoring the woman in the blue dress, so as not to appear obvious, he greeted the administrative assistant for the firm.

"Hello, Chantel, so nice to see you again," he said and reached out and shook her hand.

"Hi, Damian," she replied. Damian was a big fish, and no matter how hard she baited her hook, she had never been able to gain his interest. She was curious why he had crossed the room to say hello.

"Are you enjoying your evening?" he asked. Then, feigning as if he did not realize he had interrupted them, he said, "I'm sorry, ladies. Pardon me, I did not mean to interrupt." His eyes quickly scanned the group, still avoiding eye contact with the woman in blue standing directly next to him. He noted she was wearing a Tiffany fragrance and smelled positively edible.

He hadn't moved away, and Chantel felt compelled to make introductions. Going slowly around the small group of women, she introduced him to everyone. The names went in and out of his head as he shook hands and smiled charmingly while he waited patiently for her to reach the woman at his side.

Chantel stepped in front of the woman in the blue dress, and Damian finally turned to face her. Apparently she hadn't paid close enough attention to him either. She pegged him to be a rich playboy who was used to women falling over him and maintained her conversation with the woman next to her. Finally she turned to look at him as he faced her for the first time. Their cordial smiles immediately froze in place. Agnes's eyes frosted over, and Damian's eyebrow arched quizzically.

"Agnes Garfield, I would like you to meet Damian Adams. Damian is the regional sales director for our West Coast region, and Agnes is a tax attorney with Martin and Claymore," Chantel said and turned her attention back to the group.

"Martin, Claymore, and Garfield," Agnes corrected. "I made partner last month."

"Congratulations," Damian said politely. He chided himself; he knew her body was familiar, intimately familiar.

"So, your name is Damian?" Agnes asked with thinly veiled agitation.

"Yes, it is. May I offer you a drink, Ms. Garfield?" he asked in an attempt to draw her away from the group.

She didn't want to have a public discussion with him any more than he did with her. She had a lot of questions, and she wanted answers. She agreed to go with him. They walked toward the bar. They were a stunning couple. He was tall and elegantly handsome. She was tall, beautiful, and statuesque. He placed a hand on her elbow to guide her through the throng of people. She flashed him a quick warning look.

"It isn't as though I haven't touched you before," he said quietly. "Lighten up."

Damian regained his footing a whole lot faster than she did. When he thought about it, he realized it was only sheer luck he hadn't run into her before now. She'd been using his services for almost six months. They traveled the same business circles. He stepped up to the bar and ordered a Cosmopolitan for her and another Sapphire martini for himself. They walked in silence to a secluded corner.

"You're a tax attorney?" he asked.

"You have a real job?" she retorted and took a sip of her drink.

"Touché," he said. "You're looking extremely attractive this evening. Could we perhaps call a truce for tonight?"

"I'm not sure, *Mike*. You've been taking quite a bit of my

money for the last several months. It does not appear you even need it. So why do you do it?" she asked.

"It's a job, and you've been getting quite a bit for your money," he countered smoothly. "For obvious reasons, you can stop calling me Mike."

She stared into his hazel eyes and wondered why she hadn't noticed before how attractive he was. His smile, when he smiled, was magnetic. He looked extremely handsome in his finery, and he smelled very good. She studied the cut of his tux and calculated the cost of the expensive material. He had good taste as well.

He was making nearly the same mental assessment of her. When she wasn't filled with attitude, she was a very attractive woman. He always appreciated her well-formed body, but he was taking a second look now. She usually wore her hair tied up. He liked it down and loose like she had it tonight. It made her appear softer, more feminine. He always thought she was smart, but a partner in such a prestigious law firm he would not have anticipated. He wondered what had turned her into such a bitch with men. Why was she so bitter?

"Well, then, Damian." She leaned in close to him and whispered, "Tell me what led you into a life of crime?"

"I'll tell you, if you tell me why a hottie like you has to pay to get fucked," he whispered back in her ear.

She leaned away from him and fixed him with an angry glare. This was not working. He had an answer for everything. She couldn't gain the upper hand, and she didn't like it at all. Maybe she should get up and walk away. Yes, that was a good idea, she thought. Just walk away from him. She remembered the last time she was with him. Looking at him tonight, she reluctantly admitted she wanted him. She wanted him badly. Agnes shook her head slightly and took a bigger gulp of her drink than she intended. She gagged on the liquid. Turning away from him, she coughed several times. Tears stung her eyes as she fought to catch her breath.

Damian immediately realized what was happening. He took her drink from her hand and began massaging her back. She wasn't choking. She had taken in too much air with the drink. A good belch was all she needed.

She continued to walk in a circle, trying to cough up the excess air. In a few minutes she emitted a very unladylike belch. Damian handed her a glass of water, and she took a few sips. She coughed a few more times and then was able to stop. She smiled at him weakly, embarrassed by the incident.

"God don't like ugly, sweetheart," he said and returned her smile. He handed her a handkerchief from his pocket.

She dabbed lightly at the corner of her eyes and handed it back to him. "I'll agree to the truce, for now," she said. "I have to get to my table. They will be serving dinner soon." She cradled the water glass in her hands and started to walk away.

Damian reached out and touched her arm. "I'd like to continue our conversation after dinner."

She hesitated for a moment, and then replied, "I'll meet you in the martini bar later." She walked away and made her way back to her table. Damian watched her for a few moments and then sought out Trevor at their table.

Two hours later he was sitting in the martini bar nursing another drink, when she slipped onto the stool next to him. He nodded in her direction to acknowledge her presence but said nothing. He signaled the bartender in their direction. "What would you like?" he asked her.

"Just a glass of water with a slice of lime, please," she replied. The bartender quickly prepared her water and set it in front of her. She wasn't sure what kind of mood Damian was in because he wasn't speaking. She thought he would have so much to say after dinner. But he sat there pensively staring into his drink, barely acknowledging her presence. "I thought you wanted to continue our conversation?" she queried.

He turned in his seat to face her. Allowing his eyes to travel the length of her body from head to toe and settling back in on the deep V-neck in the front of her gown, catching an eyeful of her tempting full breasts, he replied, "Yeah, I thought about it, but then I decided it would be a waste of my time. I don't feel like trading barbs with you for the rest of the night."

"Oh, well, then I guess I'll be on my way," she said, slipping off the bar stool and reaching for her small evening bag on the counter.

His hand closed over hers on the counter. He leaned in close to her so only she could hear him. "I didn't come here to talk, and neither did you. We both know where we plan to end the night. If you want to get started, then I'm ready," he said and stood up. He reached into his wallet and laid a few bills on the bar. He placed his hand on the small of her back and guided her out to the hallway.

Agnes didn't care for his assumption. She especially didn't like that he was correct. Upsetting him now would only result in her going home alone. She really didn't want to go home yet. She silently followed his lead.

He guided her toward the elevators. While waiting for the doors to open, he leaned down and planted a soft kiss on her neck. She stiffened and looked around to see who might have seen him. There was no one else in the corridor. They stepped into the empty elevator, and Damian pushed the button for the eleventh floor. He deliberately backed her up against the wall of the elevator and moved in for a kiss.

Agnes watched as his face descended toward hers. She was surprised. He'd never kissed her before. His lips on hers were soft and gentle. His kiss was sensual but not insistent. The doors opened, and he moved away. He took her hand and pulled her from the elevator and led her down the hallway. Silently she followed. He slipped his key in the lock of his room and opened the door for her to precede him inside.

She stepped inside and immediately admired the room. It

was decorated in yellow tones. The walls were painted in a pale yellow, with the exception of the wall at the head of the bed, which was decorated with floral patterned wallpaper. There was a small gold antique desk next to the bed. It was luxurious and yet comfortable. She walked to the bed and ran her fingers along the sleigh-style footboard.

Damian walked up behind her and slipped his arms around her waist. Burying his face in her neck, he began nibbling on her neck and ear. His hands slid up her rib cage until he was cupping her breasts in his palms.

Agnes stood motionless. Her thighs were tingling, and she was unprepared for the sensations he was creating in her body. She didn't like him controlling the pace of the evening as he had been doing thus far. When his hand slipped inside her dress and cupped her naked breast, she emitted an involuntary gasp of pleasure. He captured her nipple between his thumb and forefinger and rolled it playfully. With him still continuing his exploration of her neck, Agnes could feel her body throbbing in reaction to his touch.

"I'm not paying you," she said breathlessly in an attempt to shock him and remind him of who she was.

"Sweetheart, tonight you are going to wish you were," he replied, undeterred. He continued to caress her breast while with his other hand he began unzipping the back of her gown. It was a short zipper that started right at the top of her rump. Once he unzipped it he slipped the side straps off her shoulders, and the gown fell to the floor in one heap. He stepped back to look at her. She was naked under the dress except for a black lacy thong that disappeared between her firm round butt cheeks. Growling under his breath, he easily lifted her off the floor and laid her down on the bed.

Agnes watched as he began removing his bow tie and vest. The muscles rippled across his chest as he unbuttoned his shirt. Her eyes strayed to the bulge at his crotch. Eagerly she waited for him to remove his trousers. He was fully erect by the time his pants dropped to the floor. Taking only a moment to put on a condom, he climbed onto the bed with her.

His hands again began their exploration of her body. He relished the feel of her silky-smooth skin under his hands. She'd never been completely naked with him before, always preferring to keep some barrier between his skin and hers. Tonight he intended to take full advantage of the situation. He kissed her again. This time his tongue poked and probed until she opened her mouth.

She accepted his tongue in her mouth and enjoyed the taste of him. She soon found herself joining in the dance as his tongue enticed hers into a tango of their own. His hand slipped between her legs and found her wet and ready. Not in a hurry this evening, he slid the lacy thong over her hips and down her long legs. He tossed it aside and allowed his fingers to touch and explore her feminine areas. Flicking the tiny protrusion of her mound, he drove her to quick, short orgasms.

Her body arched and bucked as she tried to move away from his insistent fingers as the next orgasm crested. The pleasurable feelings were taking over her mind, and she was trying to get away, to regain control.

He rolled over on top of her and parted her legs. Sliding easily into her, he began slowly stroking in and out. Agnes matched his rhythms, and she sucked her lips to prevent any pleasurable noises from escaping. Damian pulled the rigid peaks of her breasts into his mouth and began softly nipping them.

Agnes flailed wildly in the bed, looking for something to hold on to. She needed something to grab, to squeeze. Damian grabbed one of her flailing hands and planted it firmly on his butt cheek. She tried to pull it away, and he replaced it again. He continued driving his body deeper into hers. Agnes gave up and placed both her hands on his buttocks. It was firm and smooth under her fingers. Raking her long nails across his ass, she was pleased to hear him hiss aloud. It also heightened his excitement.

He rolled over on his back and lifted her to a sitting position on his groin. She cried aloud as the length of his rod completely filled her. It was so deep she could feel it pressing against the inside of her belly. Holding her breath, she tried to relax and find her groove. With his hands firmly planted on her hips, he lifted her up slightly and eased her back down, showing her how he wanted her to move. She rocked back and forth on his rigid member. She was receiving more pleasure than she could remember. She still felt in control or at least cognizant of what was happening. Unexpectedly, he began tweaking her clit. Arching wildly, she tried to get away from his fingers, but her bucking only caused her vaginal muscles to tighten their grip on his organ. She tried to shove his hand away from her clit. She was having difficulty thinking.

"Mike, stop," she said loudly. She hoped it would bring him back to reality. Halt him for a second.

He quickly flipped her over on her back again, this time driving his shaft deeper inside. He knew her game; this time he wasn't playing it. Her head games were useless on him tonight. This was his dime, not hers. He captured her mouth and began kissing her passionately. With one hand under her buttocks, he lifted her and pounded furiously.

Agnes felt herself pushed to the brink of orgasm time and time again. She fought giving in to it. She would not give him that satisfaction. She refused. She pulled her mouth away from his. "Mike, stop," she said again.

He stopped for one second to look at her. She looked angry and frightened at the same time. He knew she wasn't afraid of him. She was afraid of her own body. He knew she didn't want to climax. But then he wouldn't have done his job. He slipped his hand between his body and hers and rubbed her clitoris. "What's my name?" he demanded.

"Mike," she spat through gritted teeth.

"Try again. What's my name?" he said with slow deliberateness. Slowing down, he started grinding in and out of her body with deep, purposeful movements. He could feel the juices of her body spilling over his fingers. "What's my name?" He repeated, sucking on her nipple.

His multitasking was driving her crazy. With his finger on her clit, dick in her vagina, and mouth on her tit, she gave up. She didn't have the will to fight anymore. Her body convulsed in the most explosive orgasm she'd ever experienced. Involuntarily, her mouth opened and she screamed, "DAMIAN!"

Satisfied, he finally came and collapsed on top of her. Rolling away, he pulled her onto his shoulder and breathed deeply for a few minutes. She surprised him by not pulling away. She rested her head on his shoulder and placed her hand on his chest.

"I hate you," she said quietly.

"That's okay. I hate you, too," he said and kissed the top of her head.

Agnes arrived at her office on Lakeshore Drive the following Monday to find a huge bouquet of tropical flowers sitting in the middle of her desk. The stunning arrangement of orange, red, yellow, and purple transformed the feel of the stark office. There was a long credenza behind her desk, which ran under the huge bay window. The window provided a perfect frame for a scenic view of the Chicago River. Very few pictures adorned the office. There were framed works of art, but very little of a personal nature except for the picture on her desk of two small children. The children were her brother's fraternal twins, Ashley and Daniel. She slowly walked into her office and placed the briefcase on the desk. Unable to resist, she leaned in and inhaled the sweet fragrance of the flowers. She looked around the arrangement for a card but found none.

Her secretary Pam poked her head in the door. Her boss had

been the recipient of flowers before but never a bouquet this extravagant. The usual corporate thank-you arrangements were pretty common in their business; the style of this bouquet had romance written all over it.

"Good morning, Miss Garfield. Those are gorgeous flowers," Pam said.

"Do you know where they came from?" Agnes asked, deliberately ignoring Pam's compliment.

"No, ma'am. A courier brought them. I did inquire about the sender, but he said it was an anonymous gift," she replied.

"Okay, thank you," Agnes answered and looked pointedly at Pam, dismissing her.

Pam frowned as she closed the office door behind her. *That woman could suck the joy out of a gorgeous spring day*, she thought. She probably didn't even deserve the guy who sent them to her, and Pam was certain it was a man.

Agnes moved the arrangement of flowers to her credenza. She took one last whiff of the heady aroma and sat down at her desk. An involuntary smile crept to the corners of her mouth. She knew the flowers were from Damian, and she knew he knew she would know this, which is why he didn't feel it necessary to attach a card. She removed her suit jacket and hung it on the coatrack in the corner. Reluctantly she admitted she was pleased. She was also very wary. Bad memories of relationships gone terribly wrong were never very far away. She rubbed her right elbow tentatively and felt the jagged three-inch scar through the thin fabric of her blouse. She remembered what had happened the first time she trusted a man.

She was fifteen and an honor-roll student. Agnes maintained a straight-A average, and her teachers were already predicting she would be the valedictorian for her graduating class. As a promising tennis player and scholar, a world of options lay open before her. College scouts had been following her progress since she was an eleven-year-old phenom winning local and state competitions for her age group. The scouts were easy to spot because most of the adults in attendance were parents or coaches. When an outsider showed up at a tournament, the parents eagerly looked for a college logo on the shirt or notebook to find out where they were from. Agnes began receiving letters of interest when she was fourteen from several Ivy League schools. When it became clear her height was too much of a challenge for other girls her age, she began competing in higher age rankings. At fifteen, her six-foot frame was lean and athletic. Her naturally auburn hair was worn in a French braid tied at the end with a ribbon to match every outfit. She was a stunning figure, even at an early age.

One day as she had walked to the gym to meet Ricky, she thought about the conversation she'd had with her parents the night before. Tears pricked the corners of her eyes as she remembered the disappointment on her father's face and the tears her mother had shed. There was plenty of anger and even more accusations. How could she have been so stupid? Hadn't they warned her about getting too involved with boys at her age? She wasn't even allowed to date—where and how had this happened? What was she thinking? Her stupidity had compromised her future; hadn't they raised her to be better than this?

She had sat there silently in the living room staring at her tightly clasped hands in her lap. Their barrage continued. Her father stormed out of the living room, slamming doors and knocking over one of the dining chairs in his wake. Her mother cried silent tears of lost hopes and dreams.

After her father's stormy departure, Agnes rose from her seat on the couch and knelt down in front of her mother. Placing her hand on her mother's knee, she implored her to understand. She'd never seen her mother cry before, and now she was the cause of her mother's distress. The tears trickled down her mother's chin and fell on the back of her hand. Her mother refused to look at her. Desperately she wanted her mother to understand, woman to woman.

"Mom, I can still go to college. I can still play tennis," she said urgently.

Her mother looked down at her daughter. She was so beautiful with her fresh-faced optimism. She was so naive. She had no clue how her actions had just changed the entire course of her life. Her mother could feel the anger beginning to boil in her stomach. The world had been her oyster, and because she couldn't say no to some boy, she had foolishly thrown it all away. Thrown away all the money and time they had devoted to giving her the best possible chances at a future. All the sacrifices they'd made so she would have a chance at a better life. So she would have more opportunities than they did. It was all over because she couldn't keep her damn legs closed. A fury unlike any she had ever known clouded her mind, and before she could stop herself she lashed out.

The unexpected openhanded blow sent Agnes sprawling across the living room floor. Tears of pain and shock sprung to her eyes as she tried to regain a seated position. Her mother rose from her chair and towered above her. Her fists clenched tightly at her sides; she had no sympathy for her daughter.

"You stupid, stupid girl! You've ruined everything! I told you to stay away from boys. I told you time and time again they were no good. But you're so damned smart! You think you know everything! Well, look at you now! Pregnant at fifteen! Who's going to fix this mess? Who's going to take care of this baby? You? How?"

Agnes sat there with her head bowed and tears streaming down her face. Her mother had never lifted a hand to her in all her fifteen years. Why couldn't she understand it wasn't his fault? Ricky loved her, and she loved him.

Evelyn Garfield took a deep breath in the middle of her tirade. Her eyes cleared, and she looked down at her daughter on the floor. The rage inside slowly ebbed away, and she was left with a feeling of immense sorrow. She wanted to comfort Agnes, to tell her it would be fine. But she couldn't, not at this moment in the midst of all this pain. She just couldn't. She stepped around Agnes and walked into her bedroom and closed the door.

Agnes sat on the floor of the living room for two hours, hoping one of her parents would come back to console her. She heard her father come back into the house, but he never passed through the living room. The room darkened as night settled in; still she waited. She jumped at every sound, but they didn't return. Reluctantly she stood up and walked upstairs to her bedroom. She lay down on the bed, curled her body into a fetal position, and pulled a pillow to her face to muffle the sobs.

The following morning Agnes had entered the kitchen to find her parents seated at the kitchen table. The room was devoid of the usual aromas of coffee and bacon she was accustomed to. The lack of the normal smell indicated her mother wasn't cooking today. Her mother's hands were clasped around a half-empty, lukewarm cup of tea. Her father sat silently at the head of the table. For reasons she could not fathom, her parents suddenly looked older this morning. She guessed they were just tired from lack of sleep like she was. She didn't want another scene like the night before and mumbled a quick "Good morning" as she made a beeline for the back door. Her mother's voice, soft and low, halted her progress.

"Sit down, Agnes," she said.

She hesitated with her hand on the doorknob. She wanted to open the door and bolt out into the yard. Run as fast as she could away from them. She didn't know these people. Where were her parents who loved and supported her every minute of her life? The parents who took care of every little pain and made things better? These old, worn-out-looking people were strangers, and she just wanted to get away from them.

"I'm late, Ma. I got practice this morning," she replied and turned the knob to open the door.

"Agnes Diane Garfield, sit down," her father's voice boomed across the kitchen. He saw the frightened look appear on his daughter's face and lowered his voice. He continued, "We all need to have a talk about this situation. Practice can wait today."

Agnes slowly walked to the kitchen table. The short five-foot distance seemed like a walk through a prison on her way to the gas chamber. She pulled out a chair on the opposite side of the table and sat down. She concentrated on the mosaic of in-laid tiles on the top of the oak dining table while she awaited her execution.

"Agnes, your father and I are very disappointed with your predicament. There is no getting around this. However, we are your family, and in spite of how it may have seemed last night, we love you very much," Evelyn said and reached across the table for Agnes's hand.

Tears of shame and relief welled in Agnes's eyes as she held tightly to her mother's hand. For the next two hours they discussed, as a family, how to address her pregnancy and ways to make it possible for her to continue her tennis and college career. Agnes would have the baby, and her parents would raise the child while she went to school and resumed her tennis training. They would work it out. Everything would go on as planned, with a slight deviation.

It was with this knowledge of her future secured that Agnes waited for Ricky to show up at the gym. She was happy and excited. They could have their baby and still be together. Although she had not worked that part out with her parents, she knew Ricky would be as pleased, too. She remembered he hadn't said very much when she had told him she was pregnant. He had only asked if she was sure.

She smiled as she remembered how all the girls had envied her when Ricky first began talking to her. Ricky Evans was a senior, and she was just a sophomore. At seventeen he was already six foot five. He was gangly but was gaining muscle every day from the weight-training program the coach had him on. He was a good-looking young man with a sepia complexion and dark honey-colored eyes. She was proud to be his girlfriend.

She peered out the window of the second-floor stairwell and watched as Ricky crossed the courtyard, headed for the gym. His gym bag was slung over his shoulder. She noticed he did not look too happy, but she was sure she could cheer him up with her good news.

The heavy metal door to the school clanged shut as she heard him enter the building. The gym was farther down the hallway on the first floor, but they always met here on the second floor before his practice. On Saturdays, like today, the school was relatively empty except for the athletes. This was the place where they had shared their first kiss. It was her first kiss, but she knew it wasn't his. She didn't care; he was her man now. She felt the familiar tingling sensations as she remembered the first time his hand had slipped under her shirt and cupped her small budding teenage breast.

Agnes could hear his shuffling gait as he walked passed the stairwell headed to the gym. Had he forgotten they were meeting today? She raced down to the landing of the first flight of stairs and called his name. He did not respond. She called again and then went all the way down to the first floor. He was almost to the gym door. She ran down the hallway and grabbed his arm.

"Ricky, did you forget about meeting me?" she asked.

"Uh, yeah, got a lot on my mind," he replied as he looked around to see if anyone else was watching them. The hall was still empty.

"I have important news," she said excitedly and began pulling him toward the stairwell. He frowned and shook his head.

"More news? I got to get to practice. Maybe later," he replied. The last thing he wanted to hear was more of her news. Hadn't she done enough damage already? Getting pregnant—how dumb could she be? Girls were supposed to take care of these things! His mom had warned him about girls trying to trap him just so they could get some of his money. He was going to the NBA, and no one was going to mess with that. His mom would kill him if she found out about Aggie being pregnant.

"But it's good news, Ricky. I promise. Come with me, please. Just for a few minutes," she begged. She was eager to tell him what her parents had said. She was also hoping he would give her a kiss or two. She always felt better after one of his hugs. She eagerly led him up the first flight of stairs and then stopped.

"No, not here," he said. On this level anybody entering the building could hear and see them. "Let's go farther up."

They climbed to the second-level stairwell, where Agnes eagerly slipped into his arms. She pressed her face against his chest and breathed a deep sigh of relief. Ricky did not return her embrace. He held fast to his gym bag.

"So what is it? What's your news?" he asked as he turned to look out the window.

"My parents said I could keep the baby, and they will help me to go to school. Isn't that great? I can still go to college and play tennis and everything. And—and we can still be together," she finished excitedly.

Without turning around, he responded, "I was thinking maybe you could get rid of it, like an abortion or something."

Shocked by his suggestion, she hesitated and replied incredulously, "I can't do that, Ricky."

"Why not? Girls do that shit all the time. It's not like it's a real baby or something. Not yet anyway," he said as he turned to look back at her.

Agnes backed away and sat down on the steps leading up to the third level. This couldn't be happening. He was supposed to be as happy as she was. It was their baby, and he wanted to kill it.

"It *is* a baby Ricky. It's our baby, and I want to keep it," she said firmly.

"Why?" he shouted, losing the little patience he had. His mother was right. He glared at her. "Why can't you be like the others and just handle your business? I thought you were supposed to be so damn smart, Miss Honor Society. Well, how'd you get pregnant?"

"How?" she screamed back at him. "You damn well know exactly how I got pregnant, Ricky." She'd been helpless in front of her parents' anger, but how dare he blame this one on her. He was the older one. He was the one with all the experience. She stood up angrily and confronted him. "And just how many other girls have you gotten pregnant, Ricky Evans?"

"Don't matter. None of them was as dumb as you," he spat back. "I don't care what you do. The baby probably ain't mine anyway. You ain't fucking up my career. I'm going to UNLV and getting the hell away from here, you and that fucking baby."

Agnes wondered why she'd never seen the real Ricky before. He didn't care about her. It was just like her parents told her. Boys only wanted sex; they never owned up to their responsibilities. They warned her not to expect too much of this boy, who had gotten her pregnant, because he wouldn't be around. They assured her they would take care of everything as a family. She hadn't believed them; she thought Ricky would do the right thing. She had defended him to them, and now, as she listened to him, she realized they had been right. He had used her. She had never been so angry in her life. With all her fifteen-year-old righteous indignation she pointed her finger in his face and slipped into a lingo she knew he would understand. "This is your baby, and everybody's gonna know it. That's what they have paternity tests for, ya ignorant asshole. So you better go tell yo mama she gonna be a granny real soon."

She turned away from him on the landing and started down the stairs. Ricky turned angrily away from the window. This bitch was not going to ruin everything he had worked for, and his mother was not going to find out anything about this. Fear, rage, and demons he couldn't control propelled him from his position at the window. Just as her foot was about to settle on the second step from the top of the stairwell, Ricky pushed her.

Her body hurtled into the wall as she tried to grab the iron railing to catch herself but missed it. Her foot slipped off the step, and she heard her ankle pop from the jolt on the cement steps. Her knees buckled from the pain, and she tumbled, arms flailing, head over heels, down the remaining ten steps. Agnes landed with a thud at the bottom of the steps on the first landing. She was not moving. Her right arm lay at an awkward angle from her elbow down.

As Ricky watched horrified from his position at the top of the landing, a small trail of blood began trickling out of her shorts, pooling on the floor beneath her. Panic set in as he grabbed his gym bag and raced down the stairs. Gingerly stepping around her broken body, he raced to the first floor. Breathing deeply, he leaned up against the wall in the hallway. He took one last look up at the landing where Agnes lay crumpled and headed to the gym for practice.

Agnes was found by a custodian an hour later and rushed to the hospital near death. She lay comatose for three days. When she regained consciousness, her parents were by her side. She learned she'd lost the baby, broken her ankle, shattered her right elbow, and would never play competitive tennis again. Ricky eventually was charged with aggravated assault, which ended his chances of an NBA career. Agnes learned the hard way that men only wanted to use you for sex or whatever else they could get from you. Once you threatened their perfect worlds, they took it out on you and stole from you the things you treasured most. Men were not to be trusted. Over the years her parents did nothing to deter her from this line of thinking. They wanted Agnes to be secure and confident in her own abilities and taught her never to rely on a man for anything. She took this lesson to heart.

The memories faded with time, and the pain was almost gone except on cold winter or rainy days, when the ache in her elbow and ankle would remind her. Nine years later the tragedies of the events were a distant memory when she met William Jeffrey Scott.

Agnes got up from her desk and wandered to the flowers on the credenza. She lifted a petal to her nose and inhaled deeply. The scent was intoxicating. *Daddy was right*, she thought. He never trusted Will, and I shouldn't have either. He told her the only man she could truly trust was him. So far he had been proven correct.

Her mind shifted to the night of the ball. She could see Damian smiling at her. He was so handsome, so passionate, and he brought desires to the surface long ago suppressed. After all these months that she had been having sex with him, she had never let down her guard. Yet as she watched him the other evening across the ballroom floor, she saw a totally different side of him. She saw someone who was charismatic, debonair, intelligent, and well respected amongst his peers. She saw a successful businessman, not a gigolo she paid for sex. Damian was someone who under different circumstances at a different point in her life she would have been very attracted and vulnerable to. Those days were long gone. In the hotel room she had dropped her guard and allowed him to take her to a level of passion she'd never known. Once her guard was lowered in the privacy and safety of that room, they had made love over and over until the wee hours of the morning. Damian made love to her as if he cherished every inch of her body. He had dozed off finally, and she took that moment to make her escape. She didn't want to face him, or maybe she didn't want to face herself, in the cold light of day the following morning as she slipped out of the room and had the concierge call a cab to take her home.

Today he had sent such a beautiful bouquet of flowers. This told her he did not regret the night he had spent with her. She felt a pin pierce her heart, and a tear trickled out of the corner of her eye. It was too late, too late to change the effects of years of hurt. She couldn't change who she had become or how she felt. Agnes stared out across the Chicago River and said softly, "And I can't trust you either."

Damian sat thoughtfully in his office. His hands were clasped together, with his index fingers resting on the tip of his nose. A frown puckered his brow as he pondered his most recent purchase. What possessed him to send the extravagant bouquet of flowers to Agnes? It was not that he wasn't the type of man to send flowers, because he was. He knew deep down she wasn't going to appreciate the reminder of their evening together. She'd shown a little chink in her formidable armor, and he knew right now she was regretting it.

She intrigued him. He had been servicing her for six months and never really looked at her. He had to admit, he never really looked at any of them. He more or less looked through them. They were just bodies in need of carnal satisfaction, and he was paid to provide it. He did not have to know them, be attracted to them, or even like them, and he certainly did not have to care about them. All he needed to maintain was his ability to perform, and this he did.

Agnes had gotten under his skin the other night. He had been forced to see her in a different light. She was gorgeous when she wasn't trying to break his balls and control the flow of their encounters. In any other circumstances, she would have been the type of woman he might have pursued. Maybe he would have pursued her for the wrong reasons. He would have pursued her to break down those control barriers she held on to so steadfastly. He would have seduced her, claimed his victory, and moved on. But they had an unlikely history now. She'd challenged him, and he'd won that battle. He wasn't so sure he would win again. He wasn't sure he needed to win again.

"Agnes—uh," he said aloud. "What an awful name for such a beautiful woman." He rolled back from his desk and reached for his suit jacket on the valet stand in the corner. It was time to push all thoughts of her out of his mind. He decided he had no desire to be the one to break down her barriers of resistance. He didn't need that kind of headache. As he slipped the jacket onto his shoulders and left his office, he said a mental good-bye to her. He knew she'd never call him again.

14

Twenty minutes away on the other side of town, Marissa was about to make a fatal error. Toby was growing suspicious of Marissa's constant late hours at work. She'd been snapping at him, and he didn't like it at all. He'd been forced to put her in check on a few occasions in the last couple of weeks. A quick smack to her cheek reminded her who was the boss in his house. The fact that he had been unable to locate her on several occasions didn't sit too well with him either. Her explanations didn't sound right, and he could always tell when she was lying, because she wouldn't look him in the eye. He was tempted to take some time off work and follow her around to see what she was up to, but it was the busy season, and he couldn't afford to miss the overtime. So he stewed while he waited for her to slip up. It was only a matter of time.

Marissa was putting the last dish into the cabinet when Toby entered the house. His mere presence annoyed her lately. She couldn't get Steve off her mind and spent quite a few hours lately driving around hoping to catch sight of him. She'd gotten lucky on a few occasions and spotted his car in the downtown area. Often she would hang out as long as she could, and once or twice she'd caught him walking back to his car. Afraid to approach him, she watched from afar. Her heart swelling with love, she knew she only had to get away from Toby, and Steve would be hers. However, she did not want to scare him off in the meantime and kept her distance.

She knew Toby was becoming more and more suspicious of her behavior. Tonight she decided to be extra nice to him to throw him off track. She'd fixed one of his favorite meals and was very solicitous to his every demand.

"Can I get you a beer, honey?" she asked as Toby walked past the kitchen into the family room.

Toby raised his eyebrow at the word *honey*. He wondered what had gotten into her tonight. She was being too damn nice. Heck, he could use her good mood to his advantage. She hadn't been putting out lately, and he could use a good fuck. There was always one damn excuse after the other.

"Yeah, sure, I'll take a beer. Bring it in here for me," he called from the family room.

Marissa took out a cold beer and uncapped it for him. She carried it into the family room as he requested. She bit back her repulsion when she saw him reclined on the sofa, his pants unzipped and his organ in his hand. He stared at her, silently daring her to say no, and worked his hand up and down the shaft.

"Come on, baby. I got something for you tonight," Toby coaxed, intently watching the expression on her face.

Marissa handed him the bottle of beer and obediently knelt down next to the sofa. She told herself she'd done this a hundred times before and to just get it over with, but her body wouldn't move.

Impatient and tired of her hesitation, Toby put his hand on the back of her neck and pushed her face against his engorged rod. He put the beer to his mouth and took a drink as her lips closed around his shaft.

Marissa silently prayed he'd jerk off right there on the sofa and leave her alone for the rest of the night as she applied herself to the task at hand. She gagged several times as he tried to shove his organ deeper into her mouth. Finally she stopped and moved away from him at the sofa. She hoped he would finish the job on his own.

Toby grabbed her hand as she tried to walk away and pulled her back to his side. He roughly shoved his hand up her dress and fondled her private parts. Marissa was careful not to push his hand away and smiled down at him while trying to evade his hands.

"I was gonna do a load of laundry," she said, hoping there were enough dirty clothes in the hamper to justify this.

"You can worry about that later," Toby said, sitting up on the couch. "I want you to take these clothes off now," he continued and slipped his hand inside her panties.

"Oh, Toby." Marissa giggled nervously as she complied with his request and stepped out of her panties. She reached behind her back and unzipped her housedress.

Toby watched while she let the housedress fall to the floor. Roughly he grabbed her breasts and squeezed and then pulled down the front cup of her bra to expose one breast. He latched on to her nipple and sucked while she struggled to get her arm out of the straps that were cutting into her shoulder.

Still smiling in spite of her inner feelings, she tried to transport her mind elsewhere. She couldn't let him see how disgusted she was at his roughness. Why couldn't he be gentle and loving like Steve?

Toby dropped his pants and stood with his organ jutting forth like a battering ram. He laid Marissa down unceremoniously on the sofa and slipped between her open thighs. She stared at the ceiling above their heads while he pumped and ground his body into hers.

A silent tear rolled out of the corner of her eye, and she

brushed it away. Why couldn't he be more like Steve? Why couldn't he be Steve filling her body with his love machine? *Steve, where are you?* she wondered as she raised and lowered her hips appropriately to match Toby's rhythm. She closed her eyes and thought of Steve. He was so fine. His hands brought fire to her body. Relaxing into her fantasy, she pictured Steve touching her, kissing her, and filling her body with his magnificent form. *Steve*, her mind cried out, and a genuine smile crossed her lips. *Steve*, she thought, as she began to roll her hips and her feminine juices began to flow.

Toby noticed the change in Marissa almost instantly. When she rolled her hips and thrust herself upward to match his downward thrust, he rose up and began to watch her face while continuing to stroke in and out of her body. Her usually dry vaginal cavity was suddenly getting mighty wet. He watched the secret smile cross her face as she licked her lips and continued to rock him in and out of her body. She had never been this involved. He wanted to see how far she would go.

Marissa kept her eyes tightly closed, deep in her own fantasy. Steve was making love to her again, and it was all that mattered. Steve withdrew his organ from her body and sat back on the couch with the jutting rod upright in his hands.

"Sit on it, baby," Toby said eagerly, but it was Steve's voice she heard.

"Oh, yes," she gushed as she straddled his hips and the stiffened rod eased up into her body. "Oh, yes," she cried aloud as she tightened her vaginal walls around his rod like the books told her to do. She rocked deeper and deeper into his crotch, determined to take every inch. *Steve, it's so good*, her mind whispered in absolute joy.

When her body began convulsing in orgasmic pleasure, Toby knew for sure his wife had been fucking someone else. He watched as she winced and cried out in sheer pleasure and did her utmost to squeeze every inch of his stiff dick. He couldn't remember the last time he heard her say anything during sex, and here she was moaning and panting like a porn queen. The very thought of Marissa with another man infuriated him. Yet it excited him at the same time. Some other man's dick had been where his was right now, and his mousy little wife had learned a few new tricks in the bargain. Rage filled his body as surely as semen filled his rod. His orgasm was growing so intense, he fought to keep it back. He knew he would explode any minute with her constant rocking. The juices from her body were slipping between his thighs.

"Marissa," he called softly to gain her attention. She continued her moaning and rocking.

"Marissa, touch yourself, baby" is what she heard Steve say. Happily she slipped her hand between his belly and hers and began stroking her clitoris. Her orgasmic screams resounded in the room as she bucked and arched, clenching the stiff rod between her thighs.

"Marissa!" Toby's angry voice jolted her back to reality. Her eyes flew open. No deer stuck in a pair of fast-approaching headlights could have looked more alarmed. Her hand flew to her mouth. It was too late to cover, and she was too inexperienced to know how.

"Who you been fucking?" he demanded. His hands clamped down tight on her thighs, preventing her escape.

"Nobody, Toby, nobody. I swear!" she cried out. She tried to wiggle away, but his fingers dug viciously into the soft flesh of her thighs.

"You think I'm fucking stupid don't you?" he spat, and his hand connected hard with her cheek. "Lie to me again, bitch. You ain't never moved like that before."

"I read it in a book, Toby. I swear I did. I was just trying to make it better for you," she pleaded and covered her face to ward off another stinging blow.

Toby shoved her to the floor and stood over her. Furious

with her lies, he yanked her off the floor by her hair and slapped her again. The blow sent her sprawling to the sofa. Toby continued to scream and rant.

"Make it better for me. You coming like there's no tomorrow. Yeah, I was thinking how good you was till I saw your face, and I knew you was thinking of somebody else. Somebody done fucked you real good, ain't they? Who is he?" he demanded.

Marissa tried to scramble away, but he trapped her in the corner of the sofa. She continued to protest and proclaim her innocence.

"There's nobody, Toby. I promise there's nobody," she begged, tears streaming down her face.

Toby was enraged beyond anything he had ever felt in his life. His dick was still erect and throbbing, his wife was screwing another man and enjoying it, and he was the one taking care of her. He'd teach her to go out there and make a fool of him. He was a man, and she damn well was gonna know it. He would make sure she didn't think of anybody else when she was fucking him. He grabbed her roughly and shoved her again against the back of the couch.

Marissa pleaded for him to calm down. When he grabbed her hand and pushed her face into the back of the couch she finally thought he believed her. *He's going to keep fucking me, he must be calming down* were the frantic thoughts racing through her mind. She took a deep gulping breath. Once he came he would feel better, she was certain. He just needed to come. That's all. His hands grabbed her roughly around the hips and lifted her so her butt was poised high in the air. *Doggy style*, she thought, and she barely had a second to breathe a sigh of relief when Toby forced his engorged rod into her tight, unyielding anus. Her bloodcurdling scream filled the room as pain ripped through her body. Toby continued to pound his message into her. *She better never again think of another man while she was fucking him.*

15

Olivia and Desmond entered the courtroom for Trevor's arraignment the following morning and made their way to the bench behind the defense table. Trevor was not yet in the courtroom. Desmond had given Trevor's clothes for the arraignment to the court deputy earlier in the morning, and then he and Olivia walked to a local establishment for breakfast. Olivia did not have much of an appetite and spent an hour just picking at a muffin and nursing a lukewarm cup of decaf. Desmond tried to cheer her up and told her she must be strong for Trevor. It would only upset him if she appeared distraught in the courtroom. Now she sat quietly looking around the courtroom. It was large and very intimidating. The dark decor and atmosphere lent itself to the severity of the circumstances that had brought them here.

Damian entered the courtroom with Trevor's attorney, and they made their way up to the bench to sit with Desmond and Olivia. They sat through a few arraignments and cases before Trevor was finally brought in through the side door. The attorney rose and entered the small gate to join him at the table.

Trevor smiled weakly in Olivia's direction and made his way to the defense table. Olivia smiled bravely back at him and noticed how tired and drained he looked. He was still handsome in his dark business suit. The proceedings went very quickly as the prosecutor presented his evidence for the charges of second-degree manslaughter and requested no bail. The defense countered with Trevor's lack of any criminal history, community standing, and the prosecutor's failure to provide concrete proof he had actually killed Toby Matheson. Mrs. Matheson was still comatose and unable to corroborate or disprove Trevor's account of the events. He requested bail until trial. The prosecutor countered with the fact that Trevor was a successful executive with the wherewithal to flee the country; therefore, he was a possible flight risk.

The judge released Trevor on bail until the trial. However, the bail was set at one million dollars. A gasp escaped Olivia's lips when the judge set bail. Surely this would mean Trevor was not leaving with them today. She looked up questioningly at Desmond. He grimaced back at her. Trevor turned to look at Damian standing behind him. Damian nodded his silent assent to an unspoken agreement between them. Trevor then smiled at Olivia.

"I'll see you later," he said. As he turned away and glanced briefly around the courtroom, he saw a familiar figure in the back of the room. Her face almost completely shaded by the large floppy hat she wore, her bright Caribbean-blue eyes smiled warmly at him. She mouthed the words *It will be okay.*

Heartened by her unexpected presence, he returned her smile. The bailiff tugged at his arm to lead him out of the courtroom. He shook his head slightly as he allowed the bailiff to lead him back to the holding area. He'd thought he would never see her again, and after all this time, Paige had come to lend her support.

The brief exchange of glances did not escape Olivia. She turned and watched the slender young woman exit the courtroom. Suddenly she wanted to know who she was and what she was to Trevor. She excused herself from Desmond and Damian and hurried out of the courtroom to see if she could catch her. The floppy hat wasn't hard to follow. Paige was just turning the corner when Olivia exited into the hallway. She scurried after her. Meanwhile, Paige—unaware she was being followed—pulled the hat from her head and tousled the loose curls and continued walking. Olivia caught up with her just as she stepped out into the fresh brisk air of the November afternoon.

"Can I talk to you for a minute?" she said as she matched Paige's steps.

"Excuse me?" Paige replied and looked around nervously. She wasn't ready for anyone to question her. She only wanted to let him know she knew he was innocent. That's all.

"You came to see Trevor, didn't you?" Olivia asked. Paige did not respond. "Look, are you his coworker, girlfriend, or what?" she pressed.

"What does it matter?" Paige answered evasively and started to walk away.

Olivia took a good look at the woman in front of her. She was very beautiful, certainly the kind of woman who would have gotten Trevor's attention. But he had never mentioned her. Or had he? "Are you Cynthia?" she asked. Maybe this was the ex he told her about.

The frown passing across her face told Olivia she was not Cynthia. "No, I'm not. Now if you will excuse me I have somewhere to go," Paige replied coldly.

"I'm sorry. I don't know many of his friends out here, that's all. And you seem to believe in his innocence. He's always been like a brother to me, and I was hoping to find another female friend of his to talk to. My fiancé and Damian don't understand how I feel right now. I thought another woman might," Olivia countered, hoping to get her to open up.

"I understand your plight. However, I really didn't know him that well. He was just an acquaintance, and I was in the area today. That's all there is to it. I wish him the best of luck. I'm certain he didn't do anyone any harm," Paige replied and walked away.

Olivia stared after her, puzzled. No one would go out of his or her way to support an acquaintance. There was more to the relationship between Trevor and this woman, and she wanted to know what it was.

Desmond drove them back out to Trevor's house. Throughout the ride, Olivia questioned him on the bail proceedings. She wanted to know if they had to put up the whole one million or only 10 percent. Could they use Trevor's house as collateral? She was desperate to find a way to get him out of jail at least until the trial. Desmond did the best he could to keep her calm. He assured her he was sure something could be worked out.

She was beginning to drive him a little crazy, and while he empathized with her and understood her concerns, he was beginning to think it was time for him to get back to work. He'd been gone for several days, and there wasn't much more he could do here.

Olivia was standing at the kitchen sink filling a teacup when she heard the front door open. Assuming it was Damian, she didn't turn to acknowledge him. She was still harboring feelings of resentment for his part in Trevor's situation. The sound of Trevor's voice behind her startled her, and she dropped the cup into the sink, where it shattered on impact.

"Hey, big sis," he said wearily.

Olivia whirled from the counter and flew into his arms. Burying her face in his shoulder, she burst into tears of happiness. Trevor lifted her in his arms and gave her the hug she had been longing for since they landed in Chicago. Desmond moved to the sink to clean up the broken teacup. Damian followed Trevor into the kitchen and headed for the refrigerator to get a much-needed beer.

"How, what?" Olivia stammered as she tried to understand why he was standing here with her now. "Oh, I don't care. I'm so glad you're home."

"Yeah, me, too. For now at least," he said, releasing her and accepting a cold beer from Damian. "Folks, I know I have a lot of explaining to do, but first I need a shower. So if you will excuse me for a short while, we'll talk later." He took a swig of his beer and left the kitchen. His heavy footfalls could be heard from the kitchen as he made his way up the front staircase.

Olivia looked over at Damian. As angry as she had been with him, he had brought Trevor home. She didn't even care how he did it. She was grateful. She smiled across at him and said, "Thank you."

Damian nodded his head in response and walked into the family room to turn on the television. Olivia moved to stand next to Desmond at the sink, who was nursing his own bottle of brew. She smiled weakly up at him and moved easily into his embrace. Sighing deeply, she felt truly relieved and hopeful for the first time.

"Hey, how come nobody offered me a bottle of beer?" she asked brightly to lighten the sullen mood of the men.

"My bad," Damian called from the other room.

"I'll get you one, sweetheart," Desmond replied. "Go have a seat in the family room, I'll join you in a minute."

Olivia entered the family room and sat down on the sectional opposite Damian. He continued to scroll through the channels for something to watch. Desmond brought her a glass of beer and then excused himself to attend to some business matters.

Desmond retreated to their bedroom and made a few phone calls inquiring about flight availability. He booked a return flight home the following day. Olivia had Trevor and Damian to take care of her now. He could leave her in their hands. He tried hard not to become jealous of her relationship with Trevor, but he didn't think even she had realized how much Trevor meant to her until this happened. He could see in Trevor's eyes she was much more than a big sister to him. He wondered why Olivia never saw it. Maybe he should just consider himself lucky and not stir the pot. He wasn't planning on losing Olivia to anyone. He trusted her to work through her feelings, and it would be best if he were not here as a distraction.

On his way back downstairs he stopped by the master suite to have a brief talk with Trevor. He let him know Olivia was aware of his other activities, so there was no reason for him to attempt to hide it any longer. He advised him to tell her the truth.

"Anybody hungry?" Trevor asked as he entered the family room fifteen minutes later. "I'm starved. I made dinner reservations. So, after we talk, if you all don't mind, I'd like to get some real food." He smiled his usual enigmatic grin and received the nod of approval from all.

He sat down on the sectional next to Olivia and placed his hand on her knee. "I'm sorry for dragging all of you into this mess with me. I promise you right now before God, I did not shoot that man. I can only hope all of you will continue to support and believe in me because I really am innocent." Trevor took a deep breath before continuing. Olivia attempted to jump in, but he silenced her. "It's a long story, so let me get it all out before I lose my nerve," he continued.

"I'd been working this business for a while, and I was honestly growing tired of it. I guess I should have quit a little sooner than I did—then I would not have been in a really bad situation I couldn't control. I met this woman named Marissa a few months ago. She was a good paying customer, but I noticed she was getting a little too attached. So I told her I wouldn't see her anymore. She didn't take the news too well, but I never paid her any mind after that last afternoon. Then Cynthia called and said she was in town, so we met for dinner. . . . That's when things got crazy." He leaned back on the sofa and began to re-count that night's events.

He had met Cynthia at Allen's American Café on West Huron Street. Entering the dimly lit restaurant, he was greeted by the hostess. After he confirmed his reservation he proceeded to the bar to see if she'd arrived already. Prompt as usual, Cynthia was seated at the bar. He hadn't seen her in almost two years. She was still as beautiful as he remembered. She was five feet nine inches tall with a voluptuous thirty-six, twenty-four, thirty-six figure. Her bittersweet, dark chocolate complexion, narrow features, and high cheekbones told of her Ethiopian heritage.

He approached the bar and greeted her with a light kiss. "You're looking beautiful as usual. Life must be good to you," he said.

"I've been doing okay," she replied with a smile. Her eyes took in his black silk shirt, black trousers, and tan sport coat. The black shirt really accented his complexion. She could tell he was still in great shape. "You're as handsome as ever. Still working out, I see."

"Always," he replied. Cynthia stood up, and he escorted her to the dining room.

Halfway through dinner, Trevor was startled to look up and see Marissa standing next to their table. A chill ran through his body. This couldn't be good. "May I help you?" he asked casually.

"I need to speak with you," she said urgently.

"I'm sorry, but as you can see I am occupied right now," he replied and turned his attention back to Cynthia, who was openly staring at him with a quizzical look on her face.

"Steve, please. I really need to speak with you," Marissa pleaded. She fidgeted and glanced furtively around, hoping she wasn't attracting too much attention.

"I'm sorry, miss. I can't help you," he said firmly.

"Steve . . ." she whispered and began to cry.

"Who is this woman, and why does she keep calling you Steve? What is going on here?" Cynthia hissed, embarrassed by the scene Marissa was making.

"Excuse me," he said to Cynthia. Placing his napkin on the table, he stood up, took Marissa by the arm, and led her out of the dining room. Afraid his intuition about Marissa was proving valid, he stopped in the lobby and turned to face her. "What do you want?" he demanded.

"My husband found out about us," she cried.

"Us? What us? There is no us. You mean he found out about you. This has nothing to do with me," he replied and decided it would be better to take this conversation outside. He pushed through the front doors and pulled her outside with him. He walked a few steps away from the entrance.

Marissa removed her dark glasses. Even with the illumination of the dull street lamps he could see the bruising on her cheek and purple swelling of her right eye. "Shit!" he exclaimed and turned away from her. How could a man inflict this kind of injury on a woman he was supposed to love, no matter how angry he got?

"I'm scared, and I don't know where to go," she wailed.

"Don't you have family?" he asked.

"He'll find me if I go there. My parents are too old to have to deal with him," she replied. "Can I go home with you?"

"No!" he said a little more loudly than he meant. But the idea of taking her to his house was out of the question. He lowered his voice. "No, I can't take you home. How did you find me anyway?"

"I was just driving around, and I saw your car. I checked a few other restaurants till I found you," she said and looked away. She realized how desperate her behavior sounded, but she was scared for her life.

He wondered how she knew his car but decided at this point

it was too late to worry about that. "Stay here. I'll be right back," he said and returned to the restaurant.

Two blocks away in a darkened car, Toby watched the scene unfolding. "So that's the motherfucker who's been screwing my wife," he said aloud. "You ran right to him, you dumb bitch. Just like I thought you would." He fingered the steel barrel of the 9mm pistol resting between his thighs and continued to watch.

Trevor walked back to the table, where Cynthia waited with an angry expression on her face. He took out his wallet and laid a hundred-dollar bill on the table. "I'm sorry, Cynthia. I have to go."

"What is going on, Trevor?" she demanded. "Who is that woman? She really doesn't look your type."

"It's not what you're thinking. She's an acquaintance. She's frightened and in trouble. I'm trying to help her, that's all. I'll call you tomorrow," he said and walked back out to the street.

Marissa was waiting exactly where he'd left her. He walked up and took her arm. He asked where her car was and followed her down the street. She handed him the keys, and he got in the driver's seat and pulled away from the curb and headed west.

Down the street, Toby started his car and eased into traffic a few cars behind them. His hands tightly gripped the steering wheel, and his eyes were filled with rage as he plotted his next move.

Inside Marissa's car, Trevor wondered where he should take her. Taking her to his house was out of the question. He already suspected she'd been stalking him. He didn't want her or her problems following him home. He decided it would be best to take her to a hotel and headed toward Franklin Park.

"What happened tonight, Marissa?" he asked. He wanted to know the whole story of what drove her to seek him out and screw up his evening.

"He raped me, and then he beat me," she cried. After she escaped the house, she decided to say it was rape. Foolishly she didn't want Steve to think she was a willing participant in a sex act with her husband. She reasoned if he thought she was forced into it, he might be more willing to protect her.

"Raped you? He's your husband. What do you mean?" he asked.

"He wanted to have sex, and I didn't. So he forced himself on me. I tried to pretend I was enjoying it. Then he said I was doing it too good, better than usual. He said I must have been thinking of someone else. And I was. I was pretending he was you," she said and looked at him sadly. "I denied it, and he didn't believe me, so he started calling me names and hitting me. I tried to fight him off, and he just got madder. I started screaming for help, even though I knew no one would hear me." She began to weep.

Trevor's jaw set as the anger surfaced. He did not say anything but stared straight ahead. They were almost at the hotel.

"He said if I wanted to scream he was going to give me something to scream about, and he made me bend over on the side of the sofa. I thought he was just going to do it, you know, doggy style. But he . . . he . . . It hurt so bad!" She burst into tears and could not continue.

He knew exactly what she was talking about. He felt sorry for her. How could she have stayed married to such a pig? No wonder she was seeking sex outside her marriage. Who would blame her? He pulled into the drive of the hotel and advised her to stay in the car. He went inside and secured a room for her. Within a few minutes he returned and got back into the car. He drove around to the back of the hotel where the room was located. He handed her the key and told her to lock herself in and not to call anyone.

"Could you walk me to the room? Please, I won't take up any more of your time tonight, I promise. I really appreciate what you did for me tonight," she said.

"Look, Marissa, you have some decisions you need to make. First you could call the police and file a rape complaint against your husband. But if you plan to do that, you should do it right away while there is still evidence of the crime. If you're not going to call the police, then you should at least contact the local domestic-abuse crisis center for help. You can't hide forever. You need help. The room is paid for the week, so you have some time to think about this," he advised.

"Thank you, Steve. I know I need to make some decisions. A few days here should be good enough. How will you get home tonight?"

"I'll call a cab from your room. It can take me back into town."

They emerged from the car and walked up the stairs to her room. She opened the door and stepped into the room. Trevor followed her inside. Just as the door was closing, Toby burst into the room. He swung the gun wildly into the back of Trevor's head.

Caught off guard, the sting of the gun sent fireworks off in Trevor's brain. Momentarily stunned, he dropped to his knees. Toby rushed past him and straight for Marissa. She screamed and tried to dart into the bathroom, away from him. He snatched her by the back of her hair and yanked her back into the room. Shoving the gun into his waistband, he spun Marissa around. Shooting her was too simple, too easy. He wanted her to pay for making a fool of him.

"Lying cunt. Fucking bitch!" He spat in her face. "I'll teach you to fuck around on me." He punched her in the face.

Marissa felt her cheekbone crack as she fell to the floor in extreme pain. Barely able to remain conscious, she tried to drag herself across the floor away from him. He stood above her and kicked her in the side. Lights flashed in her head, and she felt herself gagging on her own blood.

Trevor jumped Toby from behind, and their bodies slammed

into the wall. Pushing off the wall, Trevor punched Toby several times. Toby staggered and then seemed to remember his gun and pulled it from his pants and fired at Trevor. His first shot missed as Trevor ducked and dove for his legs, knocking Toby to the floor. The gun was knocked out of his hand and skittered across the floor.

The gun landed in front of Marissa, and she reached out and pulled it to her chest. She tried to raise the gun and fire it, but her vision was blurred, and she couldn't distinguish the two figures as Toby and Trevor continued to battle. Sirens could be heard wailing in the distance. Trevor hoped they would get here in time.

Toby managed to get free as the two men squared off again. He reached down quickly and tried to pry the gun away from Marissa. She held on to it with all her waning strength. As Trevor came at him again, he kicked Marissa in the face, breaking her nose. Pain exploded in her head. Toby reached down with both hands to pull the gun out of Marissa's hands. He grasped the barrel firmly and pulled. Her finger was still curled around the trigger. With the the last vestige of will in her body, she squeezed the trigger. Marissa descended into the darkness of unconsciousness. The bullet tore into Toby's stomach, and the force of the blast sent him flying into the bathroom. He landed on the cold tiles with the gun still in his hands. Trevor raced to the bathroom door and looked down at Toby, gurgling blood and staring incredulously up at him.

The police burst into the room and ordered Trevor to freeze. He raised his hands above his head and stood still. The police immediately entered the room and handcuffed him. One officer checked Marissa's condition and called for an ambulance. The second attended to Toby.

Realizing he was dying, Toby made one last attempt to kill Trevor. Through his gurgling lips he managed to spit out a last few words.

"He . . . raped . . . my . . . wife," he said and coughed a few times and died on the cold bathroom floor.

The officer looked up at Trevor. "Take him in, and book him," he said.

"He's lying," Trevor said, shaking his head. He knew it was useless to argue with them at this point. He allowed himself to be led out of the room to the waiting squad car.

The ambulance rushed into the parking lot while Trevor sat in the backseat of the squad car. He hoped Marissa would be okay because she was the only one who knew the truth. He saw them carrying her out on a stretcher as the police car pulled out of the parking lot on its way to police headquarters.

"Next thing I knew, I was sitting in Cook County jail. I don't know how she found me. I hope she makes it because I need her to corroborate my story. I never touched the gun. But nobody was checking that out. It was another black-on-black crime. I don't even think the police really care what happened. Toby Matheson was a sick man, and I have no idea why she stayed with him so long. But his sickness led her into having this kind of sick obsession with me and nearly got me killed," Trevor finished.

There was silence in the room as everyone pondered what they had been told. For Olivia it was confirmation from Trevor, himself, that he had been providing women with sex for money. She felt sick to her stomach at the thought of it but tried not to let it show. She didn't know what to say to him.

Desmond contemplated the story from a legal perspective. The evidence would certainly clear him; it was only a matter of time. His fingerprints would not be on the weapon. He hadn't raped the woman, and DNA would surely prove this to be the case. He breathed a tentative sigh of relief. Maybe it would never get to trial, and Olivia could come home that much sooner.

Damian, who had heard the story before but without all the

extra details, was ready to get something to eat. It had been a long day, and he wanted a change. He stood up and looked around the room.

"I don't know about anyone else, but I'm ready to roll. There is nothing else we can do tonight. Tré is home, and we need to enjoy the moment. I'm driving, so let's go." He walked across the room and stood in front of Trevor. Trevor rose from his seat and clasped him in a tight hug. They had exchanged hugs at the jail when Damian posted his bail, but this was different. That was a *thanks for getting my ass out* hug. This was the embrace of two men who had been together through thick and thin since their college days and would always be there for one another. It was an expression of the bond and love they had for one another, and it brought tears to Olivia's eyes as she realized Damian would never have intentionally done anything to harm Trevor. She was ashamed of her previous accusations to the contrary.

"Let's go," Trevor said as he turned to Olivia and grabbed her hand. He pulled her close to his side and tousled her hair. "Enough sadness for tonight," he added as the four of them left the house and piled into Damian's car for the trip downtown.

The conversation at dinner centered on old basketball stories and childhood memories. They steered clear of current events. After dinner Desmond pulled Olivia out onto the dance floor for a little one-on-one reconnection when their favorite slow jam was played. Damian and Trevor were sitting in the booth surveying the crowd when Agnes stopped by to say hello. At first Trevor did not recognize her, and then the memory suddenly came flooding back and he remembered where he'd seen her before. He assumed she must have seen the papers and was stopping by to gloat. She seemed bitchy enough to do it.

He was shocked when she smiled warmly at Damian and said hello. He was even more shocked when Damian returned the greeting. Trevor became immediately suspicious. "What the heck is going on here?" he demanded and looked accusingly at Damian. The rule said no fraternizing with the clients. He knew the look in Damian's eyes meant he'd been with this witch and not in a professional way.

"Easy, Trevor. Take it easy. Agnes is the one who got your attorney. So ease up a minute. She helped me out when I needed to find a good attorney for you," Damian said.

"I didn't mean to upset you, Trevor. I just wanted to say I'm glad to see you. Damian, I'll talk to you another time," Agnes said and moved off into the crowd.

"What is going on, Damian?" Trevor demanded.

"Look, man, it's cool. She's an attorney, and I needed an attorney. I didn't know who else to call at the time. She helped us out. Leave it at that," Damian replied.

"D, I've known you for, what, fifteen years? I know that when you look at a woman like that, something has happened between the two of you. You told me she was all business."

"Well, you know what? I can't be right all the time. Your girl's coming back, so drop it, okay?" he said as Olivia and Desmond returned to the table.

Trevor looked at him quizzically and shook his head. "I'll be damned," he said as the irony of the situation dawned on him. Damian had warned him about getting soft, and look who got hooked. He laughed out loud and took a sip of his drink. Damian glared at him across the table and smiled into his own drink.

16

The morning after Trevor's arrest, Damian was sitting in his office scrolling through his Rolodex trying to find the name of a good attorney. He'd never needed one before, and it wasn't like he knew any criminal attorneys. The firm's lawyers were out of the question. He also knew he needed someone discreet. No matter how much client-and-attorney privilege there was supposed to be, he wasn't trustful of everyone. He was getting extremely frustrated when his secretary stepped into his office and advised him Ms. Garfield was on the line. He wasn't taking calls this morning, and at first the name did not ring a bell. He was just about to turn her away when he realized who she was.

The secretary put the call through, and he answered right away. "Damian Adams," he said.

"Damian, this is Agnes Garfield," she said.

"Hello, how can I help you?" he asked.

"I'd like to help you, if I can. I happen to know several excellent criminal attorneys, if you want a few names," she replied.

"Agnes, you're a godsend. I was racking my brain trying to

figure out who to call." He breathed a much-needed sigh of relief into the phone.

"Can you meet me for lunch?" she asked.

"Sure. You name the time and the place. I'm there," he said emphatically.

"How about Pili Pili at two o'clock? I'll make some phone calls before I get there to see who's available," she offered.

"Thanks, Agnes," he replied. "I'll see you at two." He smiled as he hung up the receiver. For Agnes to call and offer to help was totally unexpected. He hadn't seen her since the ball a few weeks ago. Every now and then she would cross his mind, but he quickly dismissed any thoughts of contacting her.

Agnes replaced the receiver on her end and took a deep breath. Damian had been a constant thought these past few weeks. She tried to keep in the forefront of her mind the image of him as a prostitute and not as the Damian she met the night of the ball. Curiosity was getting the better of her. Why would a successful businessman prostitute his body on the side for money? Maybe he was a reckless gambler and deeply in debt and needed the extra funds? No, he seemed too in control to be so careless. Why? When she saw the article in the paper about Steve, whom she now knew to be Trevor Calhoun, another successful businessman, she was really curious. It also gave her the excuse she needed to call Damian. She looked forward to their lunch meeting. In the meantime she better see whom she could find to help him out. She opened her day planner and began flipping through the pages of business cards for criminal attorneys.

Damian arrived at the restaurant at one forty-five. He'd made a two o'clock reservation, and he knew from past experience how Agnes felt about waiting for anyone. She was doing him a favor today, and he was not about to antagonize her.

Agnes arrived ten minutes later. She was dressed in a tan wool business suit with a V-neck chocolate silk blouse. She accented the outfit with an African beaded necklace and matching earrings. Chocolate designer pumps accented her long, slim legs. Her hair was pulled up and away from her face in her usual French roll. Damian wore a charcoal-gray sport jacket with an ivory crew-neck silk sweater and black slacks. As the couple followed the hostess to the booth Damian requested, they were oblivious to the stares of the other patrons. Other patrons who surely noticed what a striking pair they were.

Once seated, Damian ordered martinis for them both, and Agnes reached into her purse and pulled out a business card. She slid the card across the table to Damian. The name on the card read *Marcus Carpenter, III.* There were so many degrees noted after his name, Damian could not help but comment on them.

"What's with the hieroglyphics after the brother's name? I assume this is a brother?" he asked, smiling. The waitress returned with their drinks, and Damian requested more time for them to peruse the menu.

"Marcus graduated from Harvard Law School and was awarded a Rhodes Scholarship to Oxford. He is an excellent criminal attorney. I'm surprised you haven't heard of him. Oh, yes, and he is black," she replied.

"Yeah, now that I think about it. I have heard the name before. How do you know him?" he asked. Then he realized how the question sounded. He had no right to ask how she knew him, if she dated him, or anything else. "Never mind. Will he take the case?"

"Luckily, he is available, and, yes, he said he would take the case. He is going out to see Trevor this afternoon. I hope you don't mind my arranging it, but he is the best, and when he said yes, I gave him Trevor's name. All I told him is Trevor is a friend of a friend. I did not admit to any personal knowledge of him," she replied and looked for confirmation from Damian that this would remain their secret.

"Thanks again for taking care of it. Hopefully our true associations will never come to light. I promise to keep you out of it. It's the least I can do," he said. He took a sip of his martini and wondered again why she was offering her assistance. Surely, being associated with him at this time was dangerous. In her position, could she stand the scrutiny of people who would want to know how she knew him?

"You're frowning. What's on your mind?" she asked. The unspoken questions were clouding his features.

"I'm not sure why you're here. Or why you called me this morning. Surely you would want to stay as far away from this situation as possible. Why get involved? Don't get me wrong— I appreciate your help more than you know—but aren't you taking a really big chance?" he asked.

He was right, and she knew it. She couldn't tell him she'd been hoping to bump into him again or thought he might call. She had put her reputation in a precarious situation by meeting him today. The information could have been passed through a phone call. There was no need for her to be sitting here across from him now, except for the fact that she wanted to see him. However, she couldn't admit it to him.

"I guess I didn't think things through very well. I thought you might be in need of some help, so I called. That's all," she replied and sipped her drink.

Damian didn't believe a word of it. He had no doubt she planned her days from *A* to *Z* a week in advance. There was no way she didn't think it through. Yet for some reason she chose to ignore the danger.

"Are you ready to order lunch? Since I obviously don't have to call this lawyer right away, I have some time on my hands," he asked.

"Sure, my next appointment isn't until four thirty," she said and picked up her menu. She selected a Mediterranean salad.

"Great," he replied and ordered her salad and a grilled salmon for himself.

During lunch they talked about their college years. He told her he met Trevor at basketball camp as a youth, and they both ended up at Duke on full scholarships and had been friends ever since. He asked about her family. She told him about attending Harvard, where she'd met Marcus Carpenter. She told him about her parents, brother, niece, and nephew. They didn't delve into the events that brought them both together, or their history. Agnes excused herself at four to attend her next meeting and thanked Damian for the lunch. He likewise thanked her for her assistance. She gave him her business card as they parted, and he slipped it into his jacket pocket as he escorted her outside and hailed a cab for her. He didn't talk to Agnes again for almost a week.

A couple days after his lunch with Agnes, Damian had returned home from Trevor's house, having explained to Olivia Trevor's relationship with the victim. He'd maintained his cool when Olivia confronted him and blamed him for Trevor's predicament. In the aftermath of her rage, they had all sat down and discussed the situation rationally. She seemed to accept it was not his fault. However, he felt her acceptance was only on the surface.

Alone in his home on the other side of the Forest Glen development, he wondered if it was more his fault than he admitted. Trevor had told him weeks earlier that he didn't want to be in the business anymore. He was beginning to feel for the women, and it wasn't a good sign. Instead of accepting his uneasiness and allowing him to gracefully exit the business, Damian had pushed him to continue. He'd admonished him about getting soft. They'd sworn to look after one another, to protect each other, and he had let Trevor down. He'd missed the signs, and, as a result, Trevor had allowed a client to get too attached. She'd stalked him, and he didn't even notice—didn't notice until it was too late. Now look at the situation: Trevor was locked up with a possible murder charge pending and he would lose

his job for sure; even though the firm hadn't moved to disassociate themselves yet, Damian knew it wouldn't be long before
Westmoreland and Phelps moved to protect their reputation.
Yes, ultimately it was his fault. He let his best friend down, and
there was no way around it. He forgot that this was fun-and-
games money. They each commanded six-figure salaries. They
didn't need this income to survive. He was the one who forgot
that part. He couldn't imagine someone getting tired of this
kind of easy money. He blamed himself, even though he knew
Trevor would never blame him. He poured a shot of vodka and
chased it with an ice-cold beer.

He carried the beer up to his bedroom and hung his suit
jacket in the closet. He had spoken with Marcus late this evening,
and Marcus had assured him Trevor would be cleared. He said,
unfortunately, it was going to be a while before they could resolve everything. First of all, Marissa was still in a coma, and
they were uncertain of her prognosis at this time. Second, the
DNA would undoubtedly show Trevor had not raped her, but
the Chicago police could possibly be slow in obtaining the results. There would be an arraignment, and he anticipated if bail
were granted it was going to be incredibly steep. He advised
Damian to make whatever arraignments he could to prepare for
that eventuality.

Damian spoke with Claudette immediately after getting off
the phone with Marcus. She preferred to remain anonymous
but would certainly provide the bail if they needed her assistance. He assured her he would call only as a last resort. He was
certain as long as the judge was reasonable, he and Trevor could
cover the bail from their own assets.

Stretched out on the California king-size bed, he stared at
the ceiling. His thoughts were crowding in on him, and he wanted
to talk. Yet his lifestyle did not provide for close friends, and,
other than Trevor and, by default, Olivia, he wasn't close to
anyone. His parents were deceased, and he had no siblings.

Restless, he scrolled through the channels on his wall-mounted plasma television. He rolled off the bed and tried to remember what jacket he had been wearing the day he had met Agnes for lunch. It took him only a few minutes to retrieve her business card from the inside pocket. He knew her business number would be listed, but he was hoping a cell-phone number was there as well.

He hesitated and then dialed her number. What would she do? Hang up on him? It wouldn't be the first time a woman had hung up on him. He doubted it would be the last. She answered on the second ring.

"Hello."

"Hey, Agnes, it's Damian," he said as he looked up at the ceiling, waiting for her response.

"Yes, Damian?" she replied. Her voice was cold and non-committal. She rose from her seat at her antique Louis VIII desk and wandered over to the window. A cloudless night sky stared back at her.

He was a little surprised by the lack of emotion in her voice. It was like she was talking to a total stranger, not a woman who had come to his aid just a week ago. "Am I calling at a bad time? I didn't mean to disturb you," he replied.

Agnes looked at the phone in her hand and shook her head. She was annoyed. Annoyed with him and annoyed with herself. She had thought he would call sooner, which was why she had given him her number in the first place, and she was annoyed with herself for setting expectations for his behavior and then allowing it to disturb her when he didn't do what she wanted.

Her hesitation in answering was beginning to get on his nerves, which were in short supply as it was. He regretted obeying the impulse to call. He paced back and forth in his bedroom.

"Agnes, look, I'm sorry I bothered you. Have a good night," Damian said.

His agitated tone broke into her mental deliberations and snapped her quickly back into the present.

"Damian, I'm sorry. I was in the middle of reviewing a case, and my mind drifted," she lied. She sat down on the cushioned edge of the window seat.

"Then you are busy," he said. "I'll talk to you another time."

"No, really. I needed a break. What's on your mind?" she asked, unable to stop the warmth from creeping into her voice. She liked his telephone voice; she always had.

"It's going to sound crazy, but I just wanted to talk," he said and sat down on the side of the bed.

"About anything in particular?" she asked. She recognized the tone in his voice. She heard it often enough in her own when she just needed to be distracted from all the things going on in her head and she didn't care what she talked about. It was at those times she called on her brother. He was the only man she trusted since her father passed two years ago.

"No, not really," he said.

"Well, I have a funny story to tell you," she said and relayed a tale about a client who had some serious IRS issues.

Damian laughed in spite of himself. He lay back on the bed and rested his arm behind his head. She continued to regale him with tales of misguided clients who tried to avoid paying the IRS and ended up in her office hopeful she could straighten out the mess they had created.

"Hey, I just want you to know I file my taxes on time every year." He laughed.

"On all your income, Damian?" she asked quietly.

He stopped smiling and realized what he'd said. Of course he didn't pay taxes on his illegal activities. It was a cold dose of reality in what had been an otherwise pleasant conversation. Although there was nothing accusatory in her tone, it raised a wall between them. It reminded them both of their true association.

"I'll have to plead the fifth. Forgive me for not answering," he replied with ease.

"Since it's out there in the open now, can I ask you a question?"

"Sure, shoot," he said. The tone of the conversation suddenly took a very serious turn, and he wondered what was on her mind.

"Why do you do it?" she asked.

He thought about evading her question, pretending he didn't know what she meant. But it was pointless. He had called her tonight, not the other way around. He figured after six months of paying for his sexual favors, she at least had a right to ask.

"It was fun. In the beginning anyway," he said.

"Fun? How was it fun?" she asked. This wasn't the answer she was expecting. There had to be more to it than that. She wanted to believe there was more to it than just fun. She wanted to find a way to justify her participation, and fun wasn't covering it. He had to have a better reason, something more noble than fun.

He sensed her agitation with his answer. He really didn't want to drag the conversation on the path she was taking tonight. He needed a diversion from his thoughts, and she provided it. But he wasn't up to her psychoanalysis tonight.

"Agnes, I gotta run. I have an early morning conference call, and I need to get some rest. I appreciate you taking the time to speak with me this evening," he said.

"Sure, Damian, any time," she replied. She wasn't going to get any more out of him tonight and chose not to press the issue.

"Sleep tight," he said and hung up the phone. He laid the phone on his nightstand and proceeded into his master bath for a shower. He was glad he had called, but he wasn't sure reaching out for Agnes was a good idea. Then again, he didn't have to pretend with her. She knew who he was and what he did—

rather, used to do. His days of prostituting his body for money were over.

"Same to you," she replied and closed the lid on her cell phone. She sat back in the corner of the window seat and pulled her knees to her chest. Leaning back against the wall, she stared at the star-laden sky outside her penthouse window. Damian Adams was a dangerous man. He made her want things she'd given up on a very long time ago. On top of all of that, he was a male whore. She needed to remember that, no matter how handsome or professionally successful he was.

Fresh out of Harvard Law School, a young Agnes was eager and determined to make her mark in Chicago. Once she recuperated from her injuries, Agnes focused on her school studies. She had little tolerance for the gossip that spread quickly around the high school. While some schoolmates empathized with her situation, many blamed her for Ricky's imprisonment and loss of an NBA career. He'd been a hometown hero, and his mother vocally blamed the little tramp that tried to trap him with a baby for ruining his life. It became so bad at one point her parents transferred her to a private boarding school to finish out her junior and senior years.

Agnes was very much a loner during her college years. She avoided relationships like the plague and spurned the advances of her male schoolmates none too politely. Fiercely dedicated to becoming a successful lawyer, she spent most of her time studying. Her academic excellence paid off when she was offered an internship with a well-known law firm downtown. If she could prove herself, this could lead to a full-time position with the firm. Agnes tackled every assignment given to her with unbridled enthusiasm. She spent countless hours at the law library on research projects. She was diligent in her pursuit of information. It didn't take long before the firm's top attorneys were requesting her assistance on their cases. Agnes was in her glory. She was learning more and more every day and filing away for future use all the tips and pointers the attorneys shared with her.

Six months later the firm brought in a young man from NYU also as an intern. He was charismatic, handsome, and charming. His name was William Jeffrey Scott, Jr. Will, as he preferred to be called, came from a long line of family lawyers and appeared well connected. Many in the office speculated that his internship was an arrangement between family friends. Will gave the appearance of being very humble in spite of his connections. He went out of his way to endear himself to the office staff and to make friends with his peers.

Agnes was irresistibly drawn to his magnetic personality. At twenty-four she was still single and available, and although she had not previously been attracted to Caucasian men, Will was quite the package. He was six foot two inches tall with dark, wavy brown hair and cobalt-blue eyes. His pale, slightly olive-tinted skin always seemed to have a perpetual year-round tan. He had an athlete's body and was an avid racketball player and golfer—the sports where big deals were often made after a duel or battle.

It did not take long for Will to assess who his greatest competition was for the next full-time slot with the firm. Agnes was initially resistant to his advances, but his persistence finally wore her down, and she agreed to go on a date with him. He wasn't like any of the men who had approached her in the past. Will was determined to win her over, and he wined and dined Agnes in ways she had never known before. He took her to all the best restaurants and stores. Agnes was from a middle-class family with middle-class values and tastes. Will showed her a different side of life. The first time he spent fifteen hundred dollars for a dress at Saks Fifth Avenue and four hundred dollars on Charles Jourdan shoes, she was hooked. This was how she wanted to dress; this was how she wanted to live. While

Agnes didn't have that kind of money then, she knew in time she would. Just as soon as she made partner, she could afford this lifestyle. When they weren't working and he could manage to drag her away from her assignments, they spent all their time together. He was very romantic and would often surprise her with gifts and weekend getaways. She became intimately familiar with several Caribbean islands and the Las Vegas strip.

Agnes generally did not like to discuss the cases she was working on with anyone, but he soon wore her down and she began filling him in on her research techniques and resources. After six months of intense dating and sex, Will asked Agnes if she wanted to leave a few things at his place. She took this as a prelude to moving in and eagerly accepted. She was deeply in love and tried not to dwell on the fact that she had yet to meet any member of his family.

She remembered the weekend they drove out to Oak Park to meet her parents. Her father covered his displeasure but not surprise when he opened the door and saw her standing there with Will. He enveloped his daughter in a warm embrace and shook hands with Will. Agnes's mother was equally surprised but accepted her daughter's choice of mate. After all, they weren't talking marriage yet, so there was nothing to be alarmed about. Agnes had never brought anyone home for her parents to meet, and the first time she did, it was a white man. Her parents were very leery of young Mr. Scott.

They spent a cordial afternoon together speaking of work and their vacations. Little mention was made of the future, which her father found strange. He would remark to his wife after their departure that he did not trust Will with his baby. He did not like his eyes. She would agree there was something not quite right about him.

Agnes was near the end of her internship. She was certain the firm would offer her a position. Will was also eager to get a full-time position with the firm, and although Agnes had been there longer, he began talking about getting the upcoming position. Agnes reminded him he had another six months or so to complete his internship, and she was certain he would get picked up as well. This wasn't good enough for him, and after several heated discussions Agnes decided it wasn't a subject they should discuss anymore.

Agnes was growing uneasy with Will's mood swings. She learned from a coworker that Will was being pressured by his family to secure a position soon. There was a merger in the works of the law firms, and they felt he would be an integral part of the deal. Because Will rarely discussed his family with her, she felt uncomfortable bringing the problem up.

She believed they had a bright future. All his friends accepted her, but after almost six months it was clear he was in no hurry to make introductions to the family. She wondered if they knew she even existed. One day Will's father unexpectedly showed up at the law firm. Will was in court assisting the attorney he was assigned to. Agnes had seen the older distinguished-looking gentleman when he was escorted to the partners' offices but had no idea who he was until she overheard two coworkers discussing him in the ladies' room. She was not only shocked and appalled by what she overheard, but a huge knot formed in the pit of her stomach.

An attorney with the firm was giggling as she told another attorney, "Just wait till Papa Scott sees the woman his little heir has been keeping company with; that will curl his hair."

"I think Agnes is going to be a brilliant attorney," countered the other attorney.

"Maybe so, but she'll never be accepted into the family. There's no way they are going to allow him to dilute that blue-blood line with black blood," she replied.

She giggled. "Stupid, their blood is as red as ours."

"I'll bet they don't even know about her. I'd love to be a fly on the wall when they find out," she said as they walked away down the hallway.

Agnes leaned against the wall in the stall. She could hardly breathe through the pain in her chest. Usually she would have dismissed their conversation as idle office gossip, but it rang too true in her mind. She tried not to be overly concerned by the fact that Will hadn't introduced her to his family, but it was slapping her in the face, and she felt compelled to confront him about it.

When Will arrived home later that evening, she wasted no time getting to the point. "I heard your father was at the office today," she said shortly after he walked through the door.

"Yeah, he wanted to take me to lunch," he replied as he loosened his tie and removed his jacket.

"I'd like to meet him," she said and approached him in the hallway. Dressed in a T-shirt and sweat shorts, she'd pulled her hair up into a ponytail and had been working at the dining table when she heard his key in the lock.

"Uh-huh," he said and planted a quick kiss on her cheek and headed toward the bedroom.

"I'm serious, Will. I'd like to meet him. I'd actually like to meet both your parents. How about we have them over for dinner?" She followed him down the hall.

"My folks don't do things like that, honey," he replied.

She was annoyed he was brushing her off so easily. She wanted to know if this was a real issue or her imagination. "They don't do what, Will? Eat or meet your black girlfriends?" she asked.

He turned to look at her angrily. His father had been riding his ass all afternoon about making a name for himself, excelling at his internship so he could obtain a foothold in the firm. The family law firm needed this merger, and they were counting on him. He wasn't distinguishing himself enough. All his father had been hearing in the business circles was about some black female intern who was going to be brilliant one day. Why wasn't he hearing Will's name mentioned with the same distinction?

"Aggie, look. I'm really tired and not up for this fight tonight," he said, unbuckling his belt and kicking off his shoes.

"I don't want to fight. I want to know the truth. Am I ever going to meet your parents? Where is this relationship going?" she pressed.

"My parents have no say in whom I see or don't see. Nor do they have any say in what I do. Meeting them has nothing to do with you and me. It's not important," he said and turned to look at her. He could see this answer wasn't going to be good enough, and he truly didn't want to deal with it anymore tonight. He decided charm would serve him better here than continuing to fight. Aggie could fight forever. He found that out the hard way. She was like a dog with a bone when she wanted to settle an issue. That's why she would make a great attorney one day.

He smiled and crossed the room to where she was standing in the doorway with her arms petulantly folded across her chest. He slipped his hand around her neck and pulled her face close to his and kissed her deeply. With his free hand he removed the scrunchy in her hair. Her long auburn hair cascaded down over his fingers. She tried to push him away, aware he was trying to divert her attention from the question at hand.

"Will," she said as she unsuccessfully tried to avoid his mouth.

"All that matters is you and me," he said, burying his face in her neck, "and that I love you. Nothing else matters." He continued to slather her neck with kisses. He could feel her giving in to her desires and seized the moment. He slipped his hand inside the waistband of her sweat shorts and began ruffling his fingers through the furry patch of hair till he found her throbbing wet clitoris. Lightly he flicked the bulb until she grew weak in the knees.

She could feel the erect length of his penis pressing against her thigh. She didn't want to give in until she got answers, but her physical desires were ruling her head. Stepping out of her shorts, she allowed him to guide her to the bed. He pulled her

T-shirt over her head exposing a lacy red brassiere. He slipped quickly out of his briefs and joined her atop the bed. Positioning himself between her legs, he started nuzzling her navel and expertly made his way through the thick patch of hair to her sweet spot. He pulled the tiny protruding bulb into his mouth and flicked it lightly with his tongue.

Agnes could feel her bodily juices ebbing from her body as she grew limp from the orgasmic release. She entwined her fingers in his thick brown hair and pressed his face closer to her crotch. Arching her hips, she encouraged him to slip his tongue into the throbbing heat between her legs. She moaned aloud with pleasure as her body arched wildly under his onslaught while Will did what he did best. He treated her to several oral orgasms and then crawled up her body and captured her lips with his. His mouth was wet with her bodily juices as he began kissing her again. Slowly and deliberately he raised her hands above her head.

She heard a slight rustling sound and felt him slipping a silk scarf around her wrists. Each bedpost had a scarf tied around it and tucked under the mattress for those occasions like today when he was in an extra-freaky frame of mind. She didn't protest when he tied a knot loosely around each of her wrists. Her hands held tight to the scarf as he straddled her chest and thrust his penis against her lips. Following his unspoken command, she licked the smooth, dark red, mushroomlike cap with her tongue. She moistened her lips with her tongue and relaxed her jaw to allow him entrance to the warmth of her mouth. She never minded giving him oral sex, she just hated to be tied up to do it. It left her less control over the depth of insertion and didn't allow her to create her own sucking rhythm. This method also made it seem like it was being forced upon her, and she was as eager to please him as he was to please her.

He pushed and poked his penis in her mouth until she nearly gagged on it before he eased it from her sore and bruised lips.

He continued to sit astride her hips with his firm erection twitching against her cheek as he slipped on a condom. He grinned mischievously as he rubbed lubrication along the latex length of the condom.

"You want more, baby? I've got a surprise for you," he said as he slipped a cock ring on himself and climbed between her open legs, rubbing the tip of the condom against her tender nether lips. Excited by the amazing tingle of the vibrating cock ring, he clumsily tried to slide his rigid staff into her warmth.

Agnes felt a strange electric shock against her clit as his dick rubbed across her exposed passion. Her body recoiled instinctively, but the taut ropes restrained her.

"What the fuck is that?" she demanded and yanked at the scarves in a futile attempt to free herself. Pain still radiated from her clit, and she bucked her hips wildly to throw him off.

"Easy, girl, easy," he coaxed as he tried to calm her down and push his dick farther inside. "It's called a pleasure ring, and it's supposed to make it feel better for both of us. Calm down. Enjoy the sensations."

"It hurt," she hissed through clenched lips. She clamped her legs shut and effectively blocked him from gaining further access. The unwelcome vibrating sensation continued against the smooth skin of her thighs as she trapped his dick between them.

The cock ring still continued to stimulate the engorged head of his dick, and he was desperate to get inside her and explode. He kissed her neck and nuzzled her chin.

"Please, baby, let me in. It will be good, I promise. It's my fault. I shouldn't have rubbed it on you like that."

He kissed her lips and coaxed her mouth open. He ran his tongue along the edge of her teeth and kissed her passionately. Then he eased his hand between her thighs.

"Come on, baby. Open up for me."

Hesitantly she opened her legs and allowed him to shove his manhood inside. The tiny vibrator tingled deep inside the tender confines of her passion. The sensation was strange, not necessarily pleasant or unpleasant.

He could hardly contain himself with the thrill of the electric shock running across the tip of his dick. He held on tightly to her wrists and pumped and ground his way frantically toward his fast-approaching orgasm.

She held on to the silk bands around her wrists and prayed he'd come soon. The pleasure of the moment had died for her when he'd injected her with his electric love button. It didn't take long for him to reach his orgasmic peak. He groaned aloud as he came explosively. He collapsed on top of her and shuddered a few times before he laughed aloud in satisfaction. Finally sated, he untied her wrists from the bedposts and pulled her into his arms. He held her tightly and lovingly in his embrace.

"That was fan-fucking-tastic, baby," he said.

"Glad you enjoyed it," she replied. The dryness of her tone escaped him in his euphoric state.

She'd always considered Will's lovemaking to be aggressive and wild. While Agnes wasn't always thrilled with his freaky ideas, she went along most of the time. Sex with him wasn't always pleasant or fruitful for her, but he'd never intentionally hurt her. She was convinced their relationship had more depth than just sex. Therefore, an occasional episode of good sex was sufficient, and these little quirks of his were just something she had to get used to.

Agnes rested her head on his chest and brushed her fingers through the curly hairs on his chest. She hadn't forgotten their earlier conversation and still wanted answers. However, for the time being, she would leave the issue alone.

In the following few weeks, Will's apartment became a battleground. He began to pressure her to step aside from the internship and allow him to slide into the available full-time opening. She steadfastly refused. The full-time position would mean she would finally have a real salary. She did not think Will needed the money as badly as she did. After all, he was from a very affluent family that could support him indefinitely. She needed to take care of herself. When he complained about the job, she complained about being kept a secret from his family.

His father confided in him that their family firm had lost a couple of very big accounts recently, and they weren't drawing new big money clients to replace them. They needed him to get on board at Michaels, Derwood & Smith. He would have a better chance of meeting more affluent clients, which he could eventually move over to their firm. It was unethical, but it wasn't unheard of in their circles. They would try for the merger first, but if that didn't go through, this was the backup plan. Of course, none of this could begin to develop if MDS did not think he was qualified to be on their staff. The only thing standing in his way was Agnes.

He learned through the office grapevine that a decision was going to be made in the next couple of weeks. Both he and Agnes were under a proverbial microscope. She had the advantage of having been there longer, and she also had an advantage he had not anticipated. She was black. He was shocked to find out this was giving her an unbeatable edge. The firm had no black attorneys on staff. They needed Agnes, which was why they had sought her out in the first place. She would enhance their corporate image. At a time when quite a few of the influential people in Chicago were people of color, she would be an undeniable asset. Will grew more and more desperate.

Agnes arrived home one evening after a long day of work to find Will waiting for her with champagne and two dozen red roses. He told her he wanted to put all the bickering behind them. He told her she deserved the promotion, and he'd made arrangements for them to have dinner with his parents the following week. Agnes was ecstatic. Not because she won, but because it showed her how much he loved her. This was all she truly wanted: to be valued for her brains as well as her beauty.

Will would prove to be freakier in bed than ever when they made love later in the evening. He made love tenaciously to her and he was gone when she awoke the following morning. As it was Saturday, she did not have to go into work, so she dressed and went to work out at the gym. When she returned home later in the afternoon, she was greeted by a strange sound when she opened the apartment door. She stopped inside the doorway and could clearly hear the cries of a woman in the throes of passion. A sick feeling gripped her in the pit of her stomach. This could not be happening. Will wouldn't dare bring another woman into their home. He wouldn't cheat on her, but the cries of passion were constant. The low, mumbling tones of a man's voice accompanied them.

She laid her keys on the stand by the door and walked farther into the apartment. The sound was coming from the master bedroom. Gingerly walking down the hallway so as not to make a sound, she crept up on the master bedroom. She now recognized Will's voice as he instructed the woman which way to move and continuously asked if she was climaxing. Agnes's heart dropped in her chest like a thud. Steeling herself, she pushed open the bedroom door. There was no one in the bed. Stunned, she stepped into the room and saw Will sitting at his desk in the corner. He was writing in a notebook. He turned to smile at her as she entered the room.

Suddenly she realized he must have been watching one of his pornographic tapes on the television. Relief flooded through her body; without looking at the television she walked to the bed to find the remote to shut off the offending noise. She located the remote and was about to push the button when Will spoke.

"Hey, sweetheart. I think you'll like this one. Don't shut it off yet," he coaxed.

"Will, you know I hate these movies," she said, smiling at him. He was such a pervert at times.

Will rose from his seat at the desk and crossed the room. He kissed her lightly and took the remote from her hand. He turned her toward the television, and she reluctantly looked at the screen.

The room was dark, but she could clearly make out the bodies on the screen. It took a moment or two to sink in what she was looking at. The color drained from her face, and she felt sick to her stomach. The woman in the video was she. Her hands were bound, and her eyes blindfolded as she writhed back and forth in sheer carnal ecstasy. How could he do this to her without her knowledge? She averted her face, embarrassed by what she was looking at.

"Look, baby, you're missing the best part," he said as he lifted her up and forced her to look at the screen. She noticed the vantage point of the camera moved from time to time around the room. The picture became clearer when the photographer moved in for a close-up shot of her performing fellatio on Will. She was horrified to notice the camera switch hands at one point as a hand she did not recognize began fondling her private parts. Then a penis, distinctly different from Will's, was inserted in her mouth. She greedily accepted the foreign object in her mouth. The video continued to show this unknown man climbing on top of her and having sex with her. Then the camera switched hands again to show Will sliding between her open legs. The camera and photographer moved farther away, and the picture darkened again as Will removed the blindfold, untied her wrists, and pulled her on top of him.

The knot in the pit of her stomach began roiling like a bubbling volcano. She gagged on the vomit that rose through her stomach and projected out of her mouth onto the television screen. This was a violation so vile and reprehensible she couldn't comprehend it had happened to her. Not only had he photographed her most intimate moments, but there was another person in the room, and she'd had sex with this other man without realizing it while Will stood by watching. She fell to her knees and wretched until dry heaves gripped and held tight her stomach muscles.

Will casually walked to the bathroom and returned with a wet washcloth. Tenderly he knelt by her side and began wiping the vomit from her lips. Her head was throbbing, and she couldn't think. The cold cloth on her forehead brought her momentary relief. It was enough to bring back her fighting spirit. She reared back on her heels and swung her hand with all her might. The blow connected solidly with Will's cheek. She screamed like a caged tiger.

"Why? Why did you do this?" Her shock and revulsion were replaced by anger, hurt, and an uncontrollable rage.

Will recovered quickly from the blow and laughed viciously. He rose to his feet and looked down at her rocking back and forth on her knees. With slow deliberation and a venomous tone she'd never heard before in his voice, he explained.

"Because you made me," he said simply. He picked up the remote and turned off the VCR. He calmly popped the tape out of the VCR, walked to his desk, and sat down before continuing. "I asked you to step aside so I could get the appointment. I told you how important it was to me. However, you chose not to listen to me. You chose to think your agenda was more important than what I needed to do for my family."

"Obviously I deserve the appointment more than you, and you know it or you wouldn't have been so worried you couldn't get the job on your own merits. You wanted me to step aside to clear the path for you. I simply told you to earn it if you thought you were better qualified," she spat back at him. She stood to her full height of six feet, determined he was not going to beat her so easily. Her body was shaking, but it was with anger, not fear.

"I did earn it, but I just wanted to level the playing field a little. Have an ace in my corner, like you have in yours," he countered.

"Ace in my corner? Are you crazy? You're the one with all the connections. I worked my ass off for the appointment!" she screamed at him. She looked around the room for something to throw at him, something heavy that could do a lot of damage. She wanted to kill him. "You're the one who thought you could get the appointment by shoving your nose up a few corporate asses."

"I would have gotten the appointment, but apparently the fucking affirmative-action shit doesn't stop at the college level. The firm thinks they need a black attorney on the roster to schmooze a few of the local who's-who," he spat back at her and then waved the tape at her. "But I don't think they want a black whore who likes bondage and threesomes. No, I don't think it's the image they want their very public black attorney to have. So I know you will be stepping aside, so I can get the appointment. They can find another qualified black attorney after you're gone," he finished.

"You wouldn't dare. I'll say it was rape and you drugged me. I'll have you up on charges so fast your head will spin," she said. She was desperate to think of a charge she could make stick. He hadn't used any drugs on her, and it clearly showed she was a willing participant in the act, if not also the filming of it. The fact that there was obviously a witness made her sick to her stomach again.

Will watched the conflict of emotions on her face. He knew she was sorting out her options and finding little ground to stand on. He'd won. "You've lost this one, sweetheart. Why don't you try to step aside gracefully? You don't even have to leave the firm. Just tell them you don't feel ready for the appointment. The choice is yours. I really don't care how you accomplish it. But you better get it done by the end of the week because I will send this tape to the partners for their viewing pleasure. Make no mistake about that," he said and shoved the tape into his briefcase. He walked confidently out of the room. A few minutes later she heard the front door close behind him.

Agnes spent the next hour plotting ways to kill him and not get caught. Either way, her career would be over. If he showed the tape, she wouldn't be able to show her face in town, and if she killed him, well, that was a no-brainer. Realizing she was beaten, she went from room to room and collected all her belongings. She tossed them into a duffel bag and shoved all her work papers back into her briefcase. She was tempted to take the apartment key with her, but she had no doubt as soon as she was gone he would change the lock. No point in giving him the satisfaction of thinking she would try to come back. She laid the key on the coffee table and walked out the door.

She loaded her car and drove back to her own small apartment. There was no one for her to call and seek counsel from. Surely her parents had been shamed enough by her high school disgrace. They were so proud of her now and all she'd accomplished, she couldn't possibly let them find out. Her brother was also out of the question, and her work ethic left little time for female friends. She climbed onto her bed and curled her body into a fetal position, much like she had done nine years earlier, and cried until no tears were left.

Sunday, she awoke to swollen eyes and an ache in her throat and diaphragm from all the violent vomiting. She sat down at her small kitchen table and spent the day writing down all her options. She'd made a name for herself at MDS and did not want to leave. She decided to ask for a leave of absence. This would allow her to remain connected to the firm and also make way for Will to get the upcoming position. When she returned she would wait for the next available spot. She hoped he would uphold his end of the bargain and never show the tape to anyone. It was risky, but it was a chance she had to take.

The following Monday she showed up to work as usual. She proceeded to her cubicle and began sorting through the files on her desk. It didn't take long for the snickering to start in the secretarial pool. At first she thought she was being paranoid, but when one of the male paralegals stopped by her desk, her suspicions were confirmed. He leaned into the cubicle, grabbed his crotch, and swirled his tongue around his lips. He mouthed the words *Nice job* and moved away. A hysterical twitter burst out from the cubicle next to hers.

Agnes knew without question he was the other man on the tape. Tears sprang to her eyes, and she angrily wiped them away. She tried to focus on the papers in front of her. She prayed silently, hoping no one else had seen the tape. She felt sick to her stomach once again. Suddenly someone grabbed her arm firmly. She looked up in alarm. An older black woman from the secretarial pool was standing next to her chair, holding fast to her arm. She pulled Agnes from her chair and down the short hallway to the ladies' room. Once inside, she checked the stalls to make sure all were empty and locked the door behind them. She turned on a very puzzled Agnes and spoke very deliberately and passionately.

"Don't you ever let them see you fall apart," she said. "They have been waiting and hoping for a day like this since you started in this firm. Right now all it is is a nasty rumor circulating. We cannot stop rumors, but we don't have to give them merit."

"What are they saying about me?" Agnes asked quietly. She walked to the mirror. Her face, pale and drained, looked back at her.

"They said you slept with the paralegal, and that nice Mr. Scott dumped you," she replied.

Agnes breathed a sigh of relief. The wind was taken out of her sails, but it wasn't as bad as the truth. At least for now Will hadn't exposed the tape to anyone. She wet a paper towel and dabbed it on her cheeks. A slight rose tint came back into them. She took a deep breath and looked gratefully at the older woman.

"I don't care what happened between you and Mr. Scott, but you've done a good job here. Don't let these people steal your dignity or your pride. You keep your chin up and your head held high. I know you haven't done anything wrong. I know this because I am a good judge of character, and I can tell you have it by the boatloads." She smiled back at Agnes.

"Thank you," Agnes said and turned to walk back out the door. She looked back at the woman and reached out and squeezed her hand.

"You go on ahead and remember: Never let them beat you Agnes. Never give them the power. Be the master of your own destiny, is what my daddy used to tell me. He never steered me wrong," the woman said and turned to the sink to check her makeup.

Agnes walked back to her cubicle with her head held high. She sat down at her desk and pulled out her Rolodex. *Pilot your own ship,* she thought to herself. A leave of absence was out of the question now. She no longer wanted to be here, but she wouldn't give them the opportunity to drive her out. She called Marcus Carpenter III and asked if he could meet her for lunch. He agreed.

By late afternoon, with a personal referral from Marcus, she had secured a job at a firm even more prestigious than the one for which she was currently working. She returned to work and typed up her resignation. Collecting only her personal items, she put all her files in order and stopped by the partners' offices. She thanked them for the opportunity and apologized for the lack of notice.

As she walked out the door of Michaels, Derwood & Smith for the last time, she took a deep breath of the crisp Chicago air. Her affair with Will was over but thankfully not her career. She looked heavenward and said a silent prayer of thanks. The saying was true—when God closes one door, he opens a window. You just had to be prepared to take the leap of faith.

Agnes sealed up her heart and vulnerability for the last time. She vowed no man would ever again get close enough to hurt her, and she meant it.

17

Trevor drove Olivia and Desmond to the airport the morning following the arraignment. After retrieving Desmond's bag from the trunk, Trevor said his good-byes and discreetly waited in the car while Olivia and Desmond exchanged a kiss good-bye. Olivia promised to call every day and to keep him up to date on Trevor's situation.

Trevor had been dreading this moment since he got out of Cook County jail. He would be alone with Olivia, and he knew he would have to explain his activities. He planned to take her back to the house, where they could have a private chat. Then, if she were willing, he would take her out to lunch.

They didn't talk much on the ride back to Trevor's house. Olivia was deep in thought and dreading the conversation almost as much as he was. In spite of her feelings, she wanted to understand why he'd chosen to do this. She thought about Desmond and how she had sensed a little uneasiness in him when he was departing. He assured her he was fine, but she knew him pretty well and could tell something was on his mind. He'd been very supportive of her, and she was more than a little consumed with Trevor. Maybe her feelings were a little over the top, but she'd known Trevor for more than twenty years; this was something Desmond would have to try to understand.

When they arrived at the house they went immediately to the kitchen. Olivia sat down at the kitchen table, and Trevor retrieved bottles of water from the refrigerator. Seated opposite her at the table, he wasn't sure where to start. He decided it was best to find out what she wanted to know.

"I'm not sure where you want me to start," he said, twisting the cap off his water bottle.

She looked at him and then looked away, out the rear window to the backyard. Olivia was uncertain where to start with all the questions plaguing her mind; she took a sip of water, followed by a deep sigh.

"I want to understand why you would sell your body for sex. Maybe if I could understand, I wouldn't be so disgusted by the very idea," she said without looking at him.

"Livi, I wasn't standing on a street corner in the hood picking up women. I wasn't trying to support a drug habit or any of the garbage you see on television. It wasn't like that at all," he explained. The look on her face told him she was not convinced.

"How long have you been doing this, Trevor?" she asked, trying to control the anger building up inside her. Couldn't he see it didn't matter where he did his business—it was all the same immoral behavior?

He knew where this question was leading, and he could hear the agitation in her voice growing. He had no desire to hurt her, but it was perhaps the only way she would understand.

"About three or four years," he replied.

She turned from the window and stared straight at him. With slow, angry deliberation, she spoke.

"So when I came out here two and a half years ago and you offered to hook me up with Damian, were you going to pay him to 'service' me?" she asked. She needed to know and at the same time dreaded hearing his answer.

"Olivia, first of all the answer is no. I was not going to pay Damian to have sex with you. Honestly, I wouldn't have had to. He would gladly have done the deed for free. You and Damian connected while you were here. The opportunity was there, and even though you were attracted to him, you declined," he explained. She looked away again, and he reached across the table and grasped her hand before he continued. "But what you need to remember is why we ever had that conversation in the first place. I know things are different for you now with Desmond, but back then you were extremely sexually frustrated. Probably even more so than you admitted to me."

"What does this have to do with anything or what you did?" she demanded, unwilling to see his point.

"There are many women out there in the same predicament you found yourself, women who are craving sexual satisfaction and have no significant other to provide it for them. They don't want meaningless one-night stands with strangers because it's risky and dangerous. So they are reduced to finding someone discreet who is willing to provide what they need with no strings attached. Yes, it's for a fee, but the only ones who have to know about it are them," he replied. He released her hand and took another drink of water. "Can't you try to see it from the other side?"

"So you want me to think it is noble of you to fuck all these lonely old women? To take advantage of their desperation for love and attention?" she hissed. She didn't want to be angry with him, but she wasn't willing to let him off so easily. After all, look where his nobility had gotten him.

"I don't call them. They call me," he said flatly. He pushed away from the table and walked into the family room. She was refusing to understand, and there was no other way he could explain it. He knew what he'd done. Maybe he was naive to think that in some small way he was helping these women while lining his own pockets. There was no one he had to report to. He was a grown man, and she needed to accept it.

Olivia thought of the woman in the courtroom the other day. The woman she had assumed was Cynthia. She rose from her seat and moved to the entrance of the family room.

"Who was the woman in court the other day?" she asked quietly and leaned on the wall of the archway between the two rooms.

"A friend," he replied without looking at her. He knew she was referring to Paige.

"Was it Cynthia?" she asked, although she already knew the answer. She wanted to see his reaction.

He laughed aloud at the comparison and said, "No, she wasn't Cynthia."

"She is very beautiful," Olivia said, continuing to press for more information.

"Yes, she is," he replied. Then he turned to look at her. He knew he could trust Olivia not to say anything to anyone, so he told her. "She used to be a client."

Olivia's mouth fell open. She expected he would say she was an old girlfriend or new girlfriend or anything but a client. Why would a woman so beautiful have to pay for sex?

"I don't understand," she stammered and eased away from her post in the archway and walked toward the sofa.

"Yes, you do. She is a woman who paid me to have sex with her. Before you start thinking crazy wild things, there is nothing wrong with her. She wasn't kinky or a sex freak. She was just a lonely woman who had reached a low point in her life and sought some male attention. She is a prime example of what I was trying to explain to you. Just like you, she is beautiful and successful. And just like you, she was lonely and frustrated with her sex life. Unlike you, she opted to find a way to satisfy those needs. You decided to wait for your prince Desmond to come along," he finished a little more angrily than he intended.

Olivia sank down on the sofa in the family room. She remembered those times all too well. She was overwrought with her sexual frustration and, no, she hadn't waited for Desmond to come along to satisfy those urges. She'd taken matters into her own hands in a different way but had never told Trevor of her trip to Boston. When she thought back to the night in Boston, she understood clearly how these women could have paid for Trevor's attention. It was a time long ago, and she'd put the memories behind her. Now they were racing back to confront her.

She'd been celibate for five years after Eric's death when she started corresponding with a gentleman via the Internet. Before she knew it they were sending hot and steamy sexual e-mails to one another. Unfortunately, the gentleman involved was not readily available to fulfill the fantasies they discussed. As her sexual desires increased, so did her frustration level. It was at the height of her sexual frustration that she decided to escape for a week to Chicago and visit Trevor. While in Chicago, Trevor introduced her to Damian. She smiled as she remembered referring to Damian as a little bit of chocolate heaven. At Trevor's urging she'd spent a very memorable afternoon with him. He'd taken her jogging at a park near Lake Michigan. They were relaxing on a bench after their run when Damian unexpectedly kissed her. It was a kiss so simple and natural it took her breath away. He subtly intimated he was available for more if she was willing. Her body really wanted to take him up on his offer, but she couldn't imagine looking Trevor in the face, knowing she'd slept with his best friend. Instead she'd gone back to New Jersey hornier than ever and determined to take control of her own sexual needs as discreetly as possible.

She planned a sexual encounter with an unsuspecting acquaintance out of town. He was a moderately attractive business acquaintance she previously would not even have given the time of day, in spite of his relentless pursuit. He also conveniently lived several states away in Boston. She knew it wouldn't take much to entice him into her bed.

She shuddered as she relived that night in her mind. She'd been packing up her conference supplies after she'd given a seminar at a large company in Boston. On most occasions, she did the seminar as a day trip, but she knew Carl would seek her out if he found out she was in town, so she booked a room for the night. As anticipated, he approached immediately after the last session.

"Hello again," he called from his position in the doorway.

"Hi, Carl." She forced the pleasant reply.

Surprised by her friendly response, he entered the room. "How did it go today?"

"Very well, thank you," she said. She looked him over as he continued approaching her. Carl was dressed in a dark pin-striped suit. A muted tie complemented the white shirt he was wearing. He was fairly light complexioned, with curly black hair, a thin mustache, and goatee. He walked slowly up to her and then walked around, brushing her shoulder as he went by. He took the seat at the table where she was gathering her supplies. She had grimaced inwardly as he'd brushed past her. He reeked of cologne.

"Are you leaving tonight? I could drop you at the airport if you like?" he suggested.

"Actually, Carl, I'll be here overnight. I leave in the morning."

"Really," he responded with a glint in his eye. "Could I request the honor of your presence at dinner then?"

"Thank you, Carl, that would actually be very nice," Olivia replied without looking up at him. She continued to pack her briefcase.

The unexpected agreement made Carl suspicious, and he got up and then made an exaggerated effort to peek behind paintings, looking for hidden cameras. "This is a joke, right? We're on *Candid Camera* or something? Did you just agree to go out with me? Me, Carl?" he asked incredulously.

"Yes, I did, Carl. I've had a long day, and I'm hungry. You asked, and I said yes. Now, if you would like to retract the offer, I understand. I will admit I haven't been very nice to you in the past," she said contritely.

"No, no. I know the perfect place. Are you almost ready to leave?" he asked.

"Yes, I am. I have to stop by my hotel to change, if you don't mind. It won't take long," she said.

Olivia suggested Carl wait in the lobby while she went to her room to change. When she returned to the lobby twenty minutes later, Carl was seated, reading a magazine. She emerged from the elevator just as he looked up. She was wearing a red dress that hugged her figure like a glove. The bodice was cut low across her bosom, exposing plenty of her cleavage. Her smooth, rounded breasts were poised like mounds of ripe melons peaking over the top of the dress. The dress stopped at midthigh and gave him a stunning view of her legs all the way down to the red stiletto pumps she wore. She was extremely nervous and feeling nearly naked but refused to let it show. She confidently held her head high as she approached Carl.

He jumped up from his seat eagerly, took her arm, and escorted her out to his car. Once inside, he started the car and pulled off. "You look absolutely edible tonight," he said.

"I'll take that as a compliment," she replied.

"I had no idea you were hiding all this under those business suits. I might have tried harder months ago," he said slyly.

She'd smiled back at him and ignored his stupid remarks. Olivia had plans for Carl. He reached over and rested his hand on her exposed thigh. Slowly she removed his hand and placed it back on the gearshift. This was her party, not his. She remained quiet through the rest of the drive to the restaurant, allowing Carl to do all the talking. He did not seem to notice it was a very one-sided conversation.

During the dinner, Olivia looked at Carl sitting across from her and accessed his potential. He really wasn't an unattractive person. It was his playa attitude that was such a turnoff. He'd never stopped talking about himself and his accomplishments from the moment they left the office. She'd smiled sweetly and replied affirmatively to his comments. She needed to tolerate him until she completed her task—getting laid.

After dinner Carl had driven her back to her hotel. During the drive he'd casually placed his hand on her thigh again. When she did not react, he slowly tried to inch his hand higher up her thigh. She'd reached down and grasped his hand and gave it a gentle squeeze. She remembered how she'd smiled sweetly at him and held his hand in hers to stop his forward progress. He'd smiled eagerly in anticipation of things to come.

They arrived at the hotel, and he followed her to her room. While she inserted her key in the lock, he leaned down and kissed her neck and grabbed her buttocks firmly. She felt his hot, musky breath on her neck and stymied the revulsion she felt. This was business, she reminded herself. Once inside the room, he attempted to move in on her immediately. She pushed him back.

"Slow down, tiger. This isn't a race," she cautioned him while she proceeded to the closet to hang up her coat. When she turned back into the room she found Carl had removed his coat, shirt, and was working on unbuckling his pants. Damn, he was in a hurry, she remembered thinking.

His erection was already bulging against the thin nylon material of his briefs, and they hadn't even begun yet. Once his pants hit the floor, he'd moved right up behind her as she stood at the mirror removing her earrings. He'd grasped her breasts with both hands and began to massage them. He began kissing her neck, more aggressively this time, sucking and biting alternately. She could see their reflection in the mirror and feel his stiff dick pressing against her back. He couldn't wait to get her clothes off and lifted her dress up over her head and tossed it into the chair. The bra she wore that night was sheer, and her nipples were clearly exposed for his viewing pleasure.

His breathing became huskier, and his actions more assertive. He fondled her breasts, and then his hands traveled down her belly and slipped into her panties. She emitted a sharp intake of breath as his fingers touched her clitoris; she could feel the moistness growing between her legs. She didn't want to think about what she was doing or with whom. She just wanted to get laid, and at this moment in time she wanted him. She leaned over on the dresser and turned off the light. Carl stopped rubbing her clit for a moment and then easily picked her up and laid her on the bed. He continued slathering her neck and breasts with wet kisses. He raised himself up just long enough to push down his briefs. His engorged organ sprang free as he spread her legs with his knee. She pushed him back off her and handed him a condom as she struggled to remove her moist panties. He'd looked shocked at the suggestion of sheathing his penis. "You expect me to use that?" he asked, panting.

"If you expect to get this," she said and placed her hand on her crotch. She began rubbing herself, titillating him. He fumbled, but managed to slip the condom on in record time. He opened her legs wider and began pushing himself into her. She raised her hips to accept him, and as he slipped inside, they both moaned aloud in satisfaction. They pleasured each other fast, furious, and repeatedly. Olivia discovered Carl had not been such a bad choice after all. Once he got in his groove, he was a skilled lover and brought her to climax several times over the hour they spent together.

Olivia remembered that that night had not ended as he wanted it to. She had accomplished her goal of sexual release, and she wanted to be alone. He planned to spend the whole night with her. When she reflected on the final events of the night, she knew she'd been rather mean to him.

Sated and sweaty, she'd gotten up to take a shower. She returned to the bedroom to find Carl comfortably resting in the bed waiting for her.

"Thanks, Carl, you can leave now," she'd said nonchalantly.

"Huh?" he replied, confused.

"You can leave now. I need to get some rest. I have an early flight in the morning," she'd said firmly.

"Hey, babe, I'm feeling a little used here. Are you tossing me out? I thought we could spend the night together. You know, cuddle a little and do this again in the morning."

"Carl, you have been trying to fuck me for months. Lucky for you, today I felt like being fucked. Don't make more of this than it is. We both got what we wanted, and now I want you to leave."

Realizing she was dead serious, Carl had gotten out of bed and begun picking up his clothes. He stormed into the bathroom and emerged a few minutes later fully dressed.

"This really sucks, you know. You're treating me like a piece of ass. I expected better of you," he'd said angrily as he realized he'd been used.

"Why? You don't know me," she snidely replied as she followed him to the door and slammed it behind him.

"Olivia? Olivia?" Trevor called her name when she did not respond. He noticed a distant look in her eyes and realized she was deep in thought.

Her focus quickly shifted back to the present. She accepted that she was no different than these women who paid Trevor for sexual favors. Maybe they were nobler about it than she had been. She'd totally used Carl that night and justified it by believing he'd done the same to so many other women, and that it was his comeuppance for treating them all like sex objects.

"I'm sorry for being so judgmental," she said quietly. "It was a shock, but I do understand more now. I understand how the women might be compelled to call, but why did you do it?"

"Cynthia and I weren't getting along. She was out of town a

lot, and we were starting to drift apart. Damian," he paused and then continued, "I don't blame him, and I don't want you to blame him either. He met this rich woman who convinced him he could make quite a bit of money. He brought me in after a while, and I started making money, too. It was a lark. It was exciting in the beginning. Cynthia and I broke up eventually, and I had nothing to lose. You had already made your feelings about me clear and had started seeing Desmond. I really didn't care anymore. During the last several months, I've met some women who made me think about what I was doing, and I was getting restless. I started thinking of getting out of the business. I just didn't do it soon enough."

Olivia noticed the hurt in his voice when he had referred to Desmond. She'd never heard it before. Trevor was her baby brother, and it was how she always thought of him. He was a very attractive man, and she knew he'd had a crush on her when they were younger. She never seriously considered becoming involved with him once they were adults.

"Trevor, you have always been a brother to me. You know that. We talked about this before. I love you, and I always will," she said.

"I thought after Eric died, you might turn to me. But you locked yourself away from everyone. So I moved on and went to Georgia and then here. Then when I ran into you again five years later, you were still as beautiful as ever, but you were hooked on the Internet weirdo. I thought we would have another chance. But once again you didn't even consider me a possibility," he said morosely.

Her heart broke for him. Why hadn't she realized how much Trevor cared for her? She loved Desmond, and there was no way she could be the woman Trevor wanted her to be in his life.

"Do you realize how afraid I was that you were going to sleep with Damian? Even though I offered to hook you up. It was all I could do not to carry you up those stairs that night and show you how much I loved you then. But it would have scared you off. So I didn't, and I lost you again anyway," he said and moved away from the window to stand in front of her.

Olivia stood and wrapped her arms around his waist. She laid her head on his chest and sighed. "I'm sorry, Trevor. I'm sorry for being so dense. I'm sorry for causing you so much pain," she said. She started to ease away from him, when he suddenly leaned down and claimed her lips with his.

Her heart told her to push him away, but her body wanted to enjoy the sensation of his mouth on hers. Her mouth opened under the gentle insistence of his, and he kissed her deeply as he pulled her body closer to his. Hungrily she returned his kiss. Her legs began to tingle, and she grew weak in the knees. His lips moved from her lips to her neck, and she gasped aloud. Sanity returned, and she gently pushed him away from her. He did not resist and released her from his arms.

"I'm sorry, Livi, but I've wanted to kiss you for far too long," he said huskily, stepping away from her.

"I know, and I love you, too. But I love Desmond, and I can't jeopardize my relationship with him. Not even for you," she replied quietly. She did love Trevor but not in the same way she loved Desmond. She smiled as she thought of the women who had paid for what she'd just gotten a brief taste of. Small wonder they called him back time and time again. She thought it best for them to get out of the house, so she changed the subject. "Can we go eat? Because I'm starving," she said.

Trevor was grateful for the change of topic. He hadn't intended to let things go as far as they did, and he had let his emotions get the better of him. He wouldn't do it again. He felt he'd made his point, and she'd made hers. They left the house in search of food.

Trevor left the house early the following morning for a meeting with Marcus to discuss the case. Olivia had discovered during a conversation the previous night that Trevor had been sending her his client list on the computer disks over the last two years. This was the disk she was keeping safe at home and never questioned him about what was on it. Now she was very curious to find out who these women were. She ignored the voice in her head that told her she would be betraying his trust. But he'd betrayed her trust for several years—at least she was doing it in an effort to help him. At least, this was the rationale she would use if she got caught. Without mentioning anything to Trevor, she called Desmond at home and asked him to access the list for her. He was hesitant at first, but she convinced him it might be helpful to find a few character witnesses for Trevor. Desmond reminded Olivia that these women were assured of Trevor's discretion and probably would not be very happy if she contacted them. She wanted to try anyway, and it would give her something to do to help out. He accessed the disk information and sent her Trevor's list, omitting Damian's clients, in an e-mail. She accessed the computer in Trevor's office and printed up the list.

Right after her morning coffee, Olivia dialed the first number on the list. The name beside the number was Paige. She heard the unmistakable phone-company-disconnect message. No forwarding number was given. There was no last name given. She decided to move on to the next name. She punched in the numbers. This time the phone rang several times before a woman answered.

"Hello, may I speak with Naomi?" Olivia asked.

"This is Naomi," the woman replied pleasantly.

"Hi, Naomi, my name is Olivia. I'd like to meet with you to discuss a personal situation as soon as possible. It's about Steve."

The tone in the woman's voice made Naomi nervous, but when she heard his name she knew she was in trouble. Who was this person, and what did they want with her? "I think you must have the wrong number," she replied quietly and looked over her shoulder to see if Greg was nearby. She was pretty sure he was in his office, but she wasn't taking any chances.

"Don't hang up, Naomi. I understand if you can't talk right now, but I need only a few minutes of your time. I didn't want to just show up on your doorstep," Olivia implored.

"You know where I live?" Her voice cracked as panic began to set in.

"Yes, I do. Where can we meet?"

"When?" Naomi asked, fighting the tears. Greg could not find out what she'd done. He would never forgive her.

"How about this afternoon? Let's say two o'clock. You pick the place," Olivia suggested. Naomi was the first of the women on the disk she was going to meet. She didn't know where she lived, but she was sure Des could find out from the phone number. Unfair or not, she had only said it to scare her into agreeing to a meeting.

"I'll meet you at the Oakbrook Mall. I'll be waiting outside Neiman Marcus," Naomi said. Her mind immediately began concocting excuses to explain to Greg why she had to go out. She knew he wouldn't question her too much. After all, he trusted her.

"Great, I'll be there," Olivia replied and hung up. She looked over the next name on the list. This one had an address and instructions on where to park next to it. Apparently he serviced her at home. She called the number. After four rings an answering machine picked up.

"You have reached the home of Denise Jenkins. I'm sorry I can't take your call right now, but if you'll leave a name, number, and a brief message, I'll be sure to get back to you. Have a blessed day and hope to see you in church on Sunday."

Olivia replaced the handset without leaving a message. If this was a churchgoing woman, she would be even less receptive to a phone call than the last woman. She jotted down her address and decided she would stop by on her way back from the meeting with Naomi.

* * *

At two o'clock that afternoon, Olivia was standing in the entrance to Neiman Marcus waiting for Naomi. She had no idea what this woman looked like and hoped she would be able to spot her when she showed up. She'd dressed in business attire for the meeting. She hoped it would give her a certain professional edge.

Naomi watched from the doorway across the mall. She'd gotten to the mall early so she would spot her adversary when she arrived. This woman could destroy her life. It hadn't been nearly as hard to get away from Greg as she'd anticipated. He told her to enjoy herself, he needed to complete a project and felt bad he wasn't spending more time with her.

She watched Olivia pacing until fifteen minutes after two. She could tell she was growing impatient, but she didn't have the nerve to cross the mall and confront her. Suddenly she saw Olivia reach inside her purse and pull out her cell phone.

Olivia glanced at her watch: two-fifteen. She'd given Naomi more than enough time to get here. She wanted to get this over with as much as Naomi did. She wanted to check in with Desmond, so she reached inside her purse for her cell phone. As she was about to enter his speed-dial code, she saw a young woman rushing toward her. *This must be Naomi,* she thought and closed the phone. She slipped it back into her purse as Naomi approached her.

"I'm sorry I'm late," she said. She panicked when she thought Olivia might be calling her at home again to find out where she was.

"Hi, I'm Olivia," Olivia said and extended her hand. She looked at the woman in front of her. She wasn't as young as she first appeared. Olivia guessed her to be in her midthirties. She was dressed in jeans, T-shirt, and sneakers.

"Well, you already know my name is Naomi," she replied

and lightly shook hands. "I guess the best place to talk would be the food court. It's kind of noisy, and no one really pays any attention to anyone else," she said and turned so Olivia could follow her.

They walked silently until they reached the food court. Naomi selected a semisecluded table in a corner and sat down. She stared at her hands clasped in front of her on the table.

"Naomi, this is not an inquisition, and at this moment the only one who knows about you is me. And, of course, Trevor," Olivia said in an attempt to get her to relax. Naomi looked up but said nothing.

"You do know what has happened, am I correct?" Olivia asked.

"I read the paper," she replied. "I didn't pay any attention until I saw the picture, and that's when I realized who he was. I didn't know his real name."

"I'm having a very hard time trying to understand how my best friend got into this business in the first place. I hoped if I could talk to some of the women he . . . he knew, they could help me to understand. This is the reason I called you," she explained.

"What do you want to know?" Naomi asked.

"I of course want to make sure there was no violence in his association with you."

"He didn't strike me as a violent man. He was always very nice to me," Naomi replied quietly.

"Great. That's what I thought because I have known him since he was a kid, and he's never been violent at all," Olivia said, trying to ease into the question she wanted to ask. "You're an attractive woman, Naomi. You're also very obviously married." She looked pointedly at the gold wedding band and sparkling engagement ring set on her left hand. "Why would you call someone like Trevor?"

Naomi looked down at her hands. "Why should I tell you

something I've never told anyone else?" she replied and raised her eyes slowly to look at Olivia.

"Probably because I don't know you. I'm not here to judge you. I really want to understand. If I can understand what made you call him, then maybe I can understand why he did this," Olivia replied earnestly.

"It doesn't matter why I called him—why I used his services, if that's what it boils down to. It only matters that I did it, and if my husband ever found out, he'd leave me. I can't lose him," she said passionately.

"I don't think he has to find out. I certainly don't intend to tell him. Is he an invalid or something?" Olivia asked. She was fishing for clues. Naomi obviously loved her husband. This didn't make sense. Why was she sleeping with Trevor?

"No, he's not. How much longer do I have to stay here? I want to go home," she said.

"You don't have to stay. I'm not holding you hostage," Olivia replied, exasperated. This wasn't as easy as she had hoped it would be.

"Are you married?" Naomi asked as she stood up to leave.

"No, but I do have a special man in my life," Olivia replied, puzzled by the question.

"Does he make you happy?" Naomi asked.

"Yes, of course he does," Olivia replied easily and looked up at Naomi, who suddenly seemed very agitated, almost angry.

"Completely happy?" Naomi pressed. This time Olivia knew what she meant by the question.

"Yes, completely happy," she replied slowly.

"Then count yourself lucky," Naomi said and walked quickly away.

Olivia stared at her hastily retreating back. The idea of a woman having to seek sexual satisfaction outside her marriage was very sad. She wondered how she would have felt if Desmond were unable to satisfy her needs. Could she still love him as much as Naomi loved her husband? Would she stay with him and keep a man on the side? She didn't think so, but Naomi was right—she didn't have to make that choice. She collected her purse and stopped to pick up a container of lemonade on her way back to her car.

An hour later, Olivia stood on the front porch of Denise Jenkins's home and rang the doorbell. She noticed on the drive down the street that this was a very nice neighborhood, and the woman she was about to visit kept a very nice colonial home. At least from the outside, she thought. The shrubs were neatly trimmed, and the lawn well manicured. In the window was a sticker that read MOUNT CALVARY FIRST BAPTIST CHURCH.

Denise peered through the peephole and did not recognize the young woman standing on her doorstep. The woman was alone, so she probably wasn't a witness coming by to convince Denise to change religion. Denise actually enjoyed the few debates she'd engaged witnesses in when she did choose to allow them to talk to her. Still smiling from the memory of her verbal victory, she opened the door.

"Can I help you?" she asked the stranger.

"Yes, hello. I'm hoping to speak with Denise Jenkins," Olivia replied, smiling back at her.

"I'm Denise, how can I help you?" she replied, now suspicious of this beautiful young woman. She took in the neat wool suit, classic pumps, and designer purse.

"I'd like to speak with you about Trevor Calhoun. May I come in?" Olivia said quietly. Denise immediately stiffened at the name. She hadn't known his name until the newspapers last week had printed his picture in that murder scandal. There was no way she was admitting to knowing him. How had this girl found her?

"I'm afraid I don't know the name. Now if you will excuse me," she said and stepped back into the foyer to close the door.

Olivia had anticipated this reaction and placed her palm on

the door. Leaning into it, she stopped the door from closing. She knew this was not going to be easy, and Denise was reacting as she thought she would.

"Sister Jenkins, unless you would like the entire congregation of Mount Calvary First Baptist to know what you do the third Wednesday of every month, I think you can spare me a few minutes of your time," Olivia said quietly. She didn't know a thing about the church, but seeing the sticker in the window gave her the leverage she needed to get in.

Denise's heart started to race in her chest, and she saw her whole world crashing around her. This could not get out. No one could find out about him. She wasn't admitting to anything. "I don't know what you're talking about," she replied stiffly.

"Okay, let's not play this game. Your neighbors are getting curious as to why you're not inviting me in. Would you like me to walk across the street to that lady who is peeking out her window leering at us? I'm sure she would let me in. Then I can tell her about your penchant for hanging naked from chandeliers. Even if it's not exactly the truth, who cares?" Olivia said.

Recognizing a well-prepared adversary, Denise stepped back into the foyer and motioned her inside. She closed the door and led the way into the living room. Deciding to change her tactics with this woman, she offered her a cup of tea.

Olivia took in the conventionally decorated living room. Everything was in its place, and the home was spotless. Without trying, she could tell it would have passed a white-glove test easily. The grand piano was the central focus of this room, and she wondered if Denise played or if she had purchased it for its dramatic effect on the room. She noticed there were no family photos displayed anywhere. The room was appointed with plenty of artwork and antiques but nothing of a personal nature. Denise apparently kept everyone at a distance.

"Miss Jenkins, can we have tea in your kitchen, if you don't mind? It would probably be more comfortable, and I'm not here to cause you any trouble, in spite of what you might think," Olivia said.

Denise eyed her suspiciously. This girl was trying to catch her off guard. The whole kitchen scene would be too much like a girlfriend-to-girlfriend chat, and she wasn't falling for it. Then again, she did not wish to antagonize her either.

"Sure, whatever you want," she acquiesced, and Olivia followed her down the hall to the kitchen. Denise busied herself putting on a pot of tea and taking cups and saucers from the cupboard.

"First let me explain who I am," Olivia started.

Denise continued collecting tea bags and sugar and arranging them on a plate and placing them on the table in front of Olivia. She did not respond. She took out a box of shortbread cookies and laid them out on another plate. Denise never entertained, but she always imagined how she would do it if she had company. This woman was the first visitor she'd allowed into her home. Silly as it seemed, she wanted to leave a good impression.

"My name is Olivia. Trevor is my best friend. I've known him since he was literally knee-high to a grasshopper. I'm not sure how he got involved in this business, but I'm sure he didn't kill anybody on purpose. It's just not in his nature to be violent."

The teapot whistled, and Denise brought it to the table, filling two cups with hot water. She finally spoke. "What do you want from me?" She returned the pot to the stove and sat down opposite Olivia.

"Right now we're just looking for character witnesses. Women who can attest to the fact he has never been violent in his dealing with them," Olivia replied, dipping a raspberry tea bag in the hot water in her cup.

"What makes you so sure he hasn't?" Denise queried. She

wanted to gauge how well this person really knew him. She could imagine this woman was probably more his type than she was: professional, slim, and very pretty. Yes, this woman was definitely his type. She read the bio on him in the papers and was shocked to see he was a successful executive. She, too, wondered what drove him to take up servicing women as a sideline.

"Because I know him," Olivia said with conviction.

"You didn't know he was a whore?" Denise said snidely. She received the exact response she was seeking when Olivia's back stiffened and anger flashed across her face.

"You know what?" Olivia said, rising from her seat. "I tried to be nice about this and to show a little respect for your privacy. I can see now this isn't going to work. As soon as I leave here I'm calling his attorney and giving him your information. You can deal with the authorities from now on." She collected her purse and started toward the hall.

Denise panicked. As usual she had pushed someone too far. It was why she did not have any friends. She could never leave well enough alone and try to get along. She always wanted to one-up the next person. She stood quickly and blocked Olivia's exit.

"I'm sorry. I didn't mean to be nasty," she said. Olivia raised her eyebrow and stared at her. "Okay, okay. Yes. I meant to be nasty. But you're making me very nervous. This could ruin me. I wouldn't be able to show my face in public if my church or job found out about this. Please sit back down," she coaxed.

Olivia looked her up and down and walked slowly back to her seat. She understood where Denise was coming from, but she was tired of her games. She could have brought the attorney with her but thought she would talk to the women one-on-one first. See if their testimonies would even make a difference. She sat down and placed her purse on the seat next to her. Taking a sip of the tea, she decided to let Denise do the talking this time.

"He was never violent. Honestly, he has always been the utmost of a gentleman," Denise began nervously. Olivia inclined her head slightly, allowing her to go on. "I saw an ad in the *Herald* and called the service. I was very embarrassed the first time. Ashamed, I guess would be a more appropriate description, because I had to resort to such measures," she stopped and then finished, "for personal satisfaction." She took a sip of her tea to calm her nerves. She had never told anyone about this, and now she was confiding in a perfect stranger. She gulped as a stray tear found its way out of the corner of her eye.

"Denise, I am not here to judge you," Olivia said softly and reached across the table for her hand. She squeezed it gently.

"He sounded so professional on the phone and assured me of the high level of discreetness they adhered to. When he showed up the first time, I was shocked by how fine he was. I mean, let's face it, the guy's a stud. I bet tons of women flock to him all the time, and he was standing at my door waiting to make love to me," she said wistfully.

Olivia felt a little uncomfortable listening to her tale but tried not to let it show. She picked up a cookie from the plate. "Yes, he has always been handsome," she agreed.

"So once a month I have a secret lover who shows up to make mad, passionate love to me. Is that so wrong?" Denise cried. "For two hours a month, I have someone who touches me as if I am special. I have a man who loves me for me, just as I am. Even if the love part of it is all in my imagination. When I saw the article in the newspaper, I couldn't believe he could have hurt anyone either," she finished.

"Denise, with any luck you will never have to testify. Once they realize it was a mistake and an accident, they'll let him go. I promise, I will only tell them about you if we need character witnesses for him," Olivia assured her.

"I know I have sinned, and I can only ask God to forgive me for my weakness. I don't want to testify. Please, I beg of you, don't tell anyone about this. It has helped me to share this with you, and I never realized it would. As much as I counsel people to share their burdens with the Lord, I have always carried this one alone," she said, realizing her faith in the Lord would have to get her through this.

"Hopefully it won't go any further. I want to thank you for speaking with me this afternoon. Remember, we are all human and subject to human failings. I'm sure you can be forgiven for being human," Olivia said, attempting to offer what little comfort she could to this woman.

Ten minutes later she was back in her rental car and headed into town to meet Trevor for dinner. She had a lot to think about. The women she met weren't much different than she. She realized how lucky she was to have found Desmond.

18

Damian called Agnes a few nights later, and they talked for nearly an hour. Nothing personal was touched upon, but he found he liked talking to her. Soon they were speaking every night, and the calls were getting lengthier. One night they decided to stop avoiding the topic on both their minds—why Agnes was so hateful toward men, and why Damian was taking money for sexual favors.

Agnes was curled up in the window seat once again. This time the phone was pressed to her ear. She was enjoying her conversations with Damian and reluctantly admitted to herself that she looked forward to his calls. Neither of them suggested meeting; it was strictly a phone connection. It was safer this way, less tension than sitting across from one another in a restaurant. Looking up at the stars from her vantage point, she poised a question.

"Damian, have you ever been in love?" she asked wistfully. She held her breath, waiting for the answer. He was silent for a moment or two.

"Once," he answered. He shifted his position in bed. He

knew sooner or later she would ask. There were many questions he wanted to ask as well. If he brushed her off, he would have less chance of getting his own answers.

"Can you talk about it?" she asked. Keeping her own history in mind, she acknowledged there were things she preferred not to discuss. She was prepared to accept his answer if it was no.

Damian rolled off his bed and took the cordless handset with him. He hadn't talked about Felicia in a very long time. "Her name was Felicia. She was my wife," he said and made his way down to the bar in the living room to fix a drink.

Agnes sat up in the window seat and leaned her head on her knees. It never occurred to her he could have been married. She waited in silence as she heard the chink of ice in a glass and surmised he was fixing a drink.

Damian took a sip of the cognac and sat down on the recliner in his family room. He began to tell her about the love of his life, Felicia Parker.

They met in the ninth grade. Damian was from the south side of Chicago, and Felicia was from the west side. Their two schools were competing in a much-anticipated holiday tournament. Damian was starting at forward and becoming a basketball legend as a freshman. Felicia went to the game with several friends. It wasn't only the teams that were rivals—some of the students took the rivalry a bit too far. They didn't like the kids from the west side. After their team lost to the west-side school, some of the kids took out their disappointment in the parking lot by getting into fights.

At eight o'clock at night it was already dark when Felicia got separated from her friends. She rounded a corner of the building headed for her bus when she was intercepted by two girls from the rival school. In the darkness she could see she was still quite a distance from the bus. The girls accosted her and began calling her names and pushing her back and forth between them.

Felicia assessed her chances of taking on the two of them and knew it did not look good. The bigger of the two girls began shoving her farther back around the darkened corner of the building while the smaller one stood as a lookout waiting her turn to get in a few licks.

As soon as she turned the corner, Felicia bolted for the door. It was about two hundred yards behind her. She prayed the door would still be open as she ran as fast as she could toward it. The footsteps of both girls were getting closer, and she ran to the first of the row of doors and tried to yank it open. It was locked already. Panicked and with nowhere to go, she frantically tried the other doors and found them locked as well. Her tormenters, realizing they had her cornered, laughed with glee and began to approach her menacingly.

At that moment she heard the door latch behind her open. She turned quickly and bolted smack into the boy trying to exit the building. Her nose bumped squarely into his chest. Her hand flew to her face instinctively, but her mind still told her she needed to escape. The boy turned quickly and grabbed her by the hood of her coat as she tried to dart away. His hold on her hood stopped her in her tracks. He was about to ask her if she was okay when he heard the other girls outside on the stoop and quickly assessed the problem. He pulled Felicia behind him and stood between her and her tormenters.

"Ya'll need to get on the bus before it leaves, and stop making trouble," he said.

"This ain't your business, D, so move out the way," said the bigger girl. She approached him in the hallway.

Damian was already over six feet tall and stared down at this tough girl who dared to challenge him, and he laughed. He recognized her as one of the troublemakers at school and wasn't about to let her beat up this kid over a basketball game.

"Girl, I know you ain't that crazy. Now move out of the way so I can get this girl to her bus," he said and shouldered his way past her, pulling Felicia behind him.

The girl tried to get in one last lick as the couple walked by, but Felicia was able to duck the swing. Damian turned on her one last time, and she skulked away after sticking her tongue out at him.

"Where's your bus?" he asked.

"Thank you for saving me," she said and pointed to the direction of her school bus as they turned the corner into the parking lot.

"It stupid to get in a fight over a game. We lost, and I'm not any happier about it than anybody else, but it isn't worth fighting over," he replied as they approached her bus. He stood aside to allow her to get on the bus.

"Thanks again, Damian," she said and smiled gratefully.

"You know my name?" he asked and looked down at her. She was kind of cute, and he hadn't noticed before. He hated seeing senseless violence, and it was because of his feelings about it that he had stopped the budding fight, not because he'd seen what she looked like. Her hair was short and curly, and she had the biggest brown eyes he'd ever seen. When she smiled he could see braces on her teeth.

"Everybody knows your name," she answered and stuck out her hand to introduce herself. "I'm Felicia Parker."

"Nice to meet you, Felicia. Maybe I'll see you around," he said and turned to find his bus. He knew they wouldn't leave him behind. The team bus always did a head count before departing. He'd been a little bummed out when he left the gym tonight. However, he'd almost forgotten about the game now. He smiled as he reached his bus. He hoped he would see her again.

Felicia sat in her seat on the bus and watched him board his bus. Damian officially became her knight in shining armor that night. She leaned back in the seat and smiled. He was really cute, and he went out of his way to help her. She thought the beating she almost suffered was worth it because it gave her an opportunity to meet him.

Damian was from a not-so-good area on the south side of Chicago, and Felicia was from an upper-middle-class neighborhood on the west side. His parents were deceased, and he was living with an aunt who really hadn't wanted to take him in. She already had five other mouths to feed, and she could see at an early age he was going to be a big boy. In an effort to keep him out of her hair, she had enrolled him in the local PAL recreation league. It was there he developed his love of basketball.

Felicia was a popular girl at her high school. She was a member of the student union, drama club, and bowling club. Her parents were both professionals and socially active. There was very little Damian and Felicia had in common. In spite of this, Felicia began attending every basketball game she could. She and Damian struck up a friendship and began spending a lot of time on the phone. When her parents found out whom she had a crush on, they tried in vain to discourage her from talking with him.

Damian, while a gifted athlete, spent little time on his grades. He felt pretty sure he was going to get a full scholarship to play basketball in college. It was Felicia who convinced him of the importance of getting grades good enough to be selected by one of the big basketball schools. She tutored him and helped him bring his grade point average up to a 3.5. Damian wasn't stupid—he was lazy and unfocused when it came to schoolwork. Felicia changed all that.

They were both the same age, and when she turned seventeen her parents bought her a car for her birthday. She and Damian became inseparable. When Damian received the scholarship to Duke University, she was determined to follow him. Damian contemplated declaring his eligibility for the NBA draft in his junior year. Felicia convinced him not to, much to the chagrin of his aunt who saw her little pain-in-the-ass nephew suddenly having the potential to become an NBA star. Felicia explained that he needed to have a career that extended beyond a basketball court.

Damian knew Felicia was right, but the ability to make a lot of money fast was very tempting. It would mean he'd have to leave her behind if he was selected for a team. She was determined to get her degree, and she was adamant she was not leaving school to follow him again.

In the fall of their senior year, Damian proposed, and they became engaged. He would declare his eligibility for the draft after he obtained his business degree. Their wedding was planned for the summer after graduation. Wherever he was selected to go, he wanted her to go as his wife. Her parents finally accepted their union and gave them a two-week vacation in Hawaii as a wedding gift.

Their wedding day was almost picture-perfect. The sun was shining on a cloudless June afternoon. The church was filled with family and friends. Damian stood at the altar with his best man, Trevor, by his side as he watched his bride-to-be walking up the aisle on the arm of her father, and the wedding march played. She was stunningly beautiful in her designer wedding gown. The moment they saw each other, he couldn't remember ever being as happy or as proud. Her love for him shone brightly on her face as she smiled through her lace veil at her husband-to-be. He returned her smile with all the love he had in his heart. She mouthed the words *I love you*, and he did the same.

She was just approaching the front pew when her eyes closed and she went limp on her father's arm. Her father tried valiantly to hold her up as she sank to the floor. Damian raced to her side to help revive her. There was a loud gasp from all in attendance as someone screamed for a doctor. They were unable to revive her. She had suffered a brain aneurysm and died within minutes.

Damian's life spiraled quickly downward. Devastated by the

loss of his fiancée and friend of eight years, he spent his days and nights drinking. He never reported for the NBA draft nor returned the phone calls of those concerned for him. On several occasions Trevor came to his aid by saving his butt in a bar brawl.

One night Trevor woke up from a nightmare at two in the morning. He couldn't remember the dream, but the chills racing through his body told him Damian was in trouble. He scoured the city for him and wasn't sure to this day what led him to the elevated train station on State Street. He ascended to the top of the stairs and could see Damian standing on the platform precariously close to the edge. His heart stuck in his throat as he watched Damian swaying back and forth and looking down the track, waiting for the oncoming train. He quietly approached him from behind so he wouldn't be alerted to his presence. He could feel the rumbling of the approaching train under his feet. Damian leaned forward to step out onto the tracks, and Trevor snatched him back by his shoulders, and they both fell to the platform.

Damian rose quickly and turned on Trevor with all the pent-up rage that had been building for six long months. Tonight he wasn't drunk, he was just consumed with despair and loss. He decided the best way to end it all was to take his own life. Take his own life in the most violent, surefire way he could—in the path of a speeding train. He swung wildly with all his might and connected with Trevor's jaw as the train roared by. Trevor went down on one knee and came up swinging. The two battled on the platform until both were bloodied and in tears. When it was over they sat huddled together and cried. Damian cried his final tears for the loss of the love of his life, and Trevor was overcome with relief. He'd nearly lost the man he considered his brother. He knew if he'd been two minutes later, it would have been too late.

Damian turned a corner in his life that night. He dedicated

his efforts to becoming a man Felicia would have been proud of. He focused on his career. Women became a means of physical release. There was no desire to become involved again. Nine years later, and it was no different. In his heart Felicia was his wife as surely as if they'd spoken their vows to one another.

"Damian," Agnes called softly into the phone. He'd been silent for a few moments after telling her his story, and she wanted to make sure he was okay.

He stared down at the now-empty glass in his hand. He had been transported to another time and place while he told her about Felicia, unsure he wanted to come back to the present. Would Felicia be proud of the man he was today? He tried not to think about it.

"Damian, I'm sorry," Agnes said through the lump in her throat. Part of her wished she hadn't asked the question earlier, and part of her was glad she had. She knew a little more about him as a man than she had before. While her pain was of a different kind, she knew the pain of loving someone so much you couldn't imagine your life without him.

Damian roused himself on the other end of the phone. He wanted to change the subject and quickly. The past was the past, and it needed to stay there. There was nothing he could do to change the path he had walked to get to this moment with Agnes on the other end of the phone.

"What's your middle name?" he asked as he rose from the recliner and walked into the kitchen and retrieved a cold bottle of water from the refrigerator. The trip to the past had reminded him of his bad days when he had tried to drown his misery in a bottle.

She was puzzled by the question but accepted the change of subject. "Diane," she replied.

"Diane," he said, rolling her name around in his mouth. "Nothing personal, but I really don't like Agnes. Do you mind if I call you Diane?" he asked.

She laughed on her end of the phone. *Agnes* would not have been her choice either. But she'd grown used to it. She liked the idea of him calling her something different than everyone else she knew. "No, I don't mind," she said.

"Okay, well, good night, Diane," he said. He was all talked out for the evening.

"Good night, Damian," she said and slowly laid the handset down on the window seat. She knew her turn would come soon enough when she would have to answer his questions. She wondered if she could be as brutally honest as he had been.

Agnes called Damian a few nights later in a very agitated state. She'd been at a conference in town and run into Will. She tried to ignore his presence and did her best to avoid him. Over the years he'd taken several opportunities to let her know he could still destroy her if he wanted to. He warned her to watch her step. Even though she'd moved on, and become very successful, her past was lurking in the shadows, waiting to topple her at any given moment. For the most part she tried not to think about—until days like this when it was shoved in her face once again.

Damian could tell from her voice she was upset, but she refused to tell him why at first. So to allow her some time to get herself together, he decided to distract her with a different topic.

"I saw a picture of you and Marcus in the society pages yesterday," he said. He wondered if she and Marcus were an item and had done a little research on the Internet. He found quite a few social events going back a few years at which she was seen attached to Marcus's side. He thought maybe they had a thing and then broken up before she started calling Damian. When he saw the recent picture yesterday, it was clear she was still seeing Marcus. This didn't make sense.

"Yes, they always seem to catch us in the papers," she replied absently, still thinking about her encounter with Will.

"So are you and Marcus a couple?" he asked.

"Ha-ha, no, we are not," she scoffed at the idea as she paced back and forth in her living room.

"Well, pardon me for saying so, but I've seen quite a few pictures of the two of you looking pretty cozy," he said.

"Are you jealous?" she asked as she finally realized where he was heading with his line of questioning.

"Hell, no. But I was wondering why you were calling me so regularly when you got superattorney Marcus Carpenter III in your pocket. Can't the brother handle his business?" he asked wickedly.

She laughed in spite of her predicament. Everyone thought she and Marcus would be taking the stroll down the aisle—everyone except the people who really mattered, like Marcus's lover. She owed Marcus for giving her a chance to start a new career, and she helped him by appearing at social functions as his date. They explained their reluctance to commit by saying they were too career-driven to think about marriage.

"Damian, I could tell you, but then I would have to kill you," she said.

"Come on, Diane," he cajoled. Now he was really curious.

"You've met Marcus, haven't you? What did you think of him?" she asked.

"I think he's a bit of a Poindexter but seems to know his stuff," he replied.

"Do you think he could handle me?" she said seductively, teasing him.

"No way, he's a little too light in the shorts for you, baby. Hey, wait a minute!" he said as the light bulb in his head went off. "Don't tell me he's gay!"

"Yes, and you'd better not tell a soul, Damian Adams," she cautioned sternly.

Damian couldn't stop from laughing. She was parading around on a gay guy's arm, warding off all possible suitors and then paying him for his services in the meantime. He wondered if Marcus knew what their real association was, but he doubted it.

He sensed her mood was getting better, so he felt it was safe to broach the reason for her call. "What happened today? You seemed a little upset when you called," he asked seriously.

She hesitated to open up the ugly can of worms from her past. But Will had frightened her today when he threatened to take down Marcus with her as well. Apparently he'd seen the same article as Damian. Marcus's association with her would tarnish his reputation if the video got out. Although Marcus could probably disassociate himself from her and not lose a lot of respect, she would lose him as a friend. The only one she really had.

"Diane, what's wrong?" Damian asked again. He could sense her reluctance to trust him. "Hey, you know all the ugly stuff about me, and you still like me, right? Talk to me," he urged.

Slowly she began to tell him about Will, their relationship, and his constant threats to destroy her life. She was in tears by the end of the conversation. Damian assured her he felt no differently about her than he had when she initially called. He told her everyone made mistakes, and hers was in trusting the wrong man.

She felt better after telling him the truth, but it didn't remove the threat of Will. Damian told her no matter what Will did, in this day and time a whole lot of people had skeletons in their closets they overcame once exposed, and it did not destroy them. He didn't think she should put so much stock in Will's threats. It ultimately gave him too much power.

When they hung up the phone, Damian found he could not stop pacing around the house. He was angered by what she had told him. It wasn't fair that one mistake should ruin her life, nor that one man should have the power to do so. The guy was a prick, and someone needed to teach him a lesson. He wasn't motivated by feelings for Agnes, he was motivated by what he felt was an injustice. It was this motivation that took him to the West Pryor Street gym the following night.

Damian entered the gym still dressed in his work clothes. He looked around the room for a few familiar faces. It didn't take him long to spot the men he was seeking. He approached two men he knew from the block he grew up on, K-wan Price and Bootsy Murdoch. Both were hanging out in the corner of the gym talking trash when he walked up. Bootsy was the first to greet him.

"What's up, big D? You can't be planning on running the court in them five-hundred-dollar shoes," Bootsy said through half-closed lids, checking out the black Ferragamo loafers Damian was wearing.

"No, not tonight," he replied and motioned to Bootsy to step outside with him.

Bootsy was about six foot three and carried about two hundred sixty pounds. He'd spent several years in prison and was sporting muscle on top of muscles. Bootsy was wily and smart. His seven-year stint in prison didn't turn him around from a life of crime, it only taught him to be more selective in his choice of running mates. He met K-wan in prison during a brawl. K-wan stepped in and backed him up, saving him from a disfiguring beating and possibly saving his life. They were released within months of each other. Now K-wan was his faithful sidekick, and you rarely saw one without the other. K-wan was a little shorter in stature but as well built as his partner.

Damian and Bootsy grew up in the same projects, and Damian often spent the night at his apartment when his aunt was in one of her tyrannical moods. When he wasn't playing ball, Damian spent his time with Bootsy. Damian made sure he was always on Bootsy's side in a brawl because Bootsy was known to be vicious, even at an early age. It was this knowledge that made him seek him out.

"I have a job for you," Damian said as they stepped outside into the night air.

Bootsy's interest was immediately piqued. Big D never asked him for his help before, and he was anxious to know what the job entailed. Damian explained in detail what he needed, and they eagerly agreed to do the job. The only stipulation he put on the job was that no one was to be killed. However, he wanted the message to be clear and unmistakable and didn't much care how they accomplished their mission.

Will whistled as he inserted the key into the door lock of his penthouse apartment at one in the morning. As he stepped through the doorway he flipped the light switch on the wall. The room remained dark. Cursing his inept building management, he made his way into the living room in the darkness. He poured a shot of bourbon from the crystal decanter on the sideboard. Inexplicably, the hairs stood up on the back of his neck. He wasn't alone. He couldn't see anyone or hear anyone, but there was a feeling of dread creeping up his spine.

He put his glass down slowly and peered around the darkened room. A breeze blew in off the balcony. He was certain he'd closed the sliding doors when he'd left. In fact, he rarely opened them at all. The nearest phone was on the desk by the window. Slowly relying on his memory of the room, he made his way to the desk.

Bootsy and K-wan watched, amused, from their positions in the shadows of the room. The phone wire was already disconnected. As Will neared the desk, K-wan silently moved into position near the door. They correctly guessed it was where their victim would bolt to as soon as he realized the phone was dead. Will lifted the receiver and heard only silence on the other end of the line. He turned and walked quickly toward the front entrance. He saw a figure in the shadows blocking the doorway. He whirled around and ran smack into Bootsy's fist. The blow sent him toppling over the cocktail table and onto the floor.

He shook his head and assessed his situation from his position at Bootsy's feet. There was no way he could take them both. Best to find out what they wanted, and hopefully they would go away.

"I don't have a lot of money in the apartment, but I'm willing to give you what I have," he offered.

"We don't want your money," came the muffled reply as Bootsy spoke through the heavy knit of the ski mask.

The feeling of dread intensified in Will's stomach. If they didn't want money, what did they want? If they were going to rob him, they would have taken what they wanted and left before he got home.

"Where's the tape?" Bootsy demanded and kicked Will in the gut for emphasis.

"Tape? What tape?" Will gasped as he tried to regain his breath. What in the world were they talking about?

"We want the tape of the lady lawyer," Bootsy replied.

Will laughed hysterically. He couldn't believe she would send a few thugs to get the tape back after all these years. His hysteria was driven more by fear than mirth. She must have really been freaked out the other day. Well, she wasn't going to get it.

Bootsy did not take kindly to being laughed at and began to show Will how serious he was about completing his job. An hour later he and K-wan departed the apartment as surreptitiously as they had entered it, leaving behind a very battered but still breathing Will. They promised him if he'd given them the wrong tape or opened his mouth about the incident, they would return, and he wouldn't have to worry about talking to anyone again.

Agnes was surprised when her doorman buzzed the apartment a few nights later. She wasn't expecting anyone. The doorman advised her Mr. Adams was in the lobby to see her. She glanced down at what she was wearing—gray sweatpants, a navy-blue sports bra, and sneakers. Her hair was pulled up into a ponytail, and she was sweaty from exercising. She told the doorman to send him up and raced to her bathroom to wash her face before he arrived.

In a matter of moments the doorbell chimed. Patting her face with a clean towel, she hurried through the living room to open the door. She checked the peephole to make sure it was Damian and opened the door.

"This is a bit of a surprise," she remarked and ushered him into the apartment.

Damian stepped into the large marble foyer and whistled. He could tell her home was professionally decorated. Various types of art were displayed throughout the foyer and living room. The furnishings were an eclectic mixture of antique and modern pieces.

"Nice apartment. You must have paid a fortune for the interior decorator." He laughed as he moved into the living room.

"No, actually I picked out all the pieces myself," she replied, pleased with his compliment.

"Well—smart, beautiful, and talented. You're quite the catch, aren't you? Anyway, I won't stay long. I wanted to give you this in person," he said as he handed her a padded envelope.

She tested the weight of the envelope, and as she felt around the edges of the package, a chill raced through her body. Slowly she sat down on the sofa and placed the sealed envelope on the coffee table. Tentatively she reached back to pick it up again but could not bring herself to do it. It was like it was a pit of red-hot coals, and she would be burned if she touched it. She balled her hands into fists and tried to stop them from shaking. She looked up at him with tears brimming in her eyes.

"Is this . . . is this?" she started and could not finish the question.

"Yes, it is," he replied. He could see she was still frightened and embarrassed. He knew her next question. She would want to know if he'd seen it. He put her mind at ease before she voiced the question. "I didn't look at it, but you need to. Just to make sure it is the one you needed. If it's not, you let me know right away, and I'll take care of it," he said.

Relief flooded through her body, and she felt drained. Will's hold on her life was gone, and she had Damian to thank for it. She looked up at him with immense gratitude in her eyes. She rose from the sofa and slipped into his arms. She laid her head on his shoulder and whispered, "Thank you."

Damian held her in his arms for a few moments before stepping away and disengaging her arms from his waist. He held her hands in his for a moment and turned toward the exit. She held tight to his hand and pulled him back to face her.

"Stay with me tonight," she whispered huskily. She longed for the comfort of his arms and more. She owed him so much.

He smiled down at her. She was very attractive in her sweats with her six-pack abdomen exposed, no makeup, and her hair casually tied up. It was a tempting offer, but he declined.

"Not tonight. I didn't do this so you would sleep with me. I did it because it was wrong for him to use this tape to blackmail you for years. I did it because no one should wield such enormous power over another's life so unfairly." He kissed her once lightly and reached for the door handle.

"Damian," she called as he opened the door to the hallway. "Thank you again. I will never be able to repay you for this."

"You don't have to," he said and closed the door behind him.

Agnes walked slowly back to the living room and picked up the package from the table. She walked to her bedroom and turned on the television and VCR. It took her only a few moments to recognize the tape. It was the right one. She ejected it from the machine and opened the flap and pulled all the tape off the reels. Ripping it from the case, she took the mound of tape into her kitchen and piled it on the kitchen table. She spent the next thirty minutes cutting it up into hundreds of tiny pieces. She collected the pieces in a paper bag and carried them into the living room. Methodically she lit a fire in the fireplace and walked over to the bar in the corner of the living room. She poured a glass of wine as she waited for the flames to begin to glow. She opened the glass doors and tossed the bag into the fire. Then she sat back down and sipped her wine as the fears of her past went up in flames.

19

Marcus called Trevor to advise him to meet him at his office at two o'clock in the afternoon. He said he anticipated they would be getting some very good news. Trevor immediately let Olivia know and called Damian to advise him as well. The three of them were impatiently waiting at Marcus's office when he arrived at two fifteen. He apologized for being late.

Marissa had awakened from her coma, and the police were able to obtain a statement from her. She told the same story as Trevor but kept referring to him as Steve. This was puzzling, but when shown a picture of Trevor she agreed he was Steve. Cynthia's deposition was already on file, and she corroborated Trevor's claim that Marissa was already battered when she showed up at the restaurant. She also mentioned the fact that Marissa kept calling him Steve. The fingerprint analysis from the gun yielded no prints of Trevor's, and, finally, the DNA evidence from the rape kit matched Toby and not Trevor. The charges were going to be dropped. Trevor would have to appear in court tomorrow when the charges were formerly dismissed.

They all breathed a collective sigh of relief. It was finally over. Trevor hugged everyone in the room. Olivia couldn't wait to call Desmond and give him the good news. She would be coming home soon. The truth about Trevor's activities would never have to become public knowledge.

Damian excused himself to make a phone call, and Olivia followed him into the hallway to call Desmond. Trevor remained with Marcus to go over the procedures for tomorrow's court appearance. Marcus assured them they could spin the tragedy to let the press know Trevor's actions were actually heroic, and hopefully he could salvage his job.

Damian called Agnes at her office and gave her the good news. He asked if she would mind joining him for a celebratory dinner later. She enthusiastically agreed. She hadn't seen Damian since the night he stopped by her apartment, and she was eager to see him again.

Olivia called Desmond, and he told her he would make flight arrangements for her the following evening. She would go to court with Trevor, and then he could drop her off at the airport.

Damian and Olivia were standing on the curb outside Marcus's office building, each deep in their own thoughts. A gust of wind swept through, whipping up a few fall leaves. Olivia turned and smiled warmly at Damian. He opened his arms, and she stepped in and wrapped her arms around his waist. She sighed deeply against his chest. The door behind them opened, and Trevor practically bounced out onto the sidewalk beside them. Draping his arms over their shoulders, he hugged them both.

"This is what I like to see—my best friend and my best girl together again," he said.

They all laughed and turned to walk down Michigan Avenue toward the parking garage. Olivia stopped to window-shop, and Damian and Trevor continued talking while they waited for her. Through the glass in a nearby store window, Trevor saw a woman who looked remarkably like Paige. He excused himself and entered the store to see if it was her.

The woman was standing at a rack of scented candles, randomly opening the lids and taking a whiff. He walked up to her and called her name. She turned toward him and smiled. It was Paige.

"Hey, how have you been?" he asked, taking in the happiness reflected in her eyes.

"I've been very well. Thank you. And you? How are things going?" she asked.

"The charges are being dropped formally tomorrow. I'm free," he replied.

"I'm so glad to hear it. I knew everything would work out fine. I told you so." She grinned. She lifted an open candle to his nose. "Smell this. Do you like this one?" she asked.

"It's fine," he agreed as he sniffed the open candle and inhaled the sweet scent of honeysuckle. "If you're not busy, would you like to have dinner with me tomorrow evening?"

She raised her eyebrows and asked, "Are you sure? Wouldn't you rather be celebrating with your friends?"

"They are otherwise occupied tomorrow. Olivia is going back home to New Jersey, and Damian has a date. So I'll be all alone with no one to celebrate with if you say no," he replied, making a wistful face at her for emphasis.

"Okay, then, yes. I'd love to. Where should I meet you?" she asked.

"Do you want me to pick you up?" he asked.

"You can, but I've moved. So let me give you my new address," she replied and pulled a pen and paper from her purse. She quickly scribbled down her information.

Olivia entered the store to look for Trevor just as he and Paige parted company. Olivia noticed with whom he was talking, but said nothing about it when he walked up to meet her.

She wrapped her arm through his, and they departed the store, rejoining Damian on the street. Trevor suggested they grab a bite to eat.

"No, thanks, man," Damian replied. "The two of you go, and have dinner. This may be Olivia's last night here, if I'm correct?"

She nodded her head in agreement. "True, Desmond has booked a return flight for me tomorrow after the court appearance." She squeezed Trevor's arm and looked up at him and said, "You don't need me hanging around any longer than necessary."

"You're always welcome in my home. You know this, but I imagine you want to get back home, and I understand." He reached out and shook Damian's hand. "I'll talk to you later," he said.

Damian clasped his hand in return, gave Olivia a hug, and kissed her on the cheek. He wished her well and made his departure. Then he waved again as he made his way to the crosswalk and disappeared into the throng of shoppers.

Trevor took Olivia's hand in his as they strolled along Michigan Avenue. As she hadn't done any shopping since her arrival, Olivia took advantage of this afternoon to do some well-deserved shopping.

Damian arrived at Agnes's penthouse at seven o'clock for their dinner date. It was the first time they would be on an actual date. He'd made a reservation at Charlie Trotter's for eight o'clock. Her doorman was prepared for his arrival this time and buzzed him straight into the building. Damian was carrying a huge bouquet of twenty-four pastel peach roses. He reasoned that the neutral color of the roses represented their relationship, which was more than friendship but not quite a romantic one at this stage. He'd worn a classic black, three-button, wool Emenegildo Zegna suit with a crisp white collared shirt and a tan, gray, and peach woven silk tie.

Agnes left the door open to allow him to enter while she put the final touches on her makeup. She entered the living room dressed in a royal-purple, strapless, velvet cocktail dress. It fit snug across the bodice, through the waistline, and flared out slightly at her hips and stopped just above her knees. The dress had a midthigh-high slit on the right side, revealing a peek at the firm, smooth skin of her long legs. She whistled when she saw Damian standing by the window seat taking in the view from her floor. He was looking extremely handsome tonight.

Thoughts of a similar nature were on his mind when he turned as she entered the room. She was a very beautiful woman, with an awesome body. He carried the bouquet of roses across the room and presented them to her.

She pressed the velvety soft petals to her face and smiled up at him. The bouquet was gorgeous. She headed to the kitchen to find an appropriate vase. "Fix yourself a martini," she called from the kitchen. "I think I have all the ingredients you need at the bar."

Damian walked to the bar in the corner and found a new bottle of Bombay Sapphire gin, dry vermouth, Spanish olives, and a bucket of ice. He smiled as he realized she'd paid attention to what he liked to drink. He rinsed two martini glasses with vermouth, added the gin and ice to the shaker, and then shook it lightly. He filled the glasses and added two olives to each. She returned to the living room as he carried the glasses toward her. She placed her flowers on a faux stone pedestal in the corner of the room and crossed the room to meet him.

"You are very observant," he remarked as he handed her the chilled martini.

She smiled her acknowledgement and raised her glass in a toast. "Here's to Trevor and to justice prevailing," she said.

"Hear! Hear!" he commented and took a sip of his martini. She looked positively delicious, with her sparkling eyes and luscious full lips. He could feel the familiar stirring in his loins and realized suddenly that she was the last woman he'd been with and how long ago it had been. It occurred to him it was more than a month ago. *Jeez, I must really be slipping*, he thought. He'd been so caught up in Trevor's situation, he really hadn't thought about other women, and the only one he'd been speaking with on a regular basis was Agnes. He turned away and stared out the window. What was happening to him?

Agnes watched the play of emotions on his face intently. She wondered what he could be thinking about so seriously. She removed the toothpick with the olives on it from her glass, slipped an olive onto the end of the toothpick, and offered one to him.

"Don't be so serious. Not tonight," she said and put the toothpick up to his lips, cupping her hand under the dripping olives.

He pulled the first olive off the stick with his teeth and chewed it, enjoying the salty bitterness of it. Then he pulled her wet hand to his mouth and sucked the remaining olive juices from her palm while staring deeply into her eyes.

The suckling sensation on her palm caused tightening sensations in her lower regions. Laughing nervously, she pulled her hand away from his. She remembered the last time his touch had started uncontrollable physical reactions. She stepped away and took a sip of her martini.

Damian placed his glass on the sofa table behind him and moved up close to her back as she stood facing the window. He slipped his arm around her waist and gently pulled her back against his chest. He felt her relax comfortably against him. With one hand he swept her hair off the back of her neck, exposing the soft skin. He bent his head and began planting kisses along her throat.

Agnes felt her body responding to his expert touch. Her body arched forward as she leaned farther into his kisses, giving him full rein of the nape of her neck. Unconsciously, her fingers tightened on the stem of the glass. She was afraid it would slip from her hands and was grasping it tightly to steady it.

Damian continued his onslaught. He placed his palm against the flat of her stomach and reached out with his other hand and took the glass from her hand. Expertly he turned her into his arms and placed the glass on the table behind him at the same time. With her facing him, he placed one hand on her throat and slid his fingers into her hair just behind her earlobe. He continued the trail of kisses until his lips reached her trembling ones.

Agnes's breathing was ragged with anticipation by the time he finally claimed her mouth with his. She longed for the sweet taste of his tongue in her mouth. She was not disappointed as he masterfully flicked her lips with his tongue and alternately plunged his tongue into the warmth of her mouth. Agnes's body was growing feverish with desire. She wrapped her arms around his waist and then slid her hands down to his rump. She grasped his buttocks firmly and pulled him closer. The firm length of his manhood pressed against her abdomen. She slipped her hand between their hot and feverish bodies and gently raked her nails up and down the length of his shaft.

The growl that was emitted from Damian's mouth and projected from the base of his throat was akin to one of a hungry lion. He gently eased her away from him. "We can't do this right now," he said with sincere regret, and he stared at her lips, devoid of lipstick and temptingly fuller now from his kisses.

She stared pointedly at the outline of his rigid organ straining against the zipper of his pants and petulantly replied, "You started it."

"That's only because you are so irresistibly beautiful," he countered and reached over to the sofa table to reclaim his drink. He took a sip of the martini and popped one of the remaining olives into his mouth. "I think you might want to reapply your lipstick before we leave," he said casually. He wanted her out of the room. If she continued to stare at him as though he'd let her down, they might not make it to dinner, and you did not no-show for a reservation at Charlie Trotter's. They were nearly impossible to get on short notice.

She smiled at his smooth reply. Tonight was a special night for them. She'd waited this long to be with him again—she could wait a few hours more. Picking up her glass from the table, she lifted the last olive from the glass and provocatively pulled it between her lips with her teeth. She pushed the olive back out to the edge of her lips and sucked it inside her mouth slowly several times. Then she playfully rolled her tongue around her wet lips, brazenly daring him to respond. She laughed aloud and tossed her hair back over her shoulder as she carried the glass with her to the bedroom.

"Promises, promises," Damian mumbled, loud enough for her to hear, as he silently vowed to make her pay for that little performance.

Agnes stared at Damian across the table after their appetizer was served. He was so polished in his mannerisms. He'd conversed knowledgeably with the wine steward regarding the wine to be served with dinner. She wondered how a young boy who grew up in the hood had acquired such exquisite taste.

"What's on your mind, Diane?" he asked. He was proud of his ability to read people, and as much as she tried to mask her feelings, he could tell she was still plagued by questions about him.

"You have very refined tastes, and I was wondering how you acquired them?" she asked. She realized what a snobbish question it was but wanted an answer anyway.

"You can take a boy out of the ghetto, but you can't take the ghetto out of the boy?" he mocked and took a sip of his glass of wine. He continued. "I don't think either one of us was born with gold spoons in our mouths. You perhaps were born a little higher up on the economic ladder than I was, but neither one of us was born into the luxury we now afford. Could you honestly see your parents sitting here for dinner?"

"No, you're right. My parents were financially secure, and I was exposed to a lot, but I found a whole new arena to play in when I met Will. It was a lifestyle I wanted for myself. What about you?" she replied and took a bite of her appetizer.

"Felicia was from a middle-class background, and spending time with her family was my first exposure outside the hood. I liked what I saw and began imitating traits I saw in her father. When I was at Duke University, I had the opportunity to become exposed to a lot more potential wealth. When you're a ball player, you get a lot of attention, and people want to be seen with you. I was invited to quite a few high-society events. I made it my business to absorb everything I was surrounded with. My major was business, but I minored in French. I still practice speaking it now and again. Haven't been to Paris yet, but I'll get there." He smiled as he reminisced about the dialogues he and Claudette used to have when he was her favorite. He'd learned a great deal on his own about schmoozing with the upper class when he met her, but she applied the finishing coat to his high-gloss sheen. She'd toned it down to a fine matte finish—polished, but not garish or opulent. She taught him the art of subtlety. He decided not to tell Agnes about her.

Agnes leaned back in her seat as their appetizer plates were removed. She thought about what he had said. It made sense, especially since he seemed like a person who was determined to be successful. She didn't think it was his social status that had persuaded Will to give him the tape, though.

"You're too transparent, Diane. At least to me anyway," he said with a devilish smile. "There are some things you don't need to know."

She leaned forward and picked up her wineglass. She took a

sip and let the smooth, mellow taste linger on her tongue a while before speaking. Damian was an enigma to her. She wanted to know all she could about him but acknowledged it could be a dangerous proposition. What was she willing to risk to get closer to him, and did she really want to do that? This was the question that plagued her mind. Could she afford to allow him to get any closer?

"I enjoy your company, Damian," she admitted. "But I can't promise—"

"Promises aren't required," he interrupted, "of either of us at this point. I enjoy your company, and I like talking to you. Beyond that," he shrugged and then changed his mind and continued in a whisper, "well, I do like fucking you." He smiled wickedly as she blushed and looked around, hoping no one had heard him.

She realized that as reluctant as she was to admit it, she was hoping for more. She was as afraid of the possibility as she was excited by the prospect of the two of them together. A small pucker appeared between her eyebrows, and she began to lose her appetite. A shadow clouded her eyes.

Damian reached across the table and placed his hand over hers. He could tell her mood was changing, and it was not his intent to put a damper on the evening. He truly enjoyed her company, and he was very attracted to her. But he wasn't in love with her and wasn't sure he ever could love anyone again. He didn't want to raise her expectations only to hurt her again like the others. Yet he admitted he wanted to see more of her beyond tonight.

"Hey, I didn't mean to bring you down. I really didn't, but I haven't loved anyone since Felicia, and I don't honestly know if I'm capable of loving anyone else. I've been spending the last several years seeing whom I want, when I want, moved on when I felt like it, and never looked back. I don't know if I can change, if I want to change, and, most importantly, I don't want to hurt you if I can't," he told her honestly.

She looked up into his eyes across the table and understood he was trying to be honest with her. She appreciated it. For the last nine years she'd controlled every aspect of her life, including her sexual activities. She had slept with other men since Will, but only men she was not susceptible to falling in love with. There were a few she found hard to get rid of after some one-night stands, and it was then she resorted to utilizing Damian's services, never expecting the two of them to be sitting across from one another at dinner contemplating a possible future. She found she didn't care what he'd done prior to the night at the Knickerbocker Hotel, but she suddenly wanted to know what he'd done since, or, rather, whom he'd done.

"Have you been with anyone since that night?" she asked quietly and silently prayed he'd give her the right answer, an answer that would give her hope.

He thought about lying to her because he found the truth hard to believe. Diane was his friend, and he wasn't ready to lose her friendship yet. "Honestly I didn't even think about it until I was in your apartment tonight, and I guess it surprised me. I was so caught up in Tré's situation and getting him out, I guess sex wasn't on my mind. So, truthfully, Diane, you are the last woman I was with, and I can't really explain why, since it was at least two, maybe three weeks before the incident with Tré. Just don't make anything of it."

Her heart lightened inside her chest in spite of his telling her not to put any stock in the fact that the last woman he had been intimate with was she. It was all the hope she needed to hang on to.

"I won't. But thank you for being honest with me," she said and smiled. The furrow between her brow disappeared, and her eyes began to sparkle again. "I can't promise not to be a control freak and not to be bitchy once in a while because it's become part of my nature. I like talking with you and spending time with you as well, so can we just take it one day at a time and see what happens?" she asked slowly.

"I don't want—" he started.

"To hurt me, I understand. I'm a big girl. I still want to see you," she replied and started to pull her hand away from his.

"That's part of it, but I don't want to lose your friendship. So if we sleep together again and it's going to jeopardize our friendship, we can keep sex out of our association," he said. The sentence played back inside his head, and he wondered where in the hell that little speech had come from. It sounded like something he had told a few other women as he was slipping his hand inside their panties. He hadn't meant it then, but he did mean it this time. He couldn't wait to get Diane back home tonight and finish what they started earlier, but he could get laid by any number of women. If Diane was going to become too attached . . . He realized he was still holding her hand, and she was staring at him with a puzzled look on her face. *Damn,* he thought, *I'm losing it. I never spent this much time trying to talk my way out of a woman's drawers. What is wrong with me?*

"Now you're the one thinking about this too much," Agnes said. Dinner arrived, and they both breathed a sigh of relief as the conversation turned to the sumptuous-looking meals before them.

A few hours later they entered the penthouse elevator in the lobby of her apartment building. She inserted her key into the special elevator panel that would allow the elevator to ascend directly to her floor without stopping for other passengers. The doors had barely closed when Damian pulled her into his arms. Sliding his tongue easily into her waiting mouth, he sucked her into a rapturous kiss and pressed the button for the penthouse level. With her arms draped around his shoulders, he began sliding down the side zipper of her dress.

Agnes reacted to the sudden breezy feeling on her side as she caught the top of the dress as it slipped down over her breasts. She gasped and laughed nervously while trying to keep her dress from falling to the floor. He reclaimed her mouth and laced her fingers with his, raising her arms above her head. The dress fell to the floor with a soft whooshing sound. The elevator continued its ascent. He planted kisses along the baby-smooth skin of her upper arms as he worked his way up her arms to her hands. Pulling her hand to his mouth, he lightly licked the skin on the inside of her wrist.

Agnes was momentarily concerned about her state of undress in the bright elevator, but the concern quickly passed in the heat of the moment. She stood there in a one-piece, strapless, violet body shaper with black lace garter attached to thigh-high stockings. Her breasts were heaving against his chest as he plied her with kisses. He gave her a brief respite when the elevator doors opened. She bent to retrieve her gown, but he grabbed it first and guided her out of the elevator into the private hallway of her apartment. She tried several times to get the key in the lock of her door, but her hands were shaking. He stood behind her, plying her neck with wet kisses. She could feel his rigid manhood pressing against her buttocks as he pressed closer to her. She fumbled the key, and it fell to the carpeted floor. She bent quickly to retrieve it and gasped aloud as his hand slipped between her legs as she stood up.

Feeling the moistness already penetrating the undergarment she wore, he deftly unsnapped the crotch in one quick motion. Agnes finally got the key in the lock and burst into the living room. "Were you going to do it right there in the hallway?" she cried out incredulously.

Closing the door behind him, he followed her into the room. He took his jacket off and tossed it into a chair, unbuttoning his shirt as he approached her in the darkened room. "Does it matter?"

"Damian?" she queried as she moved farther away from him. He was being very aggressive, and it was making her a little bit nervous. She bent down to slip off the high heels she was wearing.

"Leave them on," he commanded, moving closer to her. The glow of the moonlight through the bay window made his hazel eyes appear catlike in the dark. He grasped her wrist and pulled her up against his chest. Running his hand along the smooth skin of her thigh, he teased her lips with his tongue.

"Damian," she started again. His touch was like fire running up and down her legs. With the snap undone on her bodysuit, the ends crept up, exposing her rounded cheeks. She wanted him as much as he apparently wanted her, but she was having a hard time making it into her bedroom. "Damian," she called again, this time louder.

He stepped away and looked into her eyes. He watched her eyes closely as he pulled off his shirt and then unbuckled his belt. He could see the hunger in her eyes. Yes, she wanted him, but she would have to realize she didn't control this part of their relationship anymore. He was a man, and she was going to have to learn it wasn't a game anymore. "Make up your mind, sweetheart, Mike is gone. Do you want Damian, or do you want Mike? Do you want some stiff dick you can boss around, or do you want me?"

She stared at him and knew what he was trying to tell her. She was only nervous because she wasn't in control of the pace. She'd never been frightened of him, and she wasn't now. She was fighting giving up control. He had controlled everything from the moment those elevator doors closed to the point she couldn't even think straight. That's why she tried to back away, afraid of where he was going to take her. It was a test—either she passed or she failed tonight. She smiled. She wasn't going down so easily; he wanted a fight, and he was going to get one.

She walked to the archway leading to her bedroom, leaned against the wall, and stared him down.

"You mean to tell me you would actually consider walking out of here with that invitingly stiff dick and not get any of this before you go?" she said as she raised her leg and placed her foot on the bench by the wall, exposing her thick triangle of pubic hair. Seductively she fingered her clitoris and dared him to walk out.

"You're playing with fire, little girl," he said huskily and quickly crossed the room to her side. She turned to walk into the room, and he pulled her back into the archway and sat her down on the bench. He stepped out of his pants and boxers, and his rigid penis sprang forward enticingly before her. He handed her a condom.

"Put it on," he said and ran his fingers through her thick hair, caressing her neck lightly.

She looked at the foil package in her hand and smiled. This was another test. She ripped open the package and held the latex condom in her left hand. With her right hand she reached between his legs and cupped his balls in her hand while she took his shaft in her mouth. His sharp intake of breath was the reward she sought. Alternately squeezing and caressing his balls, she worked her mouth up and down his shaft, lubricating it with saliva. Grasping his thickened rod, she pressed it flat against his stomach and gently pulled each pulsing ball into her mouth. She sucked gently on each before pulling both into her mouth. He could not hold back the hissing groan that escaped between his clenched teeth; it signaled the intensity of his reaction.

Damian was surprised but not shocked when she took him into her mouth. Her expert sucking was driving him crazy, and he was trying not to show it. When she took his nuts into her mouth, he fought the temptation to shove her away. The tension in his body was increasing, and he felt ready to explode.

Although in his mind he envisioned his seed spilling down her chin and onto her luscious breasts, he gently pushed her away.

"Now!" he demanded, his hands on his hips, his erection firm and ready.

Obliging him, she unrolled the condom up the length of his organ. Roughly he lifted her off the bench and pressed her back against the wall. Raising her one leg onto the bench so her high heels dug into the soft padding of the seat, he gained the access he wanted to her sweet spot. He lifted her leg up around his waist and steadied her with a firm grip on her thigh as he slid up into the wet cavity of her body.

She gasped aloud as he filled her body with his engorged, pulsing shaft. Her breathing became more and more ragged, along with his. He braced his body with his free hand on the wall above her head, while his other hand cupped her butt cheek firmly as he pumped higher and higher up the slick, wet vaginal canal.

Agnes clung tightly to his shoulders as her body thumped the wall behind her with his every stroke. Her mind was filled with thoughts of Damian and how much she wanted his body inside hers. She could feel her vulva throbbing and the juices dripping from her body as he filled her completely. Alternately tightening and relaxing her vaginal muscles, she gripped and squeezed each inch of his sizable penis. She ran her hands along the sinewy muscles of his shoulders as she felt the first wave of orgasm cresting. Her fingers dug into his muscular forearms as she began twisting and jerking to escape the electric shocks raging inside. She tried to push him away, but he stood rock solid and pressed his hips deeper into hers. The firmness of penis rubbed against her engorged and hypersensitive G-spot. The sensations created were excitingly raw and mind-numbing as he trapped her between the wall and his body. Her body convulsed as she was overcome by a violent climax. She couldn't stop the loud cries of pleasure that rolled breathlessly off her tongue. Simultaneously, he let out a deep groan of release. Thoroughly spent, she collapsed limply onto his shoulder. He leaned his head on hers for a minute and then scooped his arm under her legs and effortlessly carried her into the bedroom and laid her on the bed.

Crawling into the bed beside her, he removed her high heels one at a time. Slowly and almost methodically, he began to unsnap the garters holding up her stockings. Sated, Agnes lay in the bed and watched curiously as he rolled each stocking down to her feet and gently removed them, folded each, and placed it on the nightstand. She arched her body to assist him as he slid her bodysuit down over her hips to remove it, leaving her naked before him.

Lying next to her, he placed his palm on her stomach. Gently he caressed her rib cage and slid his hand up her diaphragm to cup her breast. Her breasts were large, firm orbs of silken pecan skin. He massaged her breasts tenderly and then circled the rigid peaks with his tongue.

She heard him groan as he opened his mouth and covered the brown nipple and sucked teasingly. The muscles of her vagina tightened and ached with each tug on her nipples. She watched as his manhood once again rose to the occasion. Mesmerized by his touch, she allowed him free rein of her body. She closed her eyes as his hand slipped between her legs and his fingers entered the wet cavity of her body. Her clitoris was pulsing, and she yearned for his touch.

Rolling over between her legs, he spread her legs with his knees. She raised her mound, eager for his fulfillment again. He opened the lips of her sweet spot and exposed the round, pink bulb. She cried aloud as his lips closed over the tiny bulb, and he tweaked it with his tongue. He alternately sucked and flicked her clit until her body writhed uncontrollably beneath him.

With the juices of her body lingering on his lips, he returned to her mouth and kissed her passionately. She wrapped her long legs around his waist as he filled her once again.

Tears of joy and confusion trickled from her eyes as she tried to understand the connection between the aggressive Damian of the living room and the man who tenderly removed her clothes and made sweet love to her again. She clung tightly to him as he climaxed once again, burrowing her face into his shoulder so he would not see her tears.

Damian eased out of her body and lay next to her on the bed. He stretched his arm above her head so she could rest her head on his shoulder. He closed his eyes and tried not to think at this moment. He didn't want to feel anything for Agnes, yet he knew he did. Flashes of her filtered through his mind: statuesque in her blue gown at the ball, choking on the drink, flashing him angry looks, and then smiling at him across the dinner table. He pictured her sitting in her window seat with the phone to her ear, talking with him, and remembered their intimate conversations over the last several weeks. She was a tigress and a kitten. She was a strong woman but still needed protection, whether she would admit it or not. Reluctantly he admitted to himself he admired her, and he cared about her.

Agnes desperately wanted to be inside his head at this moment and to know what he was thinking as he stared at the ceiling above their heads. As she lay quietly with her hand on his chest, she realized she wanted to be able to trust him. He'd acted as her knight in shining armor when he'd shown up the other night with the tape. The fact that he expected nothing in return was even more proof of the kind of man he really was. It was much more than gratitude she felt for him. She knew she would be devastated if he chose not to see her again.

"Damian," she started. She needed to ask him again about the possibilities.

His arm tightened around her shoulders reassuringly, and he

kissed her forehead softly. "One day at a time, Diane. One day at a time," he said and closed his eyes.

Agnes smiled and leaned over to plant a kiss on his lips. Snuggling into his arms again, she closed her eyes. She knew he would commit to no more than this right now, and accepting it would have to be enough.

20

As Denise Jenkins prepared for work, she reflected on her narrow escape from having her secret life exposed. Donning a chocolate-brown business suit and white silk blouse, she stared reflectively in the mahogany mirror. Her secret lover wouldn't be coming around anymore. She read in the morning papers that he was released of all charges. In fact, the press commended him for trying to protect a woman from a physically abusive husband. This was the man she liked to think she knew. The man who would risk his life to protect a woman; it was how she always envisioned him.

She had a long talk with the Lord. She confessed her sinful behavior and vowed to be more tolerant of the human failings of the other women in the congregation. Instead of treating them with disdain as she previously had, she would try to be more compassionate. Her near exposure could have cost her much embarrassment, and she would have been the center of church gossip for the next several years. She would never have been able to return to Mount Calvary First Baptist. By the grace of God, she'd been spared. It was a lesson she took to heart.

* * *

Naomi and Greg sat in the waiting room at the therapist's office. Her hand was tightly clasped in his. She'd finally gotten up the nerve to explain to Greg how seriously his problem was affecting her. He was embarrassed by his inability to satisfy her and promised to seek help. He made an appointment to see his doctor, who explained there was nothing physically wrong with him. He was able to get an erection and sustain it until shortly after penetration. He suggested his problem might be more psychological than physical. He recommended the therapist they were waiting to see this afternoon.

Naomi appreciated his willingness to do whatever was necessary to make things right for her. She knew it was a major blow to his manhood to even admit the seriousness of the situation. He told her he would rather do what he could to rectify the problem than for her to become susceptible to another man because of it. She couldn't prevent the tears from welling in her eyes as he said this. She assured him she loved him and always would, no matter what the outcome of the counseling. Her secret remained her secret.

As she sat with him in the waiting room and watched his nervous fidgeting, she was overwhelmingly relieved that he would never have to find out about Steve. She squeezed his hand and gave him a reassuring smile. He brought her hand to his lips and kissed it gently. He then retreated to his thoughts and stared at the pictures on the wall opposite their seats. Naomi sighed deeply. *Everything is going to be fine,* she thought. She realized she never loved Greg more than she did at that moment.

Paige stared at her reflection in the bathroom mirror. She loved to look at her body now. The plastic surgeon had created a new left breast, and she was amazed at the resemblance to her right breast. In the procedure they had taken a thin layer of the areola and nipple from the right breast and transplanted it on the newly formed breast mound, which was created with a saline-solution implant. Although the new breast was a little firmer and rounder, at her age her normal breast had not begun to sag yet, so the difference was visible only to her. She was astounded by the results.

She chose a V-necked, formfitting little black dress from her closet. After applying her makeup and brushing her hair, she slipped the dress over her lace brassiere and thong. The dress clung to her in all the right places and exposed just enough cleavage to titillate the male observer.

She was excited about her date tonight. She hadn't seen Trevor in many months and was so pleased to run in to him the day before. His offer of a date was an unexpected opportunity she did not want to miss. There was a very important question she wanted to ask him. He looked as handsome as she remembered, and she was honored he wanted to share his celebration with her.

She pulled a pair of jet-black ultrasheer panty hose from her dresser drawer and sat down on the bed to put them on. Finally she slipped on her black leather sling-back pumps and added a touch of perfume to her neck, wrists, and the vee between her breasts. She was ready.

Trevor arrived promptly at six thirty to pick her up. He was dressed in a tan three-button suit with a pale blue shirt and accenting tie and pocket square. He planned to take her to Tavern on Rush to celebrate the clearing of his name. When she opened the door and admitted him entrance to her new apartment, he did not miss the rising mounds of her breasts exposed by the deep neckline of her dress. He smiled to himself as he took note of what was clearly a reconstructed breast. He was happy for her and silently thankful Nina had carried out her promise to foot the bill for the procedure.

Paige offered to take his wool overcoat and asked if he would like a glass of wine before their departure. He declined. He did not want to get too comfortable in her new home because he wasn't certain of her expectations of the evening, nor of his own.

"Why did you move?" he asked as he stood in the living room, waiting for her to retrieve her coat from the closet.

"There were too many memories associated with the old apartment, and not all were pleasant memories," she said as she reflected on the one special night she'd shared with him. However, there were many more days and nights associated with her ex, and those she wanted to leave behind.

He assisted her with putting on her coat, allowing his hands to linger on her shoulders for a moment or two. He inhaled the fresh scent of her hair and very light and subtle fragrance of her perfume.

"You're looking very beautiful this evening," he remarked as he released his grip on her shoulders and stepped toward the front door.

"Thank you," she replied and looked up into his eyes, hoping he would comment on her enhanced figure. He returned her smile but said nothing as he opened the front door and walked out onto the porch.

She locked the front door behind them and followed him to his car, which was parked at the curb. After he opened the door and helped her inside, she relaxed comfortably into the luxurious supple leather of the front seat.

On the ride to the restaurant he gave her an abbreviated version of the night he was arrested. He explained the isolation and wretchedness of being imprisoned. Even though he knew he'd done nothing wrong, he wasn't sure he was really going to be free again. Memories of the cold dank cell and steel bars that kept him caged like a wild animal flashed through his mind. His grip tightened on the steering wheel, and the muscles in his jaw clenched.

"But you're out now, and it's over," Paige said, noticing the tension in his posture. She reached across and laid her hand on his on the steering wheel.

"I'll never go back. I swear they'll never do that to me again," he said and exhaled a deep breath of air.

"Have you given up your business?" she asked quietly and turned away to stare out the window while she waited for him to answer. It was the first time since seeing him again that she had acknowledged how they met.

"Permanently," he replied firmly and without hesitation. He noticed she'd turned away, and he reached out and placed his hand on her knee to get her attention. When his eyes connected with hers again, he repeated his answer. "Permanently. I made a mistake, and I have many regrets about what I was doing, but I don't regret meeting you."

"Same here," she replied and covered his hand with hers. Her blue eyes twinkled at him in the dim light of the car.

Fifteen minutes later he pulled up to the restaurant. The parking valet opened his door for him and handed him a ticket for the car. Trevor joined Paige at the curb, and, placing his hand on her elbow, he escorted her into the restaurant. The restaurant was crowded as usual, and they took a brief look around while they waited to be seated.

"I've never been here before," Paige remarked as she took in the well-dressed crowd.

"The food is good," Trevor said.

"I always said I would come here one day and sit at those outdoor tables but never took the time," she continued.

"And you should. It is fun to sit out there and people watch, especially on a nice summer evening," he said as the hostess signaled that their table was ready. He directed Paige to follow the hostess, and they proceeded to their table.

They were halfway through dinner before Paige brought up the subject of her surgery. In her fantasies she imagined he was the one who had paid all the costs, but she'd never been able to get any information from the doctors or nurses regarding her benefactor.

"Did you have anything to do with me being contacted for the surgery?" she asked quietly as she looked at him across the table. He'd just taken a forkful of food and wiped his mouth with his napkin before responding.

"Me? What do you mean?" he asked, unsure of how much he wanted to tell her. He knew when he ran into her yesterday that this conversation was going to be unavoidable if they spent any amount of time together.

"Did you pay for my surgery?" she asked bluntly.

"No, I didn't," he answered truthfully. He watched the sadness creep into her face as she looked away for a moment or two. He could see the disappointment in her eyes.

"I—I thought," she stammered. She'd thought he was her guardian angel looking out for her. All this time she'd secretly basked in the fantasy that he had cared enough to make sure she got what she needed most. Now she had to face the possibility he hadn't given her another thought since leaving her apartment that night.

"Paige, you are a very beautiful woman. I noticed that about you the very first time we met. I'm glad the surgery makes you feel better about yourself, but I always thought you were gorgeous," he said and reached for her hand across the table. Squeezing it gently, he raised it and pressed the back of her hand to his lips. The romantic gesture brought a smile back to her lips.

Still, if he hadn't paid for the surgery, then who did? She couldn't get the question out of her mind. "I'm grateful just to be alive, but when they called and offered me a chance to be a whole woman again, I couldn't say no," she explained. "They claimed to have gotten my name off some obscure list or something, and I never believed them. It happened after I met you, and I was certain you were involved somehow. I guess I wanted to believe you cared enough . . ." She looked down at his strong hand holding hers on the table.

"I admit, I did think about you after our last meeting. You were and still are a very special lady. Whoever paid for your surgery really isn't such an important factor. What's important is that you were able to get it. I can't tell you what to do, but I think it's time you let this issue go. Enjoy the rest of your life. I'm sure that's all the person or persons who took care of you could ask for." He smiled reassuringly. He released her hand and took a sip of his wine.

Paige knew he was right about not clinging to the dream of him as her benefactor. While she'd been dating other men for the last year, he was always there on a pedestal no other man could touch. In spite of the reason for their connection, he was her prince who rode up on his powerful white charger and turned her life around. First by showing her she was still very much a sensual woman even with just one breast, and second by arranging for her to have the surgery. No matter what he told her tonight, she knew in some form or fashion he was responsible.

The fact that he did not want credit for it just confirmed how much of a gentleman he really was. She reasoned if he hadn't already known about the surgery, he would have said something at the apartment when he saw her breast exposed by the low-cut dress. He would have asked questions about how and when, but he didn't ask any questions at all. If it had been anyone other than him, she could have believed they just weren't interested in her transformation. She decided to leave the subject alone. In her heart she felt she finally knew the truth. She was eternally grateful.

On the drive back to her apartment, both were deep in their own thoughts. Trevor reflected on their early conversation and the history behind their friendship. He still wasn't sure what his plans were when they reached her apartment. Paige was already thinking ahead to their arrival and anticipating he would spend the night with her. She was nervous about showing off her new body but couldn't wait to see his reaction.

Trevor pulled up outside her apartment building and got out of the car and walked around to open her door. He offered her his hand as he helped her out of the car. He followed her up the walkway to the entrance to her apartment. His mind was filled with conflicting thoughts. He was tempted to stay and make love to her tonight, but a caution light in his head was warning him it could be a mistake. He knew he couldn't give her any promises beyond tonight, and he also knew how unfair it would be to take advantage of her vulnerability.

Paige put her key in the lock and turned to face him. She reached out for his hand and clasped her small hand in his. He once again brought her hand to his lips and then cupped her chin in his hand as he bent down to place a tender kiss on her lips. She responded warmly to his kiss, parting her lips to draw him into a more intimate kiss. Sensually and teasingly he returned the ardor of her kiss. Extricating himself, he stepped away and kissed her softly on her cheek.

Paige opened her eyes and was startled to see the sadness in his eyes. Her eyes implored him to join her inside the apartment. He shook his head slowly in response. Tears welled in her eyes at what she interpreted as his rejection of her, but he spoke quickly to dispel those thoughts.

"You deserve someone who will love and cherish you for a lifetime. Whoever that man is, he'll be a very lucky guy. I know as much as I care about you and am attracted to you, that person isn't me. At this point in my life, I'm not ready to be the kind of man you need and deserve. I have to get my life together and decide where I'm going from here. Rest assured, I would like nothing better than to make love with you tonight, but it wouldn't be fair to you because I won't be here in the morning or the next day or the day after that," he explained earnestly. He kissed her briefly and turned to walk back down the walkway.

"Trevor," she called after him as he walked away. He stopped and looked back at her, standing under the lantern in front of the doorway. She was so beautiful; he wished things could have been different. "I understand, but I still want you to stay," she finished and smiled at him, valiantly fighting back the tears. She stepped from the doorway and met him halfway down the walkway.

He watched her approach and knew if she persisted he was not going to be able to resist. Her overcoat was open and revealed the black dress underneath. The soft wool clung to her body in all the right places. It had been a very long time since he made love to a woman simply because he wanted to.

She walked up to him and slipped her arms around his waist. She pressed her face into his chest and breathed deeply. He smelled so good, and the warmth of his body radiated and encased her slim form.

"I'll worry about tomorrow when it gets here, but I need you tonight," she whispered.

He started to ask if she was sure and decided he'd already explained his intentions enough. If she was still willing, and it was clear she was, he was not about to turn her down. He wrapped his arm around her, and they walked slowly back up the walk and into the apartment.

Once inside the apartment, they began the slow process of undressing one another. Although Trevor's manhood was already rising in anticipation, his movements were slow and deliberate. He methodically worked on building a slow-burning fire because he planned for it to last all night long.

He sat on the edge of her bed with her standing in front of him. While he planted kisses on each bit of exposed flesh, he slipped her dress off her shoulders and rubbed his hands along her slim waist as the dress fell into a soft heap on the floor. Her breasts were rising and falling quickly in the cups of the lace bra. Trevor pressed his face between her breasts and inhaled the sweet scent of her body.

She held his head between her breasts with both hands, gently kissing the top of his head. She inhaled a deep breath as his hands slipped down and cupped her butt cheeks, pulling her closer between his legs. He began alternately biting and kissing the soft skin of her throat as his right hand moved up her back and expertly unlatched the bra hook in one quick motion.

She wiggled out of her bra straps and let the undergarment fall to the floor. He immediately reached up to caress the soft round flesh of her right breast. Gently sucking on her right nipple, he tentatively cupped the left breast in his right hand. He paused momentarily to look up at her; he wondered if it would hurt if he gave her other breast equal attention. She pressed her left breast to his mouth in response to his unspoken question. Her left breast wasn't as sensitive to his touch as her right, but it pleased her to have him sucking on it anyway.

He rose from the bed and unzipped his pants and stepped out of them. His erection was throbbing and ready to slip between her sweet thighs. Paige took a moment to slip out of her hose and thong and then climbed onto the bed and eagerly waited for him to join her.

As he faced away from the bed to remove his boxers, she watched the muscles ripple along his back. She admired his perfect physique of broad shoulders that tapered down to a slim waist and firm, round buttocks. Her bodily juices were already flowing in anticipation.

His erection sheathed, he got into bed and wasted no time slipping between her open legs. A sharp intake of breath escaped his lips as he slid deep inside her body. Her vaginal lips closed around his firm shaft as if to trap him inside forever. He relaxed for a moment, enjoying the sensation and warmth of her body before wrapping her legs around his waist and beginning to stroke deeper and deeper into her body.

She matched his motion with a slow rolling of her hips, enhancing the pleasurable feelings they were creating for each other. Reaching up, she grabbed his face and brought it to her mouth, which he had been neglecting in his exploration of her breasts. Passionately she kissed him, inviting his tongue into her mouth and sucking the sweetness of it.

Trevor felt his climax building, and as much as he wanted to hold it off, the tension in his body had been building for weeks. He slipped his hand under her back and raised her hips just enough to slip as deep as he could into her sweet spot. His aching, throbbing dick exploded as a hot stream filled the condom. He groaned aloud as the juices flowed from his body.

Rolling over onto his side, he stared at the ceiling above him. "I'm sorry." He laughed. "I'll do better next time."

She laughed with him. Even though she hadn't climaxed, she enjoyed the feel of him inside her body. She wasn't concerned; she was happy to have given him the measure of relief he needed. She snuggled into his arms and closed her eyes.

Trevor remained still for a few minutes before excusing himself to go into the bathroom to discard the used condom. Paige was surprised and disappointed to hear the shower running after a few minutes, thinking he must be preparing to leave. She turned on her side, away from the bathroom door, and tried not to let her feelings show. She was the one who said it was okay for them to make love tonight. She was the one who claimed she could deal with his being gone in the morning. She owed it to him to be strong and not lay a guilt trip on him.

"Hey, there." His voice interrupted her reflections.

She turned to see him standing naked by the bedside. *Lord,* she thought, *what a beautiful man you have created.* She smiled demurely; he obviously wasn't leaving the apartment in that state of undress. "Yes," she answered.

"I've been waiting for you, lazy girl. Are you going to join me or not?" he asked.

Her happiness secure for the moment, Paige sprung up from the bed and swaggered boldly across the bed. Standing over him, she sweetly asked, "Were you planning to wash me?"

Wrapping his arms around her thighs, he easily lifted her off the bed and carried her into the bathroom. "I think we can share that responsibility," he murmured as he put her down on the tile bathroom floor. "You first," he said and opened the shower door to allow her to step inside.

She stepped into the very warm stream of water and let it wash down over her hair and face. He stepped into the shower behind her. She could feel his stiff rod pressing against her back as she reached for the sponge and shower gel. She diligently tried to ignore the prodding in her back every time he moved as she lathered up the sponge. She moved out of the spray and gave him room under the showerhead. In the meantime she began the sensual process of lathering his back and buttocks with soapsuds. She ran her hands along his skin, made slick and slippery from the soap.

He turned to face her in the shower, and she continued her exploratory lathering across his chest and down his stomach to his erect penis. Holding it in her hands, she gently washed the part of his body she'd come to desire so much.

Trevor leaned down and engulfed her in a rapturous wet kiss. Taking the sponge out of her hands, he took his own exploratory tour of her body, washing her lovingly and intimately as he went along.

Their senses were extremely heightened and raw by the time they rinsed off the soapsuds. He lifted her onto the built-in tile bench in the corner of the stall. Burying his face in her wet patch, he tweaked and sucked her clitoris with his lips and tongue until she cried out for him to stop. She wrapped her arms around his neck and legs around his waist as he eased her down onto his pulsing naked dick. He used the shower wall for leverage, and he made love to her again in the warm stream of water in the shower. Her moans of pleasure were fierce and frequent until he finally climaxed again.

They rinsed off again and returned to the bedroom. Slipping into bed, they nestled together, each deep in their own thoughts. Although neither said a word about it, they both were thinking along the same lines. Tomorrow would come soon enough, and they would deal with it then.

EPILOGUE

Six months later Trevor was closing the door of his home in Forest Glen for the last time. The closing was in an hour, and he would then turn the house keys over to the new owners. The probate procedures were finally complete on the execution of Claudette's will. He was now the owner of Très Chic Cosmetics and Fragrances. Because the company was privately owned, he was in total control. In her latter years, Claudette deferred the day-to-day running of the company to a board of advisers. Trevor intended to take a more active role as the new owner and would be meeting with the board early next week. He'd resigned from his position as east coast regional sales director at Westmoreland and Phelps and intended to get a fresh start in Washington, D.C.

He'd made several house-hunting trips to the Georgetown area before finding exactly what he was looking for: a three-story town house near Dupont Circle with four bedrooms and a library. He was sold when he entered the library and saw the built-in bookcases. It was a pleasant reminder of Claudette's mansion and also provided a place to display her expansive book collection.

He'd spoken with Olivia earlier in the day, and she was meeting him in Washington this weekend to help him get settled in his new place. She'd asked him about Paige and if he'd seen her. He told her they had decided it was best for both of them not to continue the relationship. He was a reminder of a time when she'd reached a very low point in her life, and while she was eternally grateful for all he'd done, it cast a pall on their association. His feelings about her were similar in nature; he didn't need the constant reminder of what he'd done and how much trouble he'd gotten into because of it. They would remain friends but wouldn't pursue anything more.

He still couldn't get used to the idea of Damian with Agnes. They were still seeing each other, and when he'd run into them on a few occasions, she did seem like a changed woman. She was always pleasant, but he couldn't shake his first impression of her and wondered what Damian had done to turn her out. Damian wasn't forthcoming with any details, which he found strange. It indicated she was more than a passing fancy for him. As long as Damian was happy, he reasoned, it was all that mattered.

Trevor had spent the last six months putting his own life in order. When Claudette died unexpectedly, he never imagined she would leave nearly everything to him. She gifted her home in Paris to Damian and made large donations to several charitable organizations. The bulk of her estate, along with her company, she bequeathed to Trevor. She had no children of her own and no relatives she felt were worthy of her inheritance. Her wishes were very specific and unchallengeable. Literally overnight he was propelled into a stratosphere of wealth he'd never in his wildest dreams ever hoped to obtain.

He accepted that Olivia would never be more than a big sister to him. He acknowledged the mistakes he'd made with Cynthia and decided he would be ready to find a steady companion once he adjusted to life in D.C. He knew from word of mouth that there were plenty of smart and beautiful black women in the nation's capital. He was looking forward to the transition.

In an effort to reconnect with his family in New Jersey, he'd flown home to make peace with them. His parents were more receptive than his sisters and welcomed him back into the fold. His sisters, fueled by jealousy, refused to believe he hadn't done something evil to convince a feeble old woman to give him everything. He laughed at the reference to Claudette as a feeble old woman. She was feisty and vibrant till the day she died. He missed her.

His parents confided they were having difficulty controlling his teenage brother, Quinton. Quinton was six foot three at fourteen and not interested in anything but girls, basketball, and running the streets. His mother feared if they couldn't set him straight soon, they would lose him. The only thing they were certain of was that he hadn't gotten into drugs yet.

Trevor spent a few hours with him the afternoon he was there and discovered that his parents were wrong. Quinton spent entirely too much time smoking weed. Quinton was a late-in-life baby for their parents, and as they approached their late sixties, they didn't have the energy to control him anymore. Trevor offered to take Quinton to live with him. He'd already contacted a private high school in Georgetown and enrolled him there. He let Quinton know in no uncertain terms he didn't have a problem knocking him on his ass if he stepped out of line. Quinton was looking forward to the change and was coming to D.C. at the end of the month.

Trevor looked back at the home he'd lived in for six years and smiled. "Look out, D.C. Trevor Calhoun is coming to town." He laughed aloud and got into his car and drove off.

Paige stood by the window in her apartment, sipping a cup of chamomile tea and looking out at the fall leaves. She loved the fall. It was her favorite time of year. Trevor was never far from her mind, and although she hadn't seen him since that night six months ago, she loved him more than ever. Accepting that he wasn't ready for a relationship was hard, but they had spoken several times since, and she was thankful they at least were able to remain friends. He called periodically to say hello. He told her of his plans to move to D.C., and she wished him well. There were things she knew she could have said to change his mind, something she should have told him, but she decided not to.

Christmas was only a few months away, and she was looking forward to it this year because she knew for the first time in a long time she would not be spending it alone. As she turned from the window, her body was framed in silhouette against the afternoon sun. She rubbed her swollen belly and smiled. "We're going to have a wonderful Christmas, little one," she said and took another sip of tea.

Please turn the page for an exciting sneak peek of
Melissa Randall's
SEXUALLY SATISFIED
coming in May 2007 from Aphrodisia!

David softly stroked my inner thigh. "I'm going to make you so wet, Gillian," he whispered. "I'm going to tease you until you're hot and excited and begging for my hard cock. Then I'm going to pump it into you, slowly at first, then faster—I'm going to make you come over and over again. And when I'm ready to come I'm going to pull my cock out and spurt all over your breasts . . . then I'll straddle your face so you can lick my balls and suck the head of my cock until I'm hard again . . ."

"Gillian? Gillian? GILLIAN!"

I was rudely awakened from my fantasy. "I'm sorry, Mr. Conley. What can I do for you?" I shifted uncomfortably in my chair to relieve the tingling between my legs. I now understood the agony felt by guys with unexpected public hard-ons.

Mr. Conley looked impatient and irritable, as always. "Please take this file up to Ms. Johnson on the 25th floor. It's urgent."

"Of course, I'll do it right away." As I took the file from him I felt like a zombie, and probably looked like one too. I'd temped as a receptionist at this accounting firm before—it ranked high on my list of mind-numbing jobs.

After dropping off the file, I ducked into the ladies room. I couldn't stand it any longer; I had to get some relief. I locked myself in a stall and unbuttoned my blouse. I pulled down my bra and rubbed my thumbs over my nipples until they stiffened. I was breathing hard, thinking of David's large hands cupping and gently squeezing my breasts. I pulled up my skirt and slid my hand down my panty hose. I rubbed my pussy through my panties and felt the deep throbbing intensify. I slipped my fingers under the elastic and caressed my swollen clit, slowly at first, then harder and faster . . . *David's cock, pumping harder and faster* . . . I came so hard it was almost painful. I pressed my other hand against my mouth to stifle my scream.

"Anita, I don't know what to do. It's been nearly a week and David hasn't called. I've almost given up. I guess it was just a one-night stand. I know I shouldn't care so much, but I'm really disappointed."

"Come on, he's a very busy guy. I'm sure he'll call. I'll bet he's been thinking about you as much as you've been thinking about him."

I laughed weakly. "Yeah, right. I guess I should be glad I had that one night with him. It's something to remember when I'm old and decrepit."

"I still think you shouldn't give up. But let's do something fun this weekend to take your mind off him. How about a club Saturday night?"

"Sure, sounds good," I replied, trying to sound enthusiastic.

"Thanks for listening, Anita. Give me a call later this week and we'll get together Saturday night."

I hung up and puttered around the apartment, trying to force David out of my mind.

"*What did you expect?*" sniped Miss Prudence. "*Of course he's not going to call. He got what he wanted from you—and it was way too easy.*"

"He was very hot for you and he still is," countered Miss Hornypants. *"He wants to see you again. Why sit around waiting for his call? You can call him."*

This obvious fact startled me out of my reverie. Of course I could call him—why hadn't I thought of it earlier? If he blew me off it would be embarrassing, but at least I'd know where things stood.

I picked up my cell phone and flipped it open. Then I remembered—I didn't have his phone number.

"He never gave it to you—a good sign that he had no interest in seeing you again." Miss Prudence sounded smug.

"Maybe not—after all, you never asked him for his number," Miss Hornypants pointed out. *"You could call his office."*

Another brilliant suggestion from Miss H. For some reason I always ended up following her advice and ignoring Miss P.

I flipped open the phone book and found Wentworth Properties. My palms sweated as I punched in the number. I negotiated my way through the automated directory and finally reached a human. "David Wentworth, please," I stammered. I half expected the operator to decline my request, but she immediately connected me. I braced myself, waiting for the sound of David's voice.

"David Wentworth's office, Elizabeth Stone speaking," said an efficient feminine voice.

"Oh . . . hi. I'd like to speak to David Wentworth, please."

"Mr. Wentworth is out of town. I'm his assistant. May I help you?"

"Um, no. I'm just a friend. Do you know when he'll be back?"

"I'm sorry, his plans are uncertain. May I take a message?"

"Uhhh . . . no message. I'll just try again next week."

I hung up abruptly. David had gone out of town without even telling me. That was it. He definitely didn't want to see me again. I closed my eyes and bit my lip, trying to push away the waves

of disappointment and humiliation. *Just let it go, Gillian...
just move on.*

It was close to midnight but I still couldn't sleep. I turned
the light on and picked up the latest Sue Grafton mystery. Kin-
sey Millhone was a woman facing *real* problems. I became completely absorbed in her story.

When my cell phone rang I nearly jumped out of my skin.
Who could be calling so late? Probably Anita or someone calling the wrong number.

I flipped open the phone. "Hi, it's Gillian," I yawned.

"Gillian, it's David."

I nearly said, "David who?" A split second later I sat bolt
upright. "David! It's so great to hear from you," I gushed.

"I'm sorry to call so late. I've been in Boston all week, dealing with this damned condo project." He sounded very tired.

"That's okay, I understand. I was awake when you called." I
felt flushed with happiness.

"I've been thinking about you a lot, Gillian. And I get hard
every time I think of you."

"Really?"

"Really. That night with you—and that morning—was in-
credible."

"Yes, it was. I've been thinking about you too," I purred.

"I'm coming back to New York tomorrow night. My flight
gets in pretty late, but I thought I could pick you up on the way
from the airport to my apartment—"

"Yes!" I blurted out.

David laughed. His laughter was so rare, it felt like a tri-
umph every time I coaxed it from him. "I look forward to it. I'll
see you tomorrow night," he said.

"Wait, David." I didn't want the conversation to end so
quickly. "I thought you might like to know what I'm wearing

right now—a black silk teddy with red lace." (I was actually wearing a faded pink cotton nightshirt with a large coffee stain on the front.)

"Gillian . . ." His breathing deepened and quickened.

"Are you hard right now, David?"

"Extremely hard."

"Good. I want you to take your cock out and stroke it for me." I waited a moment. He gave a little groan. "I'm stroking it. God, I wish you were here."

"So do I. I've pulled the top of my teddy down . . . I'm playing with my hard nipples . . ."

"Oh darling, I wish I could see you . . ."

"Hold on, I'm going to take the teddy off completely. There. I'm spreading my legs . . . and now my lips. My pussy is very warm and wet. If you were here right now, what would you do to me?"

His breathing was ragged. "I'd run my tongue all over your body . . . from your throat down to your breasts, then across your belly to your sweet pussy. I'd kiss your pussy and tease your clit with my tongue . . ."

"David, I want you so much –" I felt completely out of control. My fingers were wet with my juice. "I want your cock in me. I want you to explode in my pussy . . . I want your cum. Give it to me, David . . . give me all of your cum . . ." A cry burst from my throat as he let out a long, deep moan. For a minute the only sound was our harsh breathing.

"Oh, that was good," I sighed. "Did you like it?"

"I loved it. Gillian, I have to go now. I'll see you tomorrow night. I'll call you on my way from the airport." His tone was suddenly abrupt and distant.

"Oh, okay." I tried to hide the disappointment in my voice. *He's tired*, I told myself. "Good night, David. I look forward to tomorrow night."

I turned off the light and tried to sleep, but once again thoughts of David kept me awake. I was so excited at the prospect of seeing him again—and nervous. He was a complicated man. I'd have to handle him very carefully.